THE DOGS IN THE STREET

DARK YORKSHIRE - BOOK 3

J M DALGLIESH

First published by Hamilton Press in 2018
This edition published 2020

ISBN (Trade paperback) 978-1-80080-472-2
ISBN (Large Print) 978-1-80080-395-4
ISBN (Hardback) 978-1-80080-836-2

For Jericho

THE DOGS IN THE STREET

"No evil can happen to a good man, either in life or in death"

Plato

CHAPTER ONE

THE THUNDERING SOUND of the water filling the bathtub was barely audible over the shrieks of excitement emanating from the children. Nicola smiled at the irony. It would take nigh on thirty minutes to coax them away from the TV or their tablets and get them upstairs but once there, less than three before impatience set in at the wait to get in the water. A frustrated voice cut through as the children's mother filled their cups with squash. Chris was suffering. She felt his pain.

Leaving the kitchen, fingers looped through the handles of both cups, allowing her a free hand she flicked off the light and nudged the dog out from under her feet. Passing through the dining room, scooping up Ethan's reading book on the way she made it to the bottom of the stairs before the chime of the doorbell brought her to a halt with one foot on the first tread. The sound of splashing and laughter came from upstairs and the initial intent to ignore the caller was cast aside. Gently placing the cups on the adjacent window sill, alongside *The Lion's Paw*, Nicola stepped over to the front door.

It was still light, mid-evening and a caller wasn't unheard of although unannounced was somewhat unusual. The suited figure, viewed through the obscured glass, waited patiently hands clasped before him. Nicola unlatched the door and swung it open. Greeted with a smile the caller addressed her.

"Mrs Fairchild?" he asked, she nodded. "Please accept my apologies for calling at this time but I have a letter for your husband. Is he home?" He indicated a manila envelope clutched in his left hand.

"Yes, he is," she glanced over her shoulder up the stairs, considering whether to call out. Realising the kids would be unattended she thought better of it. "Bear with me a moment, I'll just have to swap with him. He's upstairs bathing the children."

"Certainly. I don't mind waiting."

Pushing the door to but not closed, Nicola retreated. Leaving the bedtime offerings on the window sill she trotted upstairs and eased the bathroom door open. Met with a barrage of joy from within she broke into a smile as first Ethan and then Molly flicked bubbles at their unsuspecting father who chided them with fake fury. Leaning on the door and raising her voice to be heard she got her husband's attention.

"Chris, there's someone to see you." He looked up at her, from his kneeling position.

"Who is it?"

"I don't know. Someone from work I think."

"Okay. Take over here would you?" Turning sideways, allowing him to pass, Nicola knelt alongside the bathtub as the door closed behind him. Molly threw her mother a cheeky glance before ducking her hands beneath the waves created by a plunging Ethan at the other end.

"Don't even think about it young lady," she said firmly, albeit with a smile. Muffled voices came to ear from downstairs but try as she might the subject matter was unintelligible. Not that she was bothered. Ethan yelled as Molly launched a boat full of water in his direction catching him off guard. "Behave, both of you," she stated calmly, hoping to draw a line under the impending retaliation from the eldest.

"I didn't do anything!" Ethan protested.

"You did!" Molly screamed back.

"Both of you, enough, please," their mother stated evenly. The conversation downstairs had ceased. Chris would be coming back up and she could take him up on that offering of twenty minutes of peace, a well-earned break on a day like today. He had promised her at least that after arriving home later than expected, from the office. Time passed but the door remained closed and with each minute, Nicola felt her patience ebb away. Whatever it was could wait until later, if not tomorrow, surely? Throughout the course of their nine-years of marriage, she had been conditioned to understand how the markets worked. Chris could, and notoriously did, work on well into the night but not today. He'd promised.

"I want daddy to wash my hair," Molly whined. "You get water in my eyes."

"Yeah, me too," Ethan stated.

"Me three," she replied. "I'll duck out and see where your Father's got to. Play nicely for a second."

Leaving the bathroom door open, Nicola stepped out. Not wanting to interrupt his conversation if the visitor was still present she listened. Not hearing anything but feeling a breeze blow across her from the open front door, she moved across the landing to the top of the stairs.

"Chris," she called out. No reply. "For Pete's sake," she muttered under her breath. Calling out over her shoulder as she descended addressing the children, "Popping downstairs, kids. Look after each other for a minute."

"Okay!" came a double shout from the bathroom. Reaching the first turn on the staircase she stopped. The front door rocked back and forth ever so gently. Chris sat on the floor, back against the wall open mouthed, staring straight ahead. He looked serene. All that was out of place were the two black marks on the front of his white shirt and another on his forehead above the bridge of his nose. The sound of increasing rainfall striking the mosaic tiles of the porch outside, accompanied by a drop in temperature, carried indoors on the breeze.

"Chris?" Nicola asked quietly, in a questioning tone. One of hope rather than expectation. The sounds of squabbling came from above and behind her, the children battling over something or other but the argument was lost to her. The spray of crimson on the wall above her husband now beginning to run as the force of gravity exerted itself had her transfixed. "Chris," she said once more. This time to herself.

CHAPTER TWO

"I FIND myself standing in a river. The water is almost waist high. It's fast moving but I'm steady and not in any danger. I know I should be cold but I'm not."

"What are you doing in the river?"

"Nothing. Just standing."

"Are you alone?"

"No. there are people... well, not people... bodies. They pass by all around me with the flow of the water."

"How many?"

"I don't know. Perhaps dozens?"

"Can you describe them?"

"Many are faceless or may as well be. Men, women... often children. Sometimes I'll recognise one but most of them, I don't. From time-to-time they'll speak but on the whole they're silent."

"Those that speak, what do they say?"

Caslin stared at a non-existent point on the wall as if seeing something in the distance, slowly shaking his head, "I can't make it out. They mumble. The words are drowned out by the noise."

"Of the water?"

"No, the forest. The water makes no sound but the trees lining the riverbank, they whisper and it carries on the wind.

"What do they say?"

He thought on it, "I'm not sure they say anything to be honest." There was a pause while she waited to see if he had anything else to add. He didn't.

"What do you think it all means?"

"Does it have to mean anything?"

"Usually, it does. Particularly if it's frequent and similar each time," she said, looking at him over the rim of her glasses. "Is it?"

"Always the same. Every time."

"How often?"

"Every night."

"I see."

The ringing of his phone interrupted the moment of clarity his counsellor sought to attain, much to her obvious frustration. Despite her protestations, he answered.

"Caslin," he said flatly, ignoring the stern gaze that set upon him. "I'll be right there." He said, hanging up on the caller and standing up. "Sorry. Duty calls."

"Some might say that you arranged that, in order to get out of this session."

"Now that's grossly unfair," he replied with a smile. "Particularly without evidence. Besides, you know me better than that."

"I know you very well, Nathaniel Caslin. One session a week, for the last three months. Our relationship is probably as deep as yours is with your own father. I assure you."

"I doubt that's true," Caslin said, plucking his coat from the stand and putting it on.

"Why ever not?"

"I'm here, talking to you and I can't stand *him*," Caslin replied. "Same time next week?" It was a rhetorical question. He would be there. After all he had no choice.

"You will have to take this seriously, sooner or later, Nate," she called after him. "I'm not going away."

"I don't doubt it," Caslin said under his breath.

GETTING INTO HIS CAR, he took the parking permit from the dashboard and put it back in the glove box ready for next week. Ashleigh, his long-suffering counsellor, acknowledged his wave as he pulled away from the kerb before she closed the door to her home. It was only a short drive across the city into The Mount. It wasn't often he had professional cause to go there not under circumstances such as these anyway.

The four-storey, terraced, well-to-do townhouses that made up these tree lined streets seldom had need of the police, with the notable exception of the odd burglary. Hence the reason he felt able to draw his session to an early close running the risk of yet another black mark in his abnormally, chequered-book. The scene was easy to find. The number of uniform vehicles present alongside the cordon, hastily being set up gave it away. Pulling in to park up by the growing throng of people, a mixture of passers-by and neighbours alike, Caslin got out. Acknowledging those on crowd control, he noted the arrival of a local press truck and a couple of freelancers. Ducking under the tape, he followed the direction indicated. Mounting the stone steps to the front door, he was greeted by DS Hunter and Iain Robertson, head of the Fulford Road, Scenes of Crime team.

"Not often we find ourselves here is it?" Caslin said to neither in particular.

"Sorry to call you, sir but it—" Caslin waved Hunter's apology away.

"What do we have here?" he asked, peering over her shoulder as the flash from a forensic officer's camera lit up the inner hallway.

"The home-owner, a Christopher Fairchild, has been shot dead on his doorstep, sir."

"I don't suppose we're fortunate enough to know who by?" Caslin asked.

"No, sir. This one isn't so straightforward. He had an unannounced caller this evening. It would appear there was some kind of altercation and the end result left him dead."

"Who found him?" Caslin asked, as Robertson led him inside, once he had donned the mandatory, forensic boot covers.

"His wife."

"She here?"

"Upstairs, sir. With the kids," Hunter said, her tone changing at the last. In response to his unasked question, she continued, "Two, aged three and five. They're with the mother now. We can't bring them down without passing the body... their father, so thought it best—"

"You're right," Caslin offered, kneeling before the still form of Christopher Fairchild. "What do we know about him?"

"Forty-four years old, married, father of two, as I said. He's a Senior Fund Manager for KL Global based here in York but with an office in the City."

"Known to us for any reason?"

Hunter shook her head, "No, sir. I ran him. No hits."

"Witnesses?"

"Just the wife... but she was upstairs when it happened. She initially answered the door to the caller and has given us a description of the attacker albeit a vague one. We've put it out there. Do you want to speak with her?"

Caslin shook his head. Speaking with loved ones directly following an incident such as this often proved fruitless.

"Not yet. Let's have a look at this chap first. Iain?" Robertson eased his photographer aside, enabling him to move past the body sitting at a ninety-degree angle to the front door, back to the wall.

"From what I can ascertain," Robertson surmised, "they engaged in conversation at the door. Whatever led to the attacker drawing a weapon I can't say but the first shot was into the chest causing him to step backwards. The second is likely to be the chest wound high and to the right," he leaned over, indicating it with his index finger. Caslin knelt to get a better look. "That shot spun him the ninety-degrees and as he staggered, or stumbled, back inside I believe the gunman followed him in. There's a fresh boot scuff on the carpet runner there behind you," Caslin looked and nodded, "that doesn't tie in with the victim or his wife's footwear. Then the third and final shot to the forehead. Note the high velocity spatter on the wall above and behind indicating the shooter was standing directly before him. He then fell back against the wall, sinking to the floor where we find him now. I expect he was dead before he hit the ground."

"Anything unusual about the wounds? Suggestions for the type of weapon or ammunition?"

"The first round passed through the victim embedding itself in the wall at the end of the hall," Robertson waved a hand in the general direction. Caslin looked and saw where it had been marked for analysis. "It looks like a 9mm to me but I'll confirm it once we remove the bullet. Unlikely to be a hollow point due to the size of the exit wound in the victim's back. We levered him forward before you arrived."

"The others?"

"No. The second didn't leave him. I expect it struck the rib-cage or shoulder blade, ricocheting around, doing as much damage as possible before it ran out of energy. The third was at pretty close range. You'll note the five-point star burst pattern, that the round left upon entry." Caslin turned his attention back to Fairchild and examined the head wound. "That's commonly found in these cases. The bullet fractures the skull forming the distinctive shape which translates to the outer surface of the skin. I must say that even without the headshot, he would've bled out before reaching a hospital. Your shooter's certainly no chump I'll give him that."

"Professional, you reckon?"

Robertson thought for a moment. "For starters, he policed the scene. Three shots and we've no casings. He wasn't going to make it easy for us. If it's a nine millimetre, and I'm not prone to being wrong, then it's an automatic. I'll leave speculation on motive and the emotional state of mind to you but from a forensic standpoint your man knew how to ensure this poor sod never saw another sunrise."

"How long until you can move the body?" Caslin asked, thinking of the family upstairs.

"Give me another three quarters of an hour?"

"Okay, thanks," Caslin said. Turning to DS Hunter. "Have them extend the cordon another thirty feet. The scene being this close to the front door it won't take long for the vultures outside to get access to a neighbour's house. I don't want this," he waved his hand in a circular motion, "on the front pages tomorrow morning."

"I'll do it right away."

"Before you go. What did you say he did for a living, hedge-fund manager?"

"Yes," Hunter confirmed. "Judging by his home, successful at it, too." Caslin nodded but always considered that appearances could be and often were deceptive in his line of work. Hunter made to leave, through the front door.

"Where's the DCI?" Caslin called after her. She stopped in the doorway and turned.

"No idea, sir. I've not seen him but Broadfoot's asking to see you, when you get back to the station."

With that, she was out of the door and descending the steps to the street below. Whatever the detective chief superintendent wanted with him was but a fleeting thought as Caslin climbed the stairs to the first floor. Cresting the landing, he stopped to catch his breath. Not for the first time, he felt out of shape with no good reason. Finding the family in the furthermost bedroom to the rear of the building, Caslin beckoned the liaison officer over to him.

"How are they?" Caslin asked.

"Under the circumstances, they're doing well, sir," PC Waterton said softly. Caslin knew her and respected her for the calm assuredness that she always carried when called upon. "As I understand it, sir, the children were unaware of what happened.

They were in the bath when it took place and are still none the wiser. Although clearly they are shocked about what is going on. They know their father's been hurt but nothing more."

"And the wife?" Caslin asked under his breath casting a glance over towards where she was sitting on an occasional sofa, one child snuggled under each arm.

Waterton exhaled slowly. "In a state of shock, I think. Trying to be strong for her children. Certainly nothing in her manner that strikes me as unusual."

"Okay, thanks," Caslin said solemnly. "Iain Robertson reckons we'll be able to take them out of the house within the hour. See if you can rustle up some blankets or something and we'll wrap the kids up. There's nothing down there I want them to see if we can possibly avoid it. Can you keep them entertained while I speak with their mother?"

"Yes, sir."

Caslin escorted Nicola Fairchild out onto the rear landing. The CSI team could be heard downstairs cataloguing their finds but they had a quiet moment to converse. Caslin introduced himself.

"I'm DI Nathaniel Caslin, Mrs Fairchild. I am deeply sorry for your loss," he said, real empathy in his tone. "I appreciate that this is a difficult time but I need to ask you a few questions and then I'll let you get back to your children." Nicola smiled weakly as much in appreciation of the sentiment as for Caslin's thoughtfulness. "I understand you had a caller this evening?"

"Yes, it was a little before 7 p.m., I know because I looked at the clock in the kitchen before I headed upstairs. Chris...," she paused, then. The moisture in her eyes welled up, threatening tears. "Chris was bathing the children. I was due a break from them," she broke off as if concerned she had said the wrong thing. "Not that I don't want to be around them, it... it was a rough day."

"Don't worry. We all have them," Caslin reassured her. "I have two myself. I know what it's like."

"No, no, it's my mother," Nicola explained. "She has breast

cancer and was due for surgery this morning. I went with her. It…
it's a lot to take in." Caslin felt for her even more at that moment.
To think he'd had some dark days in recent times but nothing on
this scale.

"Is your father—"

"He passed away," she answered before he finished.

"I'm sorry."

"It was a few years ago," she offered, drawing a deep breath
and steadying herself.

"Can you tell me about the caller?" She looked up, trying to
recall whilst wiping her eyes with the back of her hand. Caslin
took in her measure. Although clearly upset, understandably so,
she had managed to maintain her composure in front of her children in the most extreme of circumstances. He was instantly
impressed with her as she articulated her answer. So often
witnesses threw everything out in an apparent mind dump of
information that bore little resemblance to the evidence. Not so
with Nicola Fairchild.

"He was white, at least six-feet tall. My husband is a similar
height and size, that's why I remember that. He was smartly
dressed in a matching suit but no tie. I assumed he was from the
office and on his way home so had taken it off."

"Why would you think that?"

"He showed me a letter he had to give to Chris, so I assumed
that was the case."

"Did he specifically ask to speak with your husband?

"Yes, he addressed me directly and asked for him."

"What was in the letter?"

She shrugged negatively. "I don't know. The envelope was in
his hands, a brown one and he didn't say what was in it."

"How did he sound, was he local?"

"I don't really know. I don't think so," she said, suddenly
appearing confused, "I don't remember exactly but now you
mention it there was something about his accent. He was well

spoken or at least sounded so. Also, he was very polite. Maybe overly."

"Do you mean well educated?"

She shook her head. "No, not necessarily. He was... normal sounding... I guess but his tone, choice of words were... well... grammatically correct. I'm sorry. That probably doesn't make a great deal of sense."

"You're doing well, Mrs Fairchild. What about his face? Can you describe him to me?"

"I'm sorry, Inspector. I had my hands full, the kids were shrieking upstairs. I wasn't really paying attention."

"We can take a fuller statement later but for now anything will help," Caslin pressed. "You said he was a white male, approximately six-feet tall. What about his skin, was he tanned? Did he have any tattoos or skin condition that jumped out at you? Was he clean shaven?"

"He didn't have a beard but a day or so growth on his face. It was dark—"

"His stubble or his skin?"

"His stubble. It was greying in places so I guess he was older."

"How old would you say?"

She considered that. "Much older than you or I, possibly in his late forties or early fifties?" She glanced back towards the room where she had left the children and Caslin considered he had got all he was going to get from her, at this point.

"One more question, Mrs Fairchild and we'll leave it for tonight," Caslin said, drawing her focus back to him. "Is there anyone you can think of who might like to do harm to your husband or your family? Whether in a personal relationship or a professional one?"

Nicola shook her head emphatically. "No, not at all. We have many friends most of whom are fellow members of the congregation and certainly no enemies."

Caslin considered that. "What about your husband's work? Has he expressed concerns about anything recently?"

"Chris doesn't... didn't... really talk about his work. It is something of a family rule that we have. Once home he is home. Not that he never brings work home, he often does, but he works in his study and once out of there it's family time."

"So he hasn't got any money worries or failed business deals that you are aware of?"

"Not at all, Inspector. Christopher has been putting in the hours for the past few months but his work is demanding and he is a very driven man," she fell silent, looking to the floor. "At least, he..."

"Thank you, Mrs Fairchild," Caslin said supportively. "I'll let you get back to your family. When we are able to help you out do you have somewhere that we can take you?"

"We will go and stay with friends across the city. I've already spoken to them, they are coming to pick us up as soon as we can leave."

"It shouldn't be too much longer," Caslin said reassuringly and allowed her to return to the bedroom. Looking past her as she went in both children's heads came up and were pleased to see her enter. PC Waterton emerged to speak with him.

"I'll ensure their contact details come to you, sir, once we have them settled," she said. Caslin nodded. "Does she have any clue as to who might want to have done this?"

"Apparently not an enemy in the world. She says," Caslin stated softly. "Although, I beg to differ. They have at least one. Keep your eyes and ears open and let me know if anything useful slips out."

Returning downstairs, Caslin met DS Hunter in the hallway, "Have you seen or heard mention of a letter in a manila envelope?"

"Nothing like that as far as I know. I'll check with Iain though. Why?"

"Apparently that was the point of the visit. It could've been a ruse of some sort but we need to check. While you're at it, find out where he worked. I want to know a little bit more about how Mr

Fairchild went about earning a living. His other half was a bit too vague on the subject."

"What do you make of her?"

"I'm not sure yet. Professionals, happy families… those active in their congregational community don't usually find hitmen at their door."

"Mistaken identity?"

Caslin shook his head, "No, he asked after the target. We need to figure out why."

CHAPTER THREE

"WE'RE in a deep state of shock with this. It's difficult for everyone here. Christopher's particular brand of genius will be greatly missed. We garner a real sense of family—"

"His wife and children will no doubt share your sense of loss, I'm sure," Caslin interjected, bringing Tobias Eldridge to a juddering halt. They were making their way through the plush corridors of KL Global's offices, in York.

Eldridge replied defensively, "I certainly didn't mean to imply that our suffering is greater than…"

"Of course not. I appreciate your thoughts are primarily with the deceased and his family. What kind of an employee was he, Mr Fairchild?" Caslin asked.

Eldridge didn't falter. "Top chap, Christopher. Intelligent, popular, diligent. Everything that we look for here at KL."

"Hedge funds require a degree of ruthlessness, too. Don't they?" Caslin asked, as they passed a portrait of a suited Asian man standing in a traditionally decorated, wood-panelled room.

Eldridge slowed inclining his head in Caslin's direction. "That's one of our founding fathers, Shahram Tengku. He formed the company along with three colleagues twenty years ago, in Kuala Lumpur."

"Hence the KL of the company name?" Hunter asked.

"Quite right," Eldridge confirmed. Turning to Caslin, "You are correct, Inspector. A successful fund manager needs to know the system and exploit it for maximum return. *Ruthlessness* could be used as a crude oversimplification but I would prefer *proactive* or *resourceful* as my adjectives of choice."

Caslin didn't seek to develop the point further. "And Christopher, he hit the benchmark to qualify as successful?"

"Very much so. One of our top performers. He certainly would have been appointed to the board within the next few years with his drive and ambition. He will be sorely missed."

"It is a great loss to everyone connected with the family, I am sure."

Eldridge frowned. "How are Nicola and the children?"

"Bearing up," Caslin said. "Did you socialise with him out of the office?"

"Not a great deal. Corporate functions perhaps or the odd round of golf but not often. He worked hard but was dedicated to his family and the two don't leave a great deal of room for much else I understand."

Eldridge resumed their walk switching conversation to their newly refurbished décor. Caslin ceased listening allowing Hunter to make the appropriate sounds to indicate someone was paying attention. This place was unlike any office block he had ever attended before, thick carpets and communal leather-sofas. It had the air of a country club rather than a financial services firm.

"This is Christopher's office. His personal assistant, Alma, will assist you with whatever you need," Eldridge said, by way of an introduction. A lady stood up from behind a desk and moved to greet them. In her forties, wearing an expensive trouser-suit, she was immaculately presented but, despite her best efforts, was unable to hide the fact she had been crying. Her eyes were red and swollen, her cheeks puffy and her demeanour was of forced control almost to the point of stiffness. They introduced themselves and she escorted them into Fairchild's office.

"Is there anything in particular that you are interested in seeing?" Alma asked them.

"We're looking to build a picture of Christopher to help understand how this has happened. Who were his clients?"

"He had a small portfolio of clients both domestic and international. Mostly he dealt with larger contributors, wealthy individuals rather than collectives. Those were managed by the juniors. Although he has taken on some of our NGO related accounts."

"Non-governmental Organisations?" Caslin confirmed.

Alma nodded. "He's spent a lot of time on those accounts recently."

"What are the NGOs concerned with?"

"Two of them are refugee-assistance operations. Another, that he was very passionate about, is a human rights' group."

"And how has he been managing his client list recently? Have there been any notable failures or frictions with individuals?"

Alma shook her head, "No, not at all. Mr Fairchild is quite gifted. I've worked with him for nine years since he joined the firm and he's never missed a target. Quite the opposite in fact, he's always exceeded them."

"You must know him well," Caslin suggested, "after nine years?"

She looked away, her façade threatening to crack under strain. "Yes. He was a lovely man."

"Have you noticed anything different in him, recently... behaviour, attitude? Has he been upset? Anything at all?" Hunter asked, pen and notebook in hand. Alma's eyes flicked across at Hunter and away again, rapidly. There was something. "Alma?"

"He has seemed stressed recently but that in itself is not unusual," she offered before glancing over her shoulder towards the door as if concerned someone might hear her. "I mean, this is a stressful job. Large sums of money and the expectation of returns is a given. I'd politely suggest there isn't an account manager in this entire building who doesn't ease their nerves with something after... or even during the working day."

"What about Mr Fairchild?" Caslin pressed.

"Chris was different. At least, I thought so."

"He didn't have any... vices?" Hunter asked.

"Not like the others, he took it in his stride."

"What changed recently?" Caslin asked.

"I would still say the work wasn't getting to him but... physically, he seemed different. He wasn't one to complain but I thought he was suffering."

"In what way?"

"Stomach cramps, indigestion and such like. He would go off to the bathroom frequently. For a while, I figured he just wasn't taking care of himself but the amount of occasions he sent me out to the pharmacy for medicines—"

"Prescription?" Hunter sought to clarify.

"No, no. Off the shelf basics, indigestion tablets, antacids... but they didn't seem to make a lot of difference. I urged him to go to his doctor."

"Did he take your advice?"

She shrugged, "I don't know. He never brought it up again. It didn't affect his workload though. He was often the last one here several nights a week. If I didn't know better, I'd say his marriage was on the rocks."

"But it wasn't?"

"No, not as far as I know. He was devoted to his family. Like I said the team here manage stress in different ways. Recreational pursuits of all kinds are... commonplace. Many of which are not suitable for polite conversation."

"We appreciate your candour, Alma," Caslin said. "You disapprove?"

"I would prefer to say I'm a little old school but not naïve enough to judge."

"We'll need access to Mr Fairchild's files. Can you walk some of our colleagues through them this afternoon?"

"Certainly. Mr Eldridge has requested he be given assurances regarding data protection and that all the necessary legal paperwork is provided before you do. I think he is being thorough."

"We'll be in touch later in the day," Caslin responded, mildly irritated at the last. They made their way out. Once clear of the building, Hunter raised her concerns.

"For such a popular, decent man, someone really wanted to bury him didn't they?"

"My thoughts exactly," Caslin agreed. "When Terry Holt starts going through his business dealings later make him aware that this lot are hiding something. I expect him to find it."

"What makes you so sure?" Hunter asked as they approached their car and she unlocked it. "I mean, not saying you're wrong but—"

"Good old-fashioned instinct, my dear Hunter. Instinct," Caslin stated, opening his door. Hunter got in at the driver's side. "Tobias Eldridge got my back up."

"I noticed. You were a bit hard on him."

"He can spin all the platitudes he likes about team ethics and family values but he's a vampire, leeching off of the rest of society. I'll wager there are more sociopaths working in that building than we've met in our entire careers. Just because they don't kill anyone, doesn't make them anymore pleasant. Not in my book." Hunter cast a wry grin in his direction turning the key in the ignition. "Okay… a little more pleasant… but not much," Caslin conceded as the car pulled away.

Pondering Hunter's words as they headed back to Fulford Road in the mid-morning traffic, he asked himself, had he been too harsh? Not really. This was a murder inquiry and he had little patience for the sensitivities of a city spiv whose entire work-life was built on making little else but money. Caslin's phone rang and glancing at the screen he sighed, almost imperceptibly. He considered not answering it but caught Hunter's questioning look.

"Personal," he said, answering the call. "Hi Karen, what can I do—"

"Nate, I've been trying to get hold of you for days. Are you taking Sean this weekend or not?"

"Not sure that I can—"

"Bloody hell, Nathaniel. We moved up here to be closer to you. You promised to take a more active role—"

"And I will," Caslin interrupted. "A case has brok—"

"There always is though, isn't there?" his ex-wife replied, hanging up without waiting for an answer. Caslin took the phone away from his ear and checked the call had ended.

Glancing at Hunter, he smiled weakly, "Don't ever get divorced. Seriously, it sucks the life right out of you."

Hunter smiled back. "I'm not even married yet."

"Well, tell…" Caslin paused, struggling to recall the name.

"Steve," Hunter rescued him.

"Yes, Steve… I knew," Caslin lied, "should get a move on."

Hunter shook her head. "He's still not best pleased about the Thames Valley move."

Caslin sighed. "He'll get used to it."

ENTERING THE CID SQUAD ROOM, Caslin didn't make it to his office before he was intercepted by DC Holt.

"Broadfoot wants to see you," Holt stated.

"Still?" Caslin replied, drawing a smirk from the Detective Constable. "The DCI in yet?" Terry Holt shook his head. Caslin retreated back into the corridor along to the stairwell and up to the next floor. He was at the threshold to Kyle Broadfoot's office within a couple of minutes. He knocked and was bidden entry.

"Nathaniel," Broadfoot addressed him as he entered. "About time. I asked to see you yesterday."

"I know, sir. Sorry but I was out of the office and you had left by the time I got back last night."

"Indeed," Broadfoot said in his usual, but often misleading, disinterested tone. "I want you to bring me up to speed on this shooting in a moment but, first off, we have to discuss a point of admin."

"What's that, sir?"

"DCI Mentorn."

"Sir?" Caslin asked.

"Is on medical leave, effective immediately."

"I didn't realise he was ill, sir."

"Well, don't expect him back any time soon," Broadfoot said without elaborating further. "Which leaves me with a dilemma. Things as they are with budgets and the like, I haven't anyone available to fill his role within the next few months. Long story short, you're doing it."

Caslin was blindsided. His career path had stabilised recently having been on a downward trajectory for some time before that.

"Me, sir? I'm not sure about that."

"It's not a request, Nathaniel. I know you have every right to knock it back… and after the last time I can see why. That said, the chair was never coming back out for you, you are well aware of that fact. To put it another way, it won't do so again if you pass this up."

"With respect, sir. My career aspirations are not—"

"What they once were," Broadfoot interrupted. "However, you're getting another bite at it."

"Let's be honest, sir," Caslin said, appearing uncomfortable. "If you had someone else available you wouldn't be asking me either."

Broadfoot fixed him with a gaze. "You're a good detective, Nate. I'd go so far as to say bordering on the brilliant, if I didn't think it'd go to your head. You're also fallible. You've seen it go wrong and that makes you a safe pair of hands. As daft a logic as that may sound."

"Even so—"

"I've gone out on a limb for you in the past year, Nate. You owe me."

Caslin glanced toward the window. Broadfoot was right. "I know that, sir."

"I've read your counselor's assessment and I understand your reservations but I need an experienced hand to run that squad. You've done it before. I'm calling in the favour. You understand?"

Caslin nodded. "This will make us even?"

"Not even close," Broadfoot said without a hint of sarcasm, "and I still expect you to attend your sessions... and complete them." Caslin guessed Ashleigh had already been in touch. He wasn't angry, she was doing her job. "How are you progressing with your twelve steps?"

Caslin shrugged. "It's worked for millions... it will probably work for me."

"Good man," Broadfoot said. "Not quite a ringing endorsement but you're ticking the boxes. We'll get you there."

"You're not concerned about adding to my workload, sir?"

"You won't let me down, Nate. I know that. Now, what's the latest on the Fairchild murder?"

CASLIN LEFT Broadfoot's office with more than the caseload churning over in his mind. It wasn't the added pressure of being the Acting DCI, he could do the job standing on his head. Five years in the Met Police had proven that despite the period ending in the disgrace of demotion, transfer and the subsequent failure of his marriage. Resources were tight. A temporary situation that had now lasted the better part of a decade and with rising crime figures it was certainly not a good time to drop the ball. Particularly with someone as ambitious as Kyle Broadfoot. He was right to demand loyalty having backed Caslin when most would have discarded him.

Pushing the double doors into CID open, several faces looked to him. They knew something was afoot. Caslin didn't like the politics of man-management, preferring a rapid, surgical strike.

He brought his hands together in thunderous applause. Now all heads turned his way.

"Listen up," he said with authority. "DCI Mentorn will not be around for a while. Don't ask me why because I don't know. Long-story short, I'm Acting DCI and Hunter," he nodded in her direction, "is Acting DI. Any questions?"

Sarah Hunter remained open-mouthed for a brief moment before speaking up. "Since when?"

"Since now," Caslin stated. "Nothing else changes. Fairchild briefing in thirty minutes. Join me in your office?" he said to Hunter, walking into what was, until five minutes previously, his office. Hunter followed closing the door behind them.

"What's the story?" she asked.

"You know as much as I do," he said. An answer that didn't seem to cut much ice. "Seriously. That's what Broadfoot wanted me for. Now, you've passed your exams—"

"Yes, I have," Hunter cut him off, "and as you know, I'm starting next month, down in—"

"You still will," Caslin said. "As long as Steve goes with it. In the meantime, I need a DI and you get more experience here. Okay?"

Hunter appeared slightly perplexed but pressed no further. "Don't take this the wrong way, sir."

"Go on."

"Are you… up for this?" Caslin relaxed back into his chair. They had been through a lot together and he didn't resent the question.

"I know where you're coming from but as I said, nothing's changed. We won't have Mentorn breathing down our necks that's all."

"No, we'll have the Prince of Darkness himself."

Caslin chuckled. "Broadfoot's not that bad."

"You know he's lining himself up for Yorkshire's Crime Directorate?"

"Is he?" Caslin said. He hadn't heard that particular rumour.

"One step closer to the Chief Constable's chair. Better not screw up then."

"What is it with Mentorn? He's not been here five min—"

Caslin's phone began to ring. Glancing at the screen, he gave Hunter a nod and she left closing the door behind her. He answered.

"Hey, Jimmy. You're going to have to wait for the press conference, same as every—"

"No, it's not about the shooting. Can we meet? I need to talk to you." There was something in the journalist's tone that struck him as odd. He'd never heard Jimmy Sullivan sound like that before.

"I have a few things to do but... I'll see you in the Cellars, around midday?" Caslin offered.

"See you then."

CHAPTER FOUR

―――――――

"What can I get you, a scotch?"

"Not at lunchtime when I'm heading up a murder inquiry, no," Caslin said. "A coffee will do fine."

"Bloody hell," Sullivan said, "they're changing you, aren't they?" The barman said he'd bring the coffee over to them, so they descended into the lower section of Lendal Cellars taking a table in a quieter section. The vaulted, brick ceilings gave no indication of the time of day nor the brilliant sunshine above ground illuminating York City centre with its summer warmth. Caslin hadn't been in for a while. Temptation was best avoided altogether.

"What do you need to see me about, Jimmy?" Caslin asked as they sat down.

Sullivan looked around them nervously. "I need a favour, Nate. It's personal."

"What have you got yourself into?"

Sullivan shook his head. "Nothing like that. A colleague... a friend... may well have gotten in over her head and I'm... concerned."

"Go on."

"I know her from way back. She came to me for some local

knowledge, you know the sort of thing, asking about a few names? Anyway, I helped her out as best I could."

"All right, so what's the problem?"

"She was supposed to meet me for a drink two nights ago and didn't show. Not seen or heard from her since."

"Jimmy—"

"I know, Nate, I know. There are a million and one reasons why she bailed but I'm worried." Caslin took the moment of the barman bringing over his coffee to think on it. Jimmy Sullivan wasn't the type to make a mountain out of nothing. He was more likely to look into things on his own. That tenacity is what makes him such a strong story-hunter… and royal pain in the arse.

"What is she to you, Jimmy? You and her—"

"No," he snapped. "She's the daughter of an old friend. She's my Goddaughter."

"Does it run in the family, journalism?"

"Aye, he is… or was. He's dead now. A heart attack, years ago. I'm not the most heavily involved of Godparents but, seriously, this isn't like her."

"What was she working on?"

"She was cryptic about it. Although, acting like a cat on a hot tin-roof at the same time. Must've been something substantial. I took it that she didn't want me or anyone else lifting the story off of her."

"She knows you well, then?" Caslin said with a smile before blowing on the top of his coffee and sipping at it. Sullivan's brow furrowed.

"She was asking about a Catholic Priest living here in York. Father Callum Foley. Have you come across him?"

Caslin shook his head. "Should I?"

Sullivan returned the gesture. "Well I hadn't. I guessed she was working some historic child-abuse angle what with him coming over from Ireland and all."

"What are you suggesting about the Irish Catholics?" Caslin teased.

"No, I just mean its scandal after scandal in the Catholic Church these days. The same as with our social-care system, private schools and the Anglicans. They all tended to move them around a lot, sweep it under the carpet. Keep the shit flowing so no-one had the opportunity to smell it."

"You have a way with words, Jimmy, but you're not wrong."

"It's the profession," Sullivan said, accompanied by the briefest of smiles. "Anyway, I couldn't find anything on this priest but Emily was undeterred. She was excited. I remember how energetic I used to feel when I was about to break something huge."

"She was supposed to meet up with you the other night?"

"Aye, Sunday. Didn't show."

"You called her?"

"Of course I did but she hasn't picked up. The phone cuts straight to voicemail."

"Where was she staying, here in the city?"

"She didn't say," Sullivan met Caslin's questioning look, his frustration flaring. "I asked but she wouldn't say!"

"What do you want me to do?"

"Check it out for me."

"It's not a good time, Jimmy."

"Please, Nathaniel. You know I wouldn't make a fuss. I owe it to her parents. Her father dying orphaned her and I should've been around more back then, spent less time at the bottom of this," he said, inclining his head towards his glass as he drained the last of his pint.

Caslin sighed, "Give me what you've got."

"Thanks, Nate—"

"No promises, mind you," he added as Sullivan pushed a piece of paper, torn from a notebook, across the table towards him. On it was a hand-written mobile number and a name, *Emily Coughlan.*

"Where are we with Fairchild?" Caslin asked, now back in CID.

"As our initial checks turned up, he has no priors. Not even a speeding ticket. Privately educated. A Cambridge graduate in mathematics, who went straight into the city. He's worked for various companies from Lloyds through to several more niche financiers including KL Global where he is now," Hunter offered.

Terry Holt chipped in with results of his financial inquiries. "HMRC have nothing active on him. Fairchild submits everything on time. There's never been any referral to the Ombudsman either. The guy is as clean as a whistle. It will take some time to go through his work accounts. We're still waiting on a warrant. KL Global aren't playing ball."

"Hurry that along, Terry. I want a motive and where there's money, I usually find one. Who's looking at the family money?"

"That's me, sir," Detective Constable Kim Hardy spoke up. "He has a hefty life insurance policy with his wife as the main beneficiary. As for their personal accounts they have access to cash in their current account just north of half a million. They also own property in Spain and Croatia but I'm not done. This is going to take some time."

"Okay, maybe Terry can give you a hand with it. How did Nicola Fairchild react to us digging into their finances?"

"No issues, sir."

Caslin inclined his head. "Debts, gambling or otherwise? Anything that stands out?"

Hardy shook her head. "Not that we've come across. The mortgage is affordable bearing in mind his income levels. They have joint accounts but I'm not seeing anything unusual either coming in or going out."

Caslin felt his frustration building. Staring at the information board there was scant lead generation to it. "Come on, guys. Somebody wanted this man dead. Popular people, not involved in crime or tied heavily to shady characters, do not get shot on their doorstep. What about his wife, known associates?"

"We're working through a list given to us by Mrs Fairchild, sir.

Attendees at their local church for the most part. Again, no one has flagged up as a person of interest."

"Keep going with that. Perhaps one of the two Fairchilds were illicitly entwined with someone else and two doesn't go into three particularly well. Someone check Nicola Fairchild's movements. Where does she go, who does she spend her time with? Maybe it's nothing to do with his work. Is their marriage as perfect as it looks from the outside? It would be a first on me if it is. Close-knit communities, religious or otherwise, always have malicious chatter. Some of it might even be accurate."

"Cynical," Hunter offered, before adding, "fair comment, though."

"Backing it up a bit. The family apparently didn't hear the gunshots so that means the shooter used a suppressor. In all likelihood a professional, perhaps ex-military so put that alongside the list of friends and associates. Maybe we'll get a break there. Once you've exhausted the direct links spread the circle wider and go for known associates of associates. Anything further on the letter?"

"Nothing found at the scene, sir. We expanded the search to include neighbouring streets, bins, gardens and so on but found nothing," Hunter said flatly.

"If the contents were related it'll most likely revolve around his business dealings, sir," Holt stated. "I'll see what I can get out of his files as soon as I'm in."

"Good, Terry. Sarah," he looked to Hunter, "chase up Iain Robertson as well. I've read his preliminary report but we need something to get us going. Perhaps the ammunition used was in some way special? Keep shaking the tree, something will fall it always does. I want some movement on this and I want it now," he emphasised the last, before turning and heading into his office. Almost as an afterthought, he beckoned DC Hardy over. Lowering his voice so no-one would overhear, he took the notepaper Sullivan had given him earlier out of his pocket and passed it to her.

"Can you run this number for me? See what turns up."

"Sure. What is it I'm looking for?"

"Whatever you find. Quick as you can, yes?" he said, turning away and retreating into his office.

If she had any concerns, Hardy didn't raise them. No doubt he'd move into DCI Mentorn's in due course if the acting role became more than temporary but, for now, he was comfortable in the thick of it.

Seating himself, Caslin pored over the information they had accumulated thus far in his mind. His gut told him they'd find the strongest leads related to Fairchild's work life. His death carried the hallmarks of a professional hit not those left by a jealous husband or a rival love interest. Unable to discount anything until they knew more, Caslin was hopeful that this case would be solvable. Bringing the perpetrator in front of a court on the other hand could prove trickier. Kim Hardy appeared in the doorway.

"Got a sec, sir?" she asked quietly, unsure of whether to interrupt. A new addition to the team, Hardy had developed far in advance of his expectations since coming out of uniform. He beckoned her in.

"What is it, Kim?"

"Emily Coughlan, sir. You asked me to check her out."

"What have you got?" he asked.

"Resident of Northern Ireland but a citizen of the Republic, sir. Born in Dublin and raised in Coleraine, in the north, but registered living back in Belfast three years ago. Freelance journalist, her bio has her writing pieces for the Irish Times along with several other broadsheets here in the UK. I can't find any record of her here in York, though."

"She's only visiting, not been here long, so I'm led to understand."

"I ran the mobile number through the networks," Hardy said, looking at the notes held in her hand. "I'm presuming its hers because it isn't registered to anyone. Based on connections with the towers she's largely concentrated her time in an area north east of the city around Huntington."

"Any significant call activity in the log?"

Hardy shook her head. "Nothing that jumps out. Although she hasn't made a call since Sunday morning which does seem unusual regarding her call patterns prior to that."

"That's over two days now," Caslin mused, glancing at the clock. "What about two nights ago?"

"Let me have a look," Hardy said, bringing the call logs to the top of her clutch of papers and scanning down the entries. There weren't many. "She was in York before heading out of town. The last time her phone showed movement on the network it pinged off of a tower near Marton Abbey before another fifteen minutes later, placing her in Yearsley. After that nothing at all."

"She was heading north. When was that?"

"Early yesterday, in the direction of the Hambleton Hills. After that who knows? There hasn't been a connection since then. Either she's passed out of coverage which is very likely up there or her phone's run out of power. It might help if I knew what I was looking for or even why I'm looking," she added without malice.

"Not sure," was all Caslin added. Hardy stood silently as he thought about it. Looking back to her, he said, "All right. Have a look into Callum Foley, would you? He's a local priest." Reading her quizzical expression, he smiled. "Just check him out. Don't spend too long on it though."

CHAPTER FIVE

WEDNESDAY MORNING FOUND Caslin attending the pathology lab to hear the initial results of Fairchild's autopsy.

"I don't think I need confirmation of the cause of death," Caslin said with dark humour. Dr Alison Taylor smiled.

"You wouldn't be much of a detective if you did," she countered. "Iain Robertson's initial assessment proved accurate. The third shot killed him the moment it entered his skull. Even so, he would have died from massive internal injuries caused by the second bullet. It struck Mother Nature's bullet-proof vest, his ribcage, diverting it onto a downward trajectory through the right lung. There it caused massive damage before nicking the aorta where it connects with the left ventricle of the heart and lodging itself in his spinal column."

"That sounds bad."

"The aorta pumps the oxygenated blood from the heart," Dr Taylor clarified. "Yes, it's as bad as it gets. The haemorrhaging from that injury alone would have killed him. He'd have bled out internally in minutes."

"Were you able to retrieve the bullets?"

"Yes, both have been sent to forensics," she confirmed. "I've no idea how relevant this is but were you aware of his condition?"

"Condition?" Caslin asked. "His PA intimated that he might be ill. Why, what have you found?"

"Very ill, would be apt. Terminal to be accurate," Dr Taylor said. "I found multiple tumours on his pancreas. I'm not an oncologist but, judging by their size, I would set it at stage four. I also found widespread metastasis but I expect the pancreas was the primary cancer. Once I've retrieved his medical files, I'll confirm the diagnosis."

"How long do you think he had?"

"Impossible to say with any degree of accuracy but, in all probability, we're talking months not years."

Caslin drew a sharp intake of breath. "Do you think he was aware?"

"I fail to see how he couldn't be," Dr Taylor said stoically. "The stomach pain alone would have been excruciating at times."

"His wife never mentioned it."

"He wouldn't be the first to keep it to himself. It's not unheard of to develop the disease relatively young... processing your mortality at that age must be tough."

"To take it on alone..." Caslin said, leaving the thought unfinished. "Thank you, Alison. You'll send me your report as soon as it's complete?"

"As soon as it's ready," she replied. She stepped away, picking up her file and walking back towards her workstation. Caslin watched. As if her sixth sense felt his eyes upon her, she turned. "Something else?" she enquired, in a tone he didn't care for.

Caught without a coherent word to say, he stood openmouthed, replying with a slight shake of the head. Alison Taylor returned to her desk, tossing the file into a work tray, pulling out her stool and sitting down. Caslin chewed his lower lip as she focussed on her computer screen. Exhaling slowly, he thought better of initiating small talk and left pathology. Never one to shy away from taking responsibility for his actions, Caslin cut a dejected figure as he made his way along the corridors. Hiding behind work pressures, stress and children, lay the real cause of why he'd allowed their fledgling relationship to drop onto the backburner… fear. The reality of allowing another person to breach the hastily erected barriers he threw up after his divorce struck fear into his very core. Alison was tired of waiting, tired of playing second fiddle to the ghosts of his past. He couldn't blame her.

Walking out to his car, he pushed personal matters aside and focussed on the case. Contemplating the physical and mental state of Christopher Fairchild, Caslin considered what bearing his condition might have had on his behaviour. Knowing his days were running short why devote so much time to work? Financial security for family was a priority but early indicators showed they weren't short of funds. Furthermore, the focus his PA said he put onto the accounts of the non-governmental organisations countered the argument of money as a primary motivation. By all accounts those investments were charitable and a minimal commission was earned. It struck him as a peculiar dichotomy. Nicola Fairchild could shed light on it. Starting the car, he planned to pay her a visit.

Barely had he moved off before his phone rang. Pulling over, he answered the call. It was DC Hardy.

"Sir, local police have found a body a mile or so east of Ampleforth. It looks like a suspicious death. I thought you'd want to know."

"Why?"

"The initial description that came in on the wire is not dissimilar to that woman you asked me to look into."

"Emily Coughlan?" Caslin asked. "Are you sure?"

Hardy paused. "To be honest, it doesn't sound like it'll be that easy."

HAVING COLLECTED Hunter from Fulford Road, the journey from York to Ampleforth took three quarters of an hour. The late-afternoon traffic delayed them as they made their way through the picture-postcard villages of the Howardian Hills. On the northern edge where they merged with the North York Moors, Caslin picked up Jerry Carr Bank, a road skirting the boundary between the two. A uniform vehicle was waiting for them directing them off to the right at a fork onto a narrow lane that rapidly ascended into the hills. Half a mile from there they reached a cordon.

With the road closed the car remained where it stopped. They were led by a uniformed constable into the woods that ran the length of the lane as far as the eye could see. Moments later, Iain Robertson hailed them. The grim expression on the Scot's well-lined face ensured the early reports were to be believed.

"Brace yourselves for this one," he said, in his strong Glaswegian accent indicating for them to follow.

In a small clearing surrounded by a ring of chestnut trees, some forty feet from the road, lay a body. A more detailed description would have to wait for it was barely identifiable as such. Moving towards it, Caslin could see the remains were blackened to the point where it was difficult to discern if it was a man or a woman. The soft tissue had completely disappeared from the face and the bone of the skull was exposed. Leaning in closer, Caslin could make out tiny heat fractures crisscrossing the forehead.

"Judging by height and the slight build I would suggest we have a female," Robertson surmised. Hunter put a hand up to cover her nose, the smell of burnt flesh still lingered. Caslin surveyed the body. She lay on her back almost as if she had thrown herself backwards away from a fire. Her legs were bent at the knees, curled up to her waist and the hands were extended before her, fists clenched in a boxer's pose.

"The hands?" he pointed to them.

"That's typical of when a human body is set on fire. The coagulation of the proteins, combined with dehydration, cause the muscles to contract. It's quite natural," Robertson offered. "It doesn't indicate whether she was conscious or not."

Caslin observed the face but it was barely recognisable as such. Her features had melted, now more reminiscent of a charred husk. He couldn't imagine what she'd looked like before. The wisps of unburnt hair at the rear, protruding from the sides, all that offered any clue as to her previous appearance. Scanning the abdomen, Caslin saw her clothes had melted, blending with the organic matter. Robertson noted his interest.

"Synthetic material. They've fused with the skin under the intensity of the heat."

"Accelerant?"

"From the smell, I would say petrol is most likely," Robertson confirmed. "You'll see that her front has taken the damage but her back was largely untouched by the flames. The rear of her head still has most of the hair intact. I'm optimistic that some of the accelerant will have seeped into the ground beneath her. If so, we can get a sample for confirmation."

"Any ID?" Hunter asked, suppressing a gag reflex.

Robertson shook his head. "All we have is this. We found it in an internal pocket in the rear of her walking trousers." He lifted a transparent evidence bag. Inside appeared to be a white, credit-card sized piece of plastic. "It looks like an access key-card, probably to a hotel room."

"Any name on it?" Caslin asked, moving to take a closer look. There wasn't one but a gold logo was stencilled across the top. Embedded in the reverse was a chip. "Shouldn't be too hard to trace provided it's local."

"She wasn't carrying a purse, mobile phone, car keys..." Robertson went on. "Nothing to suggest who she is or how she got here? Stripped clean."

"What about her clothes? Synthetics suggest hiking gear," Caslin mused openly.

"It certainly could be but she wasn't hiking out here," Robertson said with confidence. "Her shoes are casual wear but not suitable for fell-walking. The soles show no evidence of vegetation or detritus collecting in the treads. The weather's been fine the past couple of days but was wet prior to that. We're standing in a natural bowl which helps the ground here retain water aided by the height of the trees shielding it from the sun. That's why the build-up of moss and fern is so concentrated." Caslin took in the area, Robertson was right. "She was either carried or didn't have far to walk before she wound up there," he pointed to where the body lay.

"Any joy with a vehicle?" Hunter asked.

Robertson shook his head. "No tracks or impressions left on the verges."

"Maybe we'll get lucky with a witness," Caslin offered. "Who found her?"

"Local farmer. He saw a plume of smoke rising through the trees out in one of his fields a couple of days ago."

"Monday?" Caslin asked.

"Aye, mid-morning, I believe. Didn't think much of it at the time but remembered today. On his way home thought he'd check it out seeing as he was passing. I'll bet now he wishes he hadn't."

"Okay. We're going to need to speak to him. Hunter," Caslin indicated she should do that. A suggestion she was only too pleased to take up. "Iain, do you have a cause of death?"

"Are you asking if she was burned in order to kill her or to cover up how she died?"

Caslin nodded, "Could've been both."

"I can't tell you is the honest answer. You see these lacerations here on the arms and again here?" he pointed to three distinct locations on her abdomen where her arms attached to her shoulders and one localised on the stomach. Caslin nodded. "They could be inflicted with a blade but, equally, intense heat can cause ruptures in the tissue where the arms meet."

"And the stomach?" Caslin asked.

"Gas expansion within the stomach can have the same effect and rupture the abdominal wall. However, I don't see any other obvious signs of trauma to the body. Without an autopsy it'd be pure speculation. I'm afraid you'll have to wait for the brilliant Dr Taylor's view on these things. How are the two of you getting on these days anyway?"

Caslin shook his head. "Not really the time or place, Iain."

Robertson chuckled. "Is it ever?"

Caslin smiled but didn't answer the question. Dispatching a uniformed constable to locate Jimmy Sullivan, Caslin, conscious of the time of day spent the remainder of the time walking the immediate area with Hunter. A detailed forensic sweep would take place at first light on Thursday but they wanted to see if anything had been dropped nearby by victim, perpetrator or anyone else. A frustrating hour passed as they found nothing of note.

Portable lights, rigged to a generator, fired up in the background illuminating the scene. Darkness was now descending upon them as the sun fell below the backdrop of the hill line. The dense woodland surrounding them brought on the gloom rapidly. Caslin thought about the isolation of this place. There was little risk of exposure. A sparsely populated rural area with infrequent through traffic. If there was a good way with which to depart from this world the fate of this poor soul was certainly not it. His thoughts turned to Jimmy Sullivan. They needed an identification and the facts were too coincidental to be ignored. He wasn't looking forward to his friend's arrival for Caslin was confident that they'd found his goddaughter, Emily Coughlan.

Taking out his phone, he saw there was no signal and headed back to the road. Once clear of the trees, he found two bars and immediately called Kim Hardy.

"How did you get on with Father Callum Foley?" he asked.

"He's not known to us, sir. He's been resident here for the last eight years since his arrival from the Republic of Ireland following appointment to the pastoral team of St. Hilda's Church, on High Petergate—"

"Cross reference where he lives and works with the known movements of Coughlan would you?"

"It is her then, out there with you?"

"We still don't know but it's likely. While you're at it, I want to know where she's been staying during her time in York. Draw a perimeter in the city where her mobile got the most hits on the tower network. Probably we'll find her at one of the hotels within it. I'm heading back soon, so you have an hour." A uniformed constable caught his attention and Caslin hung up on Hardy.

"He's here, sir."

Caslin went with the officer back to the cordon. Jimmy Sullivan stood waiting for him, hands thrust deep into the pockets of his overcoat. The flickering lights from the roof of the nearby police car highlighted his stone-faced appearance. He knew why he was there and was bracing himself for the worst.

"Jimmy," Caslin called out, approaching. Coming to stand before him, he lowered his voice so only they could be heard. "I know this is unorthodox but... are you sure you're up for this?"

Sullivan met his eye and nodded, "I'll be all right."

"Thanks for coming," Caslin said, lifting the tape and ushering him under it. "I'm sorry to put you through this. You know I wouldn't if there was any oth—"

"Let's get it done, yeah," Sullivan said with resignation. Although an unusual method for an identification, Caslin knew time was precious. The witness gave them a timeline for how long she'd been there and the first forty-eight hours were critical. Caslin assessed their killer already had more than that for a head start. Although you can cover a lot of ground in that time there was a chance he might still be close.

Caslin walked them down a freshly marked trail, drawn out by Robertson's CSI team, and into the clearing. Under portable halogens the crime scene bore an even more macabre appearance than previously. Sullivan tensed, visible even in the unearthly mixture of nightfall and artificial light. He stopped momentarily. Caslin encouraged him forward and they came to stand alongside

Iain Robertson. Recoiling from the scene, Sullivan lifted the back of his hand up and across his mouth suppressing a reflex.

"You okay?" Caslin asked, placing a comforting hand on his friend's shoulder. Sullivan closed his eyes, steadying himself. Casting a sideways glance at Caslin, he took a deep breath and nodded. Thankfully, a light breeze carried past them diminishing the intensity of the odour somewhat as they got closer. That was a small blessing against the backdrop of such a traumatic experience even for the trained officers, let alone for someone tied to the deceased. Two members of Robertson's team waited off to the left, ephemeral in their white coveralls. Sullivan stared at the body, his expression unreadable.

"Are there any distinguishing marks that might help?" Caslin asked softly, anticipating Sullivan's inability to recognise her from the front.

"She has a Celtic symbol tattooed on the back of her neck," Sullivan said, remaining transfixed. Caslin looked to Robertson who moved closer, beckoning his team to join him. Between them, they carefully levered the body onto its side exposing the rear. Robertson knelt, reached out and brushed the shock of auburn hair aside with his free hand. The action revealed a tattoo. Sullivan, guided forward by Caslin, gasped almost inaudibly and only then did he allow his head to drop. Turning away from the vision of horror in front of him, he glanced at Caslin. A simple bob of the head was enough. Caslin gripped his arm in a further show of support and inclined his head to indicate they could step away.

Neither man spoke until well beyond the clearing. Back in the blue hue of the police car's lights, Sullivan was close to tears.

"I need to know everything you do about what Emily was looking into, Jimmy," Caslin said. Sullivan shook his head, casting his eyes to the ground.

"I told you the other night. She wouldn't say," Sullivan said quietly, shaking his head. Reading Caslin's reaction as one of doubt, he emphasised his answer. "I swear. I don't know!"

"And you don't know where she was staying either?

Again, Sullivan shook his head. "I didn't even know she was coming over. I met her at a moment's notice one evening. She said she was at her hotel, so it must have been nearby in the city."

"Don't worry, Jimmy. We'll figure it out," Caslin reassured him, glancing back in the direction of the clearing where Emily met her death, a sense of determination rising within him. "I'll get to the bottom of it. I give you my word."

CHAPTER SIX

THE ORDINANCE SURVEY map was pinned to the noticeboard. A circle, marked in red, was drawn upon it. Alongside was an annotated list naming all the hotels within. There were well over fifty residences. Several were struck through. Caslin cast a wary eye over the details.

"Make sure you go with her description and not only the name," Caslin said loudly enough to be heard over the ambient noise level. "I want to know where Emily Coughlan's been since she arrived in York. I don't want assumptions. Best guess, whatever she was investigating got her killed. To figure that out we need to know where she's been, who has she been talking to? I want to know what car she drives, what she spends her money on."

The room was a hive of activity. Since Fairchild was murdered they'd worked almost around the clock for two days and now they had Emily Coughlan. Caslin felt proud. Not one member of the team was asking to leave, all were determined to get a result. So focussed was he on the information board, rapidly being updated, that he almost missed the phone ringing in his office. Running through to it, he answered before the caller rang off. It was Alison Taylor.

"I wasn't expecting to hear from you this soon," Caslin said, noting the clock passing 9 p.m. as he spoke.

"No, I've not really started yet," she said, "but I thought you'd want to know."

"What have you found?"

"Iain Robertson gave me a heads up on his thoughts but he hadn't mentioned the fingernails."

"Go on."

"In an enclosed space with intense heat and prolonged exposure they'd be consumed along with the rest of the body. Fingernails are basically keratin, the same as your hair, although obviously thicker. In this instance the outcome of the fire would cause dehydration and render them crispy but nevertheless intact."

"Your point?"

"They're missing," Dr Taylor replied. "The soft tissue of the extremities is badly damaged so I can't be sure when this occurred—"

"I'm presuming you're willing to hazard an educated guess?"

"Based on what's been done to her, conceivably we're looking at signs of torture. I'll be able to confirm it once I'm done here."

"You're staying on tonight?"

"You asked for a swift turnaround."

"Thanks, Alison," Caslin said. "Listen… about earlier—"

"Got to go. Busy," she said, hanging up. Caslin swore under his breath. Returning to the squad room, he processed what the pathologist had told him. If she was right they were in a race against time. Whatever information the killer was trying to elicit from her the chances were he was already acting upon it.

"I have a hit, sir," Holt shouted. "A woman matching Coughlan's description checked in on Friday, left the hotel Sunday afternoon and hasn't returned."

"Let's get over there, Terry."

THE LORD PERCY INN was largely a pub and restaurant affair, with letting rooms above. Set within the Shambles, at the heart of York's medieval quarter, it was a mere stone's throw from both the Minster and Caslin's apartment in Kleiser's Court. They were met at reception by the owner, Thomas Lennon, who was keen to understand how the police had been brought to his door. Ushering them out of earshot of the guest lounge, he took them past reception towards the inner lobby.

"How sure are you this is your guest?" Caslin asked.

"Oh, I'm pretty sure, despite her registering under a different name than the one you enquired about."

"What name did she give?"

"Sylvia Marshall," Lennon confirmed.

"Did you see identification?"

"Absolutely, it's policy. She had a passport."

"Did you take a copy?"

"No, I didn't think that was required."

"But it was definitely her, in the photo I mean?" Caslin pressed.

Lennon nodded. "I believe so, yes. Interesting young lady. From Northern Ireland, I understand."

"She talked to you about her home?" Holt asked.

Lennon shook his head. "No. It said so on her passport. She made quite an impression on us, I must say."

"How so?"

"Don't get me wrong, she was polite enough but not particularly communicative. Most of our guests pick our brains about where to eat, what to see and do during their visit but not her. Fussy, too."

"Fussy?" Holt asked.

"Yes, fussy. She was only here for a night before requesting a room change."

"Unusual?" Caslin asked.

"No, not in itself but to ask the following night to move again was a little frustrating. Bear in mind we only have six guest rooms and you'll understand the inconvenience."

"What reasons did she give?" Caslin asked.

"The first time, she said she didn't want to be at the front of the building, too noisy. She didn't offer a reason for the second and I must admit, I didn't ask. As I say, she was a nice girl so you make allowances, don't you?"

"Can we see her room?"

Lennon took them up two flights of stairs into the eaves of the building. There were two rooms located there and he led them to the one on the left. Taking out a set of keys, Caslin held up his hand. "If you don't mind?" he asked.

"Not at all," the man said, passing Caslin the set.

"You haven't gone for a modern, keyless system?"

"Our guests stay here for the period authenticity," he said, before adding, "provided they have an en-suite." Caslin glanced to Holt, who frowned. They were nowhere with the key-card.

"And no-one has been in here since she left?" Holt asked.

"No. She was quite insistent that she didn't want house-keeping unless requested."

"Did that strike you as odd?" Caslin asked.

Lennon shrugged. "Believe me, some of the requests we get are bizarre. That wasn't odd at all."

Caslin asked him to step away as he unlocked the room. Donning a pair of latex gloves, Caslin eased the door open. Holt entered first, flicking on the switch to the main light. The room was high in quality but low on space. Scanning the room there was a double bed, desk and chair, set alongside a large wardrobe. Upon inspection they found the latter still had clothes hanging within. The bedding was dishevelled with a hairdryer lying atop the sheets. Caslin pushed open the bathroom door, pulling the cord and turning on the light. The extractor fan started up, whirring in the background as Caslin scanned the interior. Toiletries were spread around and the overall impression left was that of a young woman preparing herself for the day ahead.

"Anything?" Caslin asked, returning to the bedroom and sliding the desk drawer out revealing a handful of tourist information guides.

Holt shook his head. "I've got nothing. No sign of a phone or laptop. Not even a paper pad."

"It looks like she was expecting to return," Caslin said, casting an eye around at her belongings. "She was tortured for something." He was disappointed.

"Maybe it was for something she knew rather than something she had?" suggested Holt.

Perching himself on the end of the bed, Caslin folded his arms and tried to imagine where he might put something that he didn't want others to find. All the while he tried to avoid the thought that either Holt was right or they were too late and the killer had already sanitised the room. Glancing to his left, back out onto the landing, Thomas Lennon waited patiently. He was itching to know what was going on. Caslin's focus moved beyond the proprietor to an occasional table opposite the stairs.

"Mr Lennon," he called, "is that a router?"

Lennon glanced behind him. "No. It's a booster. It's connected to the router on the floor below. We find the signal weakens too much due to the thickness of the walls. The rooms on the higher floors require their own connection."

"Terry, do you—"

"Leave it with me," Holt interrupted him as he reached the same conclusion.

TWENTY MINUTES later Holt returned with a tablet in hand. He was smiling and Caslin assumed the idea had borne fruit.

"There are two devices connected to this router at the moment, sir. We've managed to eliminate the other guest rooms. Only two are occupied and they are connected via a separate connection on the ground floor," Holt explained. "Take away Mr Lennon's computer and we have another that's unaccounted for. It's reasonable to assume it's here in this room."

"Let's find it," Caslin said, beginning the search all over again. Only this time they weren't looking for the obvious. Holt closely examined the furniture looking for loose panels or concealed spaces that could contain something small, a phone or tablet. He then moved to the carpets checking to see if they had been lifted giving access to the floorboards beneath.

Caslin disconnected the side panel to the bath. Illuminating the underside with a torch, he saw nothing. The floorboards here were exposed but securely fixed in place. Looking around, he noted the ceilings and walls were enclosed giving no access to a loft space or the eaves. Kneeling on the tiled floor, he sought inspiration. Holt appeared from the bedroom an air of resignation shrouding him.

"Nothing," he said flatly. Caslin sighed, leaning his shoulder against the wall. In his eyeline was the bathroom extractor fan. He stood up and crossed the room. Eyeing it suspiciously, he calculated it was barely fifteen centimetres in width. The extraction tube beyond, to vent moisture outside, would be even less than that.

Drawing the shower curtain away from the bathtub, Caslin stepped in observed by the watchful DC. Indicating for Holt to turn off the light, thereby cutting power to the extractor as they were on the same circuit, Caslin took out his pocket torch. Passing it over to Holt, the beam was concentrated on the extractor as they stood in the darkness. Caslin felt around the wall unit and realised it wasn't fixed to the wall. Easing the casing off, Caslin pulled the fan out as far as the power cable would allow. Holding the sealed unit in one hand he blindly reached into the ventilation tube with the other. His eyes lit up as his fingers curled around a small block of tightly wrapped plastic. Retrieving the package, sealed with tape, Caslin passed it down to Holt before replacing the extractor unit and stepping from the bath.

Returning to the light of the bedroom, Holt sliced through the tape with a pocketknife and unfurled what turned out to be an airtight, zip-up plastic bag.

"She's got a second mobile," he said, taking out a smartphone and showing it to Caslin.

"I wonder why she felt the need to," Caslin said aloud. Holt glanced at him.

"The other wasn't registered. Perhaps she decided to use a burner whilst in the UK?"

Caslin appeared thoughtful. "Only reason to do that is if you're concerned about someone tracking you." Holt examined the remaining contents of the bag pulling out a small notebook and offering a wry smile.

"Modern tech alongside old school," he said, passing it to Caslin. The latter could barely contain his enthusiasm as he leafed through the pages of content contained within. The optimism however, quickly faded. The notes appeared to be written in some manner of code. Flicking through to the final entry, he read the last line in the series aloud.

"M22-24D, M24DM, M25Y RF," he said, glancing over and acknowledging Holt's blank expression.

"What on earth does all that mean?"

"I've no idea but there are pages of similar entries. It has to mean something," Caslin said softly, scanning back through the pad. "Any joy with the phone?"

"Password protected, sir," Holt confirmed, having brought it out of hibernation.

"Can you crack it?" Caslin asked expectantly.

"Anything can be cracked, sir," Holt replied, with a grin. "Well, almost anything. It'll depend on the level of encryption and even once we're in, if she uses encryption software for her communications we could be stuffed."

"That's positive thinking, Terry."

"I need to get it back to Fulford Road."

CHAPTER SEVEN

EYEING A BREAK IN THE TRAFFIC, Caslin trotted across the road raising a hand in appreciation to the one driver slowing in order to avoid him. Rain was falling this morning. A marked contrast to the previous few days. Taking refuge in the vestibule of the Gothic Revival inspired St Hilda's Catholic Church, Caslin shook his sodden coat free of water.

"Quite the morning, isn't it?" a voice spoke to him, echoing in the vast space of the nave. Caslin turned to look through the open door to see who was addressing him. His eyes fell on an approaching priest greeting him with a smile.

"It is that," he replied. "I'm looking for Father Foley. Is he around?"

"I certainly am," the priest replied, encouraging him to enter. "As you can see the rain is keeping the visitors at bay. How may I help you?"

Caslin withdrew his warrant card. "DI Caslin, from Fulford Road. I'd like to ask you a few questions if you don't mind?"

"Not at all, Inspector. Whatever can I do for you?" he said, inclining his head and, with an open palm, encouraged Caslin to accompany him.

"Just routine, Father," Caslin replied, as the two men walked into the nave. The church was almost empty, two figures standing within the eastern transept were the only others present. Upon reaching the crossover the priest suggested they take a pew. Sitting down, Caslin glanced into the chancel. Open mouthed, he admired the majesty of the painted depictions of Christ hanging beyond the altar.

"It has been some time since you revisited your faith, is it not?" Father Foley asked.

Caslin broke his gaze offering the priest a wry smile. "Is it that obvious?"

"I have served my faith for nearly four decades, Inspector. Experience teaches you much in life. How to read others is one of those skills paramount to my role. May I ask why have you lapsed?"

Caslin's smile broadened as he shook his head, looking away. "I left school a long time ago. Probably a conversation for another day, Father," Caslin said, shifting the focus of his thoughts to the reason he was there. "I would like to ask you about some visitors you may have had. It would've been last week, maybe Thursday or Friday. Young ladies, perhaps only one."

Father Foley's expression didn't change in the least. "I may need a little more than that, Inspector," he said with a smile.

"Of course," Caslin accepted. "In her twenties. A compatriot of yours, I understand you are originally from Northern Ireland, is that right?"

"I am, yes. Although, I've not lived there for many years. I used to live in the Republic more recently, County Kerry, prior to moving here. Now, who was it you are enquiring after?"

"Her name was Sylvia—"

"Marshall," Foley finished for him. "Yes, I remember her. It was last Thursday evening, I believe."

"You're sure?"

"I recall the weather was far better than it is today," he pointed towards the water dripping from Caslin's coat onto the pew.

"She came to see you?"

Foley shook his head, "No, no, not that I am aware. She was seated not far from us now, very much lost in thought. I spoke with her, she appeared somewhat troubled."

Caslin was intrigued. "Regarding what?"

"I am sure a good Catholic boy, such as yourself, can understand I cannot break the covenant of the confessional, Inspector."

"Is that why she was here, to take confession?"

"It is not unusual for someone, far from their home, to seek the familial comfort that our church provides," Foley said, bringing himself upright. "Anyone travelling, tourists or businessmen alike, can experience loneliness." Caslin gazed across towards the altar, his eyes travelling up past the ornately carved stone of the windows and on towards the vaulted ceiling far above. The architecture was truly stunning. It was often argued locally that from distance, and a certain direction of approach, the tower of St Hilda's appeared to eclipse even York Minster in its grandeur.

"Would the fact that she is dead change your stance at all?" Caslin asked, lowering his eyes back to the priest. The revelation appeared to throw him if only for a moment. If Foley was aware of her death, he buried it well.

"That is dispiriting to hear," Foley said. "What has taken one so young from us?"

"Murder. In the most horrendous manner imaginable," Caslin said quietly, leaving the words hanging without offering more detail.

"There is great evil in this world, Inspector, and far fewer choosing to take up the fight every day."

"Some of us might disagree with that statement. You believe in the inherent good of mankind surely?" Caslin countered.

"I do, very much," Foley agreed. "And far be it from me to pour scorn on your profession, Inspector. However, I see God's work is far from complete. We are routinely tested and, I fear, often we fail those tests. Sometimes I consider that may be part of the plan. As a society we are becoming obsessed with the accumulation of material goods and losing sight of what is truly important."

"I can't disagree with you there. What *can* you tell me about Sylvia?"

"Not very much, I'm afraid. We had a discussion around faith. Much like you, her faith had slipped in recent years. Apparently, events were conspiring to make her re-evaluate this."

"Events?" Caslin asked.

"Regrettably, I can say no more, Inspector."

"You'll appreciate that she is dead. Murdered."

"I do," Foley said apologetically, lowering his head, "and that changes nothing. All that we discussed will remain between the two of us and our Heavenly Father. Thinking on it, though, I can see no relevance to what she told me."

"With respect, Father. I'm the detective. Perhaps the supposition is best left to me?" Foley acknowledged the point with an apologetic flick of the hand. Caslin continued, "It is our understanding she came here specifically in order to speak with you."

"So, you say. If true, that certainly comes as news to me, Inspector," Foley frowned. "She was here. She took confession and left. Although, thinking on it, she did receive a telephone call as we were bidding farewell."

"Do you know who from?"

Foley shook his head. "No, I'm afraid not. She appeared agitated though. That was very clear. Perhaps this information is of some use to you?" Caslin took one of his contact cards from his wallet, passing it across to the priest who accepted it graciously. "What about the other one?"

Caslin looked at him. "The other one?"

"Yes, you mentioned there may have been more than one visitor. Who was the other one?"

Caslin shook his head. "I was merely being thorough. Sylvia was the one we knew had been to visit you. She came alone?"

"She did," Foley confirmed.

"Just in case anything comes to mind that I might be interested in. You can reach me on that number," Caslin said, standing up.

"I still have half-an-hour before I lock up, Inspector. You and I could always discuss your faith—"

"Or my lack of?" Caslin countered.

"We all encounter moments of struggle. It is how we face them that demonstrates character. The door here is always open, no matter how long since your last visit."

"Another time, Father. Another time."

Caslin deposited a ten-pound note into the donation box as he passed through the vestibule and emerged onto Duncombe Place. Turning the collar of his coat up against the rain he made the short walk before taking the left onto High Petergate. Hunter was waiting for him. He got into the passenger side of the car.

"Well?" she asked expectantly as he wiped the rain from his face.

"If I didn't know better I'd say he was as pure as the driven snow."

"You think he's withholding?"

Caslin sucked air through his teeth. "Definitely. He genuinely seemed surprised Coughlan was dead but..."

"Did he offer us anything?"

"The sanctity of the confessional," Caslin said, shaking his head. "Coughlan wanted information on him we know that. She approached him under the Marshall pseudonym or at least that was the name Foley referred to her by. I wasn't going to drop her actual name unless I had to. It's possible she came here under a pretence and Foley's genuinely unaware of her interest in him."

"We need to find out what she knew—"

"Or thought she knew," Caslin added. That was their problem. They didn't know very much at all.

"Could he have killed her?"

Caslin's brow furrowed. "He's in his seventies. She is fifty years his junior. Could he? Yes, it's possible. Coughlan could've walked herself into that clearing. If she was already dead then I'm not so sure. He's not exactly an aging powerhouse."

"A strange way to live your life if you're into torturing young women," Hunter said denoting her scepticism. She had a point but that didn't rule him out. "What do you want us to do about Foley?"

"Let's try and dig up whatever Coughlan's investigation uncovered. I also want to find out who Sylvia Marshall is. If Coughlan has travelled on the passport then she's real. She might know something. Check with the Border Force and see what name she entered the UK under. In the meantime, we'll put someone on Foley. Kim Hardy can make a start."

Hunter exhaled deeply. "With the Fairchild case we're thin on the ground, sir."

"Better have a word with the DCI about seconding someone from uniform then."

Hunter laughed, turning the key in the ignition. Caslin cast an eye back towards the church as they set off to Fulford Road, his boyhood memories returning in flashes. The Benedictine monks and how they attempted to shape their charges couldn't seem less relevant to him now than ever.

It was 9:30 a.m. on Thursday. Emily Coughlan had been dead for three days and he was no closer to understanding why.

"TERRY," Caslin called, entering CID, "give me something on Coughlan's phone."

"It's down with tech and they're working on it. We can't bypass the security and the manufacturers are not playing ball."

"How do you mean?" Caslin asked.

"They're arguing the case for privacy."

"What privacy? Coughlan's dead."

"To help us crack the security would set a precedent."

"Bloody hell. Have they any idea what..." Caslin let the thought drop away.

"They'll keep pushing, sir but they're optimistic—"

"Optimism doesn't solve murders. Tell them to get a move on."

"I'll chase them up, sir. However, I do have this," he said, pointing to his screen. "CCTV from the lobby of the Lord Percy."

Caslin was intrigued. "That was fast."

"Lennon's worried about the business' reputation. What with rapidly approaching the end of the summer season, he doesn't want next year's bookings to be hit by some kind of stigma. He's falling over himself to be helpful."

"What am I looking at?" Caslin said, coming to stand over Holt's shoulder.

The camera angle was from an elevated position behind the reception desk, located at the midway point of the building. The entrance from the street served the lounge bar and restaurant to the left and right respectively. The camera gave a shot of the hallway in the foreground through to the main entrance and beyond. Holt moved the pointer forward. The desk was unmanned and no one was present. Holt pressed play and a figure crossed the entrance from left to right slowing as he went by before stopping. He wore a dark baseball cap, tee-shirt and jeans. Assessing him, Caslin put him in the age range of thirty to forty with an athletic build. The man glanced towards the interior of the bar but didn't enter. Casually appearing to observe the surroundings, he loitered for a minute or so before disappearing from view.

"Now, watch this, sir," Holt said, moving the footage on. Figures came and went. Judging by the time stamp it was forty minutes later when Emily Coughlan walked into reception. Leaving her room key on the desk she headed for the street before hovering at the entrance.

"Looks like she's waiting for something," Caslin offered.

"Or someone," Hunter added, appearing alongside.

"Funny you should say that," Holt replied, pointing at the corner of the image. A man came into shot at the doorway. The same man recorded earlier. The two seemingly faced off, roughly two metres separating them but the image was black and white, grainy and generally of poor quality.

"Are they talking?" Caslin said, frustration edging his tone.

"Can't tell," Hunter replied. The man stepped out of view again and within seconds, Coughlan left the building, walking in the same direction.

"They looked like they knew each other to me," Caslin stated. "It would make sense for her to hide her phone and notes if she was meeting someone she didn't trust. Otherwise she would have kept them with her. Her phone at the very least. Terry, any chance you can clean that up?"

Holt was noncommittal. "That's going to be tough, sir. Most CCTV systems worth their salt these days operate on a minimum of thirty frames per second. This one is only five. The problem I'm going to have is when I sharpen the image all I'm going to do is amplify the distortion."

"You mean it'll get worse not better?"

"Exactly," Holt confirmed.

"What about other cameras?" Hunter asked.

"Already on it. The Lord Percy doesn't have any others, unsurprisingly, seeing as this one is rubbish," Holt stated as a matter of fact. "However, this is the Shambles. A lot of shops, pubs and restaurants. I reckon we could get some joy but it'll take time to gather the footage."

"Time we do not have, Terry," Caslin said. "Get on with it. That could be the only picture we have of our killer."

"Hardy brought me up to speed on Father Foley, sir," Hunter said, as the two retreated to his office.

"What did she find out?"

"Not a great deal. He hasn't come up in any investigation we are aware of. What he told you tallies with our records. He lived in Northern Ireland before being transferred to the Republic and then on to St Hilda's nine years ago."

"Who arranged the transfer?"

"We're not sure as yet who initiated the move. However, it was arranged through the Diocese of Middlesbrough. I could chase them up tomorrow although doing so might—"

"Tip our hand," Caslin stated. "What about before, in Northern Ireland?"

"No mentions with the PSNI, sir," Hunter confirmed. Caslin slumped into his chair. Retrieving the evidence bag containing Coughlan's notepad from his desk drawer, he emptied it onto the table.

"To recap, all that we have is a mobile phone and these pages of code?" he thought aloud, flipping through the pad as he had done several times already that day. "I'm going back to Jimmy Sullivan. If he didn't know what Coughlan was working on maybe he knows who she was working for?"

"What about Fairchild?" Hunter asked. "Broadfoot will want movement by the morning briefing."

"Chase up the forensic accountants. We need them on board. They're our best shot seeing as Iain Robertson and his team have given us precious little to go on. Terry Holt is pretty good with tracking of finances. Get him on it until resources become available. How did we get on with door to door?"

"No one saw or heard anything, sir. The entrances to those houses are some way up off the street with little footfall on the path below. As you thought the gunman used a suppressor. It's looking more like a professional each time I assess it."

"We only need a thread to pull on and it'll all come apart," Caslin said thoughtfully.

"Yes, sir," Hunter replied, leaving the room. Caslin refocussed on the notepad.

"What were you up to, Ms Coughlan?" he asked himself quietly gently scanning through the combinations. The coded notepad was proving troublesome. Forwarding a copy to the National Crime Agency, he was hopeful their cryptographers would come up with something but it was a shot in the dark. Even the simplest of codes, tying numbers to pages and letters using a given novel as a key, were uncrackable without the key itself. It was simple Cold War practice but very effective.

The sequences were entered over a period of days, weeks or even months. Slight variations in the handwriting indicated entries on the move and changing ink colours suggested different pens and therefore, most likely, different times. Caslin theorised this was a journal of some kind kept over a significant period, the code recording the passage of events either destinations or meetings that took place during those times. The detail of what Coughlan was doing however, escaped him. Picking up his mobile, Caslin dialled Sullivan. The journalist answered on the third ring.

"Pint?" Caslin asked.

"Way ahead of you," Sullivan replied.

CASLIN FOUND Sullivan in Lendal Cellars absently dropping coins into a fruit machine. He took a full glass from a table alongside him passing it to Caslin before they even greeted one another.

"And don't give me any bull about being dry," Sullivan muttered, as his latest play swallowed yet another pound. "I'll not tell your sponsor." Caslin ignored the remark, accepting the drink.

"Good health," Caslin offered, taking a mouthful.

"Bollocks," Sullivan said, abandoning the machine. "Let's sit down."

The journalist was steady on his feet but, evidently, he had been going at it for a while. He brought two whisky chasers with him to the booth. Pushing one out to Caslin, he drained the other in a single, fluid motion, slamming the glass down once he'd done so.

"I would say to take it easy but I'm the last person to judge," Caslin said quietly, following suit with his scotch. Placing the glass down, he gritted his teeth as the spirit bit through. It had been a while.

"They still piss-testing you?" Sullivan asked.

"Aye," Caslin confirmed, "but not for the booze."

"They've not sucked all the life out of you then?"

Caslin smiled. "I need to know who Emily was working for, Jimmy."

"No luck there, Nate. She was strictly freelance on this one," Sullivan stated.

Caslin thought on it. "I need something to go on. You've been asking around?"

"Yeah. I've been digging in the old country," he said, referencing his roots. "Emily was rattling some cages over there. Tenacious, that one. Just like Bernadette, her mother."

"Her mother?"

"She was a union rep," Sullivan said. "Died some years ago, car crash, on her morning commute to the factory."

"So, whose particular cage was Emily rattling?"

"I'm still working on that. Although, the word is she was making contacts with those in and around the Provos," Sullivan said. "Worrying really, with it being a little off her usual patch."

"The *Provos*," Caslin was taken aback. "The Provisional IRA? What business could she have with them?"

"That's what I'm trying to find out. Let's face it the list of things she could've been writing a story about go on and on. Historic terrorism isn't really her thing, though, you know? Street-level drug-dealing or bribing local officials is probably closer to it."

"Doesn't explain what brought her to York."

"No, it certainly doesn't."

"Can you narrow it down?"

Sullivan scoffed. "You're the policeman."

"They're far more likely to talk to you than me," Caslin countered.

"On that, you have a point. Leave it with me," Sullivan replied, draining the remainder of his pint and pushing the glass across to the centre of the table and pointing at it. "Your round."

CHAPTER EIGHT

"THE BURNS WERE ANTEMORTEM, WITHOUT DOUBT," Dr Taylor stated.

"She was alive when she was set on fire. You're certain?" Caslin sought confirmation.

"The presence of smoke particles in her lungs along with the high concentration of carbon monoxide in her blood confirm it. Whether she was conscious or not, I can't say. However," Dr Taylor ushered him around to the other side of the mortuary slab, tilting the overhanging light to aid the inspection, "see this bruise covering the base of the lower skull and upper neck?"

Caslin looked. "Untouched by the flames."

Dr Taylor nodded her agreement, "Judging by the colouration it had time to manifest itself before death."

"How much time?"

"Two to three hours," she confirmed. "It isn't an exact science, more of a considered opinion. The blow would have been enough to render her unconscious."

"The fingers?" Caslin asked, looking towards her extremities still coiled like a pugilist.

"Forced extraction is still my best guess," she said flatly. "If the nails had been surgically removed for a given reason the nail matrix would have remained but I see no evidence of that. Like-

wise, if the damage was present longer, I'd anticipate the forma-
tion of a pterygium, or wing of tissue, growing over the proximal
nail fold. Although I concede it would be harder to spot due to the
extent of the damage to the surrounding tissue. I don't see one."

"Anything else?"

"Her left knee-cap was broken. Caused by the impact of a
blunt object rather than heat fractures. The damage is substantial."

"Could she have walked into that clearing?"

"That depends on when the break occurred. Prior to going
there, no. At least not without assistance," Dr Taylor assured him.
Caslin pictured the scene in his mind's eye, recoiling from it.
Emily Coughlan's last moments in this world were filled with
immense pain and suffering. "She was tortured to death, Nate."

Caslin looked up at her. "Yes. I know."

"It takes a person with a particular psychology to do this kind
of thing. Devoid of empathy, a sociopathic tendency and above
all, determination."

"Determination?" Caslin asked.

"None of this was quick, Nate," she explained. "Extracting
fingernails alone is relatively time consuming. The level of
commitment required to carry this out shouldn't be underes-
timated."

"Perhaps he enjoyed it?"

"Always a possibility but think of the location, quiet, out of the
way. The killer knew it would take a while, make a lot of noise
and ultimately needed the seclusion afforded him by the woods. I
might also suggest the method of execution was as much to terrify
as it was to consume evidence."

"You think this was more borne out of pragmatism than enter-
tainment?"

Dr Taylor nodded. "The lack of any indications towards sexual
assault push me that way. Motivating factors are often rooted in
power as you know. The physical and mental domination of
another fit this scenario but there's more to it. That this happened
where it did, the fact the petrol was brought with them. This

wasn't spontaneous, it was well planned. He knew what he was doing."

"A professional?"

"Very much so," she confirmed. "Regarding inspiration or motivation, we'll not only look at a killer's actions but also consider what was done that they didn't need to do. In this case, being doused in petrol is likely to be of equal encouragement to the actual, physical torture."

"Brutality will only get you so far?"

"Exactly. The fear of burning alive would be motivation in itself."

"You believe setting fire to her wasn't necessary?" Caslin asked.

"Possibly not. After all, there are far easier, cleaner and… quieter ways of murdering someone. I don't think this should be seen as a message to others either."

"Because the location was so isolated?" Caslin clarified.

"Yes. If he wanted to terrify others or announce his presence to the world the choice of location would've been far more public. I see the petrol as a means to an end rather than the end itself."

"A good way to hamper identification, though," Caslin countered.

Dr Taylor inclined her head in agreement. "I can't argue with that. However, she's a foreign national. Were it not for your tip, we would've struggled in any event."

"Without the tip she may have been unknown forever. The killer most likely knew her or, at least, of her," Caslin said, acknowledging her thought process. "However, there will always be a trail that links the two of them. The time it takes to uncover it puts more distance between him and her. Each and every person in between becomes a suspect before he does. The most pressing question for me is did he get what he was after from her?"

Caslin made his way back to the car deep in thought. The prospect of having two killers executing contracts simultaneously in York was troubling. The notion was statistically unlikely and nor was it corroborated by any of the evidence at hand. If both Iain Robertson and Dr Taylor were right however, then he had a far larger problem.

"WE'VE DRAWN the best image we could from the CCTV at the Lord Percy but it's not going to help us, sir," Hunter said, cutting a frustrated figure back in the squad room of Fulford Road. "The quality is poor. A white man, most likely under fifty, in a baseball cap is about it. However, I've got an idea but we'll have to go over to see someone at York University."

"I'm all ears," Caslin replied.

"Sir," Terry Holt called out to get his attention above the throng.

"What is it, Terry?" Caslin asked, seeing Holt with a handset resting against his chest.

"You've got a visitor down in reception, sir."

"All right. Sarah," he turned to Hunter, "bring the car around and I'll meet you out front as soon as I can."

Descending the stairs with the specific intention of getting rid of whoever wanted him as quickly as was politely possible, Caslin entered reception. Linda was on the desk as usual and pointed out a smartly dressed man, seated on a bench near to the main entrance. Not often was Caslin lost for words but the face waiting to greet him had exactly that effect.

"Well, I'll be damned," he eventually managed to say being utterly thrown.

"It's been a long time, Nate," the man grinned as they warmly embraced. Stepping back, standing at arm's length, the newcomer took in his old friend. "I'd say the years have been good to you but... I'd be stretching the truth." Caslin brushed the comment aside choosing not to respond in kind. Disappointingly, he couldn't say similar. The man before him was in far better shape. Standing slightly over six-feet in height and evidently taking care of himself physically, the imposing form of his old friend made Caslin feel a shadow of his former, youthful self. Aiden Reece still carried the charisma and gravitas that made him the man everyone wanted to know, if not, to be. His hair was close cut, jet-black, just as Caslin remembered and, unlike his own, bore no hint of grey. He hadn't changed a bit.

"What are you doing here?" Caslin asked.

"Business, Nate. I wish it was purely social but..." he glanced around them, "is there somewhere we can talk?"

"Sure, I have a few minutes. Let's take a walk."

The two men headed out of reception and took a short walk around the front of the building. The hum of traffic noise beyond the perimeter wall carried to them. York in summer was never quiet.

"This is probably a daft question but are you still in the service?" Caslin asked. Aiden Reece, sparking a cigarette as they walked, exhaled as he answered.

"It was still the *force* when we signed up," Reece replied.

"To some it always will be."

"Nearly ten years, now," Reece stated, returning the lighter to his pocket. "I don't miss the daily grind. I have to say."

"Daily grind, you?" Caslin laughed. "You specialised the moment we graduated from Hendon. They had you marked early on—"

"They wanted fresh faces. The bright and the bold. Sadly, that wasn't you," Reece grinned. "Happy days, weren't they?"

"What are you up to now?"

"Nothing as socially rewarding. Private sector. Company car, an expense account. Less in the way of paperwork but requiring more justification," he said with a slight hint of sarcasm. "Still, the responsibility is to a balance sheet rather than society."

"Happier?"

"I sleep better," Reece said, this time his tone was serious. "How about you?"

Caslin ignored the question. "So what business brings you to

York?" Reece stopped, took a deep draw on his cigarette and turned to face him. Caslin got a whiff of smoke on the breeze and it smelt sweet.

"Chris Fairchild," Reece stated evenly. Caslin failed to conceal his surprise.

"What's your interest?"

"Fairchild managed accounts on behalf of my employers."

"KL Global contacted you?" Caslin asked, Reece nodded. "Who is it you work for, then?"

"Renton Sands," Reece replied, acknowledging this meant nothing to Caslin. He elaborated, "Security consultancy, for private enterprise. We specialise in mitigating industrial sabotage, corporate hacks, overseas personal-security and the like. That's why I'm here, to see if we have cause to be concerned. Do we?"

"Should you?" Caslin countered. "Any reason to think Fairchild's demise is related to your firm?"

"As I said, that's why they sent me. It's standard protocol. Think what it'd do to our reputation if we, of all companies, were compromised?"

Caslin noted that was a reasonable concern. "Why you?"

"Have to put my hands up there, Nate," Reece said with a smile. "When I saw you were the investigating officer how could I pass up the trip? I flew in this morning and came straight to see you."

"Our history isn't going to curry favour with me, you know that? I won't compromise the integrity of the investigation."

"I wouldn't ask you to," Reece defended himself. "Once we know this has nothing to do with Renton, I'll be out of your hair."

"Not too soon, I hope," Caslin said warmly. "It'd be great to have a proper catch up. Where are you staying?"

"A hotel, in the city centre."

"Listen, I've got to head out somewhere," Caslin said, eyeing Hunter pulling up at the kerbside in front of the station entrance. "Do you need me to get you a ride into town?"

"No, thanks. I have it covered. Meet tonight for a drink?"

Caslin nodded. "If I have the time. You know how it is."

Reece passed him a business card. "Call me later."

They said their farewells and Caslin walked back to the station entrance, indicating for Hunter to wait there for a minute. Taking the stairs two at a time back up to CID, he walked in and collared Terry Holt.

"Check out a security company called *Renton Sands*, would you? They should show up on Fairchild's client list."

"Who are they?"

"Exactly what I want to know," he replied, passing him Aiden Reece's business card, before turning and heading back downstairs to the waiting Hunter.

"WELL, I agree that there is precious little detail in this image," Dr Malcolm Lawton said. "What exactly do you want from me?" Caslin was happy to defer to Hunter. He wasn't convinced and wouldn't seek to explain the idea.

"You study images of deep space here at the university, don't you?"

Dr Lawton nodded. "Yes, we have several courses relating to astrophysics within the faculty." They were meeting with the head of the Physics Department at the University of York in order to explore Hunter's suggestion.

"I understand even the most powerful of telescopes, earth or space-based, present images that require sharpening. I was hoping your software—"

"We don't use a software package, per se, DS Hunter," Dr Lawton interrupted her. "We take multiple images of the same section of space and then layer them on top of each other, one after another. In doing so we can build up the detail and dampen the noise... the distortion of what we see."

"Could you do this with the footage we have here?" Caslin asked, seeking to quell the excitement rising within. Dr Lawton returned his gaze to the frozen footage of the CCTV on the monitor before him. He raised his eyebrows in a thoughtful expression.

"An unusual request for me, Inspector. We can certainly try," he replied. Hunter grinned but the professor moved to curb her enthusiasm. "If you can provide us with more footage from the same camera... and if the angle of view has not been altered in the footage then... we will improve it. I make no promises—"

"That's good enough for us, Doctor," Caslin said cheerfully. "How soon could we get a result?"

"Presumably this is of some importance?"

"Significant, yes," Caslin responded.

"Well, it's the end of the week and fortuitously for you my plans for the weekend have been curtailed by a friend's illness. Bring me more footage today and if we begin straight away..." Dr Lawton said, turning his focus to the screen, "it's a painstaking process but you'll have something usable the day after tomorrow."

"Thank you for giving up your weekend," Hunter said, smiling.

Dr Lawton glanced up at her. "No sacrifice, I assure you. I enjoy a challenge."

CHAPTER NINE

HOLT RAPPED his knuckles on the door alerting Caslin to his presence. He beckoned him in.

"What have you got for me, Terry?"

"I've been working through Fairchild's accounts, personal and professional."

"Give me the headlines of his own first please," asked Caslin.

"On the surface a very successful man with all the trappings to go with it. Scratch below that and it's another story."

"Debts?"

Holt shook his head. "The opposite. Fairchild's sitting on assets worth millions. He has property in Spain, Italy and on the Adriatic coast of Croatia. Not to mention funds registered offshore that I'm still trying to pin down let alone gain access to."

"We knew they had two holiday homes on the continent."

Holt shook his head. "More than that. We're talking entire apartment blocks, high end, beach-front real estate."

"I didn't get the impression the Fairchilds were that wealthy. Inheritance?"

Holt shook his head. "No, we're looking at the archetypal working-class kid made good. His wife also comes from a middle-income family. Now a degree of wealth is expected in his line of work but this… this is exceptional."

"What's the correlation between earnings and assets?"

Holt bobbed his head enthusiastically. "Off the chart, sir. Regarding his work at KL he represents the investments of some serious clientele. Every one of those funds he manages easily hits seven-figures annually and then some."

"I'm aware of that. Anyone particularly stand out for greater scrutiny?"

Holt shook his head. "No-one who would have an axe to grind. Fairchild is good, all of his calls have seen uplifts far in excess of the trend. Not only that, he's managed it every year since he joined the firm. I've never seen anything like it."

"English, Terry," Caslin admonished him.

"This guy is either borrowing Da Vinci's time machine or…"

"He's onto a sure thing?" Caslin finished for him.

"Exactly right. It's a winning streak the likes of which I've never seen before and I've seen some."

"Can we prove it?"

Holt shook his head. "Not so far but I'll keep digging. He's covered himself extremely well. Too well if you ask me. I wouldn't be surprised if he's getting help."

Caslin thought for a moment. "Let's look at it another way then. Which of his accounts benefit the most and who owns them? Then look at what they're investing in. Putting a light on them might explain some of this."

"I'm going to need someone with real knowledge of financial—"

"I'm working on it, Terry."

Further discussion was interrupted by Hunter's arrival. "Sir, we've had a call from Thomas Lennon at the Lord Percy. He says he's had a break in."

Twenty minutes later they were met in the reception of the Lord Percy Inn by a flustered owner. He was pacing the area wringing his hands as he waited.

"You've had a break in?" Hunter asked. "Where?"

"Upstairs. Ms Marshall's room."

Caslin was stunned. "But that's on the top floor."

"I know. Come and see. I'll show you," Lennon stated, ushering them forward. The proprietor babbled details at them as they made their way up three flights of stairs. "No-one has been up there since your investigators left the other day. The top floor has its own fire door on the level below at the base of the stairs and I locked it so no-one could get up there."

The scenes of crime officers had inventoried the room and carried out a full forensic sweep before sealing it off. Lennon unlocked the fire door and Caslin indicated for him to wait there while they proceeded up to the landing of the attic floor. The police tape was still secured across the access point to Coughlan's room and only when they looked up did they see what had Lennon so spooked. Natural light was provided from an aperture in the pitch of the roof. The skylight was closed but a draught carried through a missing section of glass. Barely a hand span in width, the hole was just big enough for someone to reach through and unhook the latch.

"That's been cut, not broken," Caslin said softly before turning and calling down to Lennon. "Has anything been taken or moved as far as you're aware?"

"Not from the landing or the other room. I thought I shouldn't go into Ms Marshall's."

"You were right," Caslin said. "What made you come up here in the first place?"

"I found some roof slates in the courtyard this morning. I thought they must have come off in the wind last night. I checked the roofline with my binoculars and found the slates were missing near to the skylight. When I saw the glass had been cut I thought to call you."

Caslin and Hunter moved forward and gently eased the bedroom door open not expecting to find anyone but concerned not to damage any forensic trace of the uninvited guest. Glancing through, they saw nothing of note. Caslin looked to Hunter.

"Better get Robertson back down here. I want another fingerprint sweep and the inventory retaken. We need to know what was touched, moved or is missing."

"What would he be looking for, do you think?"

Caslin lowered his voice as if concerned someone might overhear. "I should imagine the phone and notebook. We haven't released it to the press that we found them. The key to Coughlan's movements are in there, I'm certain. Crack that code and we'll know what the hell is going on."

"Do you think we'll get lucky with prints?"

"Maybe. I figured our guy was already in the wind but he's not. Looks quite the opposite in fact. Imagine the bottle needed to break into a crime scene after the event. This is a real positive for us. He's close," Caslin said with confidence, "and we're going to have him." Hunter didn't comment. If she had, she would've done so with less conviction. In her mind, they were chasing shadows.

"THANK YOU FOR SEEING US, Mrs Fairchild," Caslin said, sipping at the coffee he had just been passed. Nicola Fairchild, seated opposite in a floral-print dress, looked every inch a broken woman. Her face was lined with the script of sleep deprivation, her shoulders sagging under the burden of loss. They were visiting the home of the family friend; the Fairchild residence remained an active crime scene.

"That's okay, Inspector. Whatever I can do to help," she replied, with a weak smile.

"I have to ask you about your husband's illness, the cancer."

"With that, I cannot help you," she replied, her tone embittered by the recently acquired knowledge. "He kept that from me."

"Can you imagine a reason why he would have done so?" he asked. Nicola met his eye briefly before focussing beyond him out of the window.

"I've no idea," she said calmly. "I've told myself it was to protect me... us... but it doesn't make any sense. He had such little time left, why he wouldn't share as much with us as he could, I don't know."

"You mean his hours at work?" Hunter asked, offering her a cup of tea provided by their host. She declined.

"We had enough money. We didn't need more. I could have sold the house. The mortgage needn't have been a burden. I don't understand any of this." Caslin observed her for a minute while drinking his coffee, struggling to decide whether she was withholding or not.

"Are you aware of your husband's overseas investments?"

Nicola looked up, meeting his eye with a wary gaze, "We have an apartment in Spain and we were thinking of investing in Croatia if that's what you're referring to?"

Caslin flipped through his pocketbook. "Four apartments in Marbella, a house in Tuscany, two further apartments in Rome—"

"No, you are mistaken," she challenged him, shaking her head.

"More property in southern Italy, Dubrovnik..."

"No, no. You've made a mistake," Nicola insisted.

"Do you have knowledge of accounts registered overseas in the British Virgin Islands for example?" Caslin pressed, aware that she was a witness and not a suspect. Not yet, at least.

Shaking her head in apparent confusion, she stammered, "I'm sorry... I don't know... what are you telling me?"

Caslin looked up from his notes. "Your husband was sitting on assets worth in excess of six-million pounds, Mrs Fairchild, over and above what you have detailed in your domestic accounts. You didn't know?" Nicola Fairchild's lips moved but no words were forthcoming. "We are trying to understand how this came about. So far, it doesn't tally with your lifestyle as presented to us or to Her Majesty's Revenue and Customs."

"I... I... don't know what you want me to say..." she mumbled. Her friend came over and knelt alongside, taking her hand reassuringly.

"Perhaps we'll leave it there, for the time being, Mrs Fairchild but if you remember anything else, please call."

She agreed and they excused themselves. Once back in the car, Hunter started the engine. Caslin looked up at the house as they moved off. The curtain, hanging in the front room, twitched as they accelerated away. Someone was watching their departure.

"What do you make of that?" Hunter asked him before answering her own question. "She seems genuine."

"I don't doubt she's lost in how everything ties in with Christopher's death but..."

"But?"

"The perfect family, the perfect life," Caslin mused openly, "and yet, six-million quid's been hidden away for a rainy day and she doesn't know anything. Nothing at all."

"You're not buying it?" Hunter asked. "One hell of an actor, if that's the case."

"Academy Award, if I'm rig—" he was cut off by his phone ringing. Caslin answered it.

"It's me. Can we meet up, later? At the usual?" Jimmy Sullivan asked.

"Yeah, about eight—" but the call ended before he could agree the time. He glanced at the screen with a puzzled expression.

"What was that about?" Hunter asked.

Caslin shrugged, "No idea."

"WHAT WAS with the cryptic call, earlier?" Caslin said, necking his scotch and turning his attention to a pint of bitter. Sullivan sat opposite him, in a booth, downstairs in the cellars. The journalist nursed his own beer which, Caslin judged, had gone flat some time previously. "How long have you been here?"

"A couple of hours."

"What's up?" Caslin asked, concerned.

"Someone I know has been in touch about Emily," he said quietly, eyes flitting around the pub as he spoke. "She was asking a lot of questions about one man in particular."

"And he would be?"

"Paraic Nelson."

Caslin shrugged. "The name means nothing to me. Should it?"

"A proper nasty bastard," Sullivan said, lowering his voice. "But there's more. We're not the only ones asking about her enquiries regarding Nelson."

Caslin was intrigued. "Who?"

Sullivan shrugged, "They didn't know or wouldn't say."

"Which was it?"

"Look. It wasn't anyone they recognised. Certainly not someone local from the old country."

"Mainland?" Caslin asked. Again, Sullivan indicated he didn't know. "This has got you rattled, hasn't it?"

Sullivan nodded. "At first I thought she was investigating a kiddie-fiddling priest. Then, I hoped it was a gang knocking out wraps on street corners but now it turns out she's poking someone like Paraic Nelson with something of a big stick. Personally, I wouldn't go near a guy like him without some serious back up. Now there's this other guy."

"You don't know who it was," Caslin argued. "It could've been another journalist. Maybe she wasn't working alone."

"I've got a bad feeling about this one, Nate," Sullivan said, shaking his head. Lifting his glass, he saw off half a pint in one go. "I do know this. In Belfast, asking unwanted questions about Nelson doesn't go unnoticed for very long."

"What aren't you telling me, Jimmy?" Caslin asked, taking a twenty out of his wallet and rising. Draining the remainder of his pint, he signalled the barman to set up another round. "What's gotten into you?"

Sullivan locked him with a stare. "You don't know your Irish history, like I do. Oh yeah, everything's a damn sight better these days but from the late seventies and through the eighties… if you had cause to come across Nelson, he'd be the last thing you ever saw."

"You think he killed her?"

Sullivan stared into the bottom of his empty glass. "I don't know… maybe. Whoever else is digging was asking the same questions as Emily had done only weeks before. If he was tracking her… and followed her here to York. I don't know… I really don't."

"You're scared—"

"Too fucking right, I am," Sullivan snapped, drawing attention from those people seated nearby. "Too right," he repeated, lowering his voice. "Nelson. Root around and find whatever it was she did… I expect then you'll know what got her killed. And to answer your next question, yes, I am worried I might be next."

"Why should you be?"

"Emily asked me for some contacts back home. I gave her a few names."

"Without asking why she wanted them?"

"Last I saw her she was writing restaurant reviews, okay?" Sullivan said curtly. "I had no idea she was into… anything… like this."

"But you don't know anything," Caslin countered.

"Yeah, I wonder if Emily said the same?"

"What is Nelson to you?"

"Back then I left well enough alone," Sullivan stated, with a sigh. "You don't have that option. Not if you're going to do your job properly."

Caslin turned and made his way to the counter, handing his money over in exchange for the drinks waiting for him on the bar. He'd never seen Jimmy Sullivan this spooked and he'd made his name crawling through gutters where no-one else dared. Drinking his scotch whilst the barman cashed the note, he looked back but the booth was empty. Catching sight of the journalist's back climbing the stairs to the exit, Caslin drew breath. Despite his closeness to the deceased, Sullivan still couldn't open up.

"Cheers," Caslin said to the barman, pocketing the change.

Taking both pints, he walked back through the bar up a flight of stairs and out into the walled beer-garden. The area was popular with patrons drinking in the evening sunshine and he found a chair at the furthest point from anyone else. Within an hour the Saturday night would be in full swing and it'd be standing room only. Putting the drinks down, he took out his mobile and called Hunter.

"Hello, sir. Where are you?" she asked. "I've been trying to call you."

"Signal's bad when I'm downstairs," he said, referring to the vaulted brick of the Cellars. "Why, what's up?"

"I've been reviewing Christopher Fairchild's movements, acquaintances, social life and so on."

"And? What have you turned up?"

"The family are big in their community, aren't they? Church goers, I mean."

"Go on," Caslin encouraged.

"Well, I was going through their phone records and once I'd checked off the office calls and cross-referenced the ones in the family contacts book, I came across another for a church, here in York."

"To be expected."

"No. Not this one, sir. It came up as a Catholic church."

"So?"

"Sir, they're Anglicans. I can't see any reason for him to be contacting this church," Hunter said, before adding, "I've no idea what it means, though, if anything but that was the only anomaly I came across."

"I guess that's one for Mrs Fairchild. No harm in asking,"

Caslin replied, equally unsure of the significance. Catching sight of a familiar face walking towards him, he acknowledged the newcomer with a wave. Glancing at the time, he returned his focus back to the phone call. "Can you do me a favour?"

"Name it, sir."

"Run a check on a guy called Paraic Nelson, anything that's on file. Currently he's in Dublin but has ties to the Republican para-militaries in Belfast."

"Will do. What's our interest?"

"He had Emily Coughlan's attention and I want to know why. And Sarah…"

"Yes, sir?"

"It's the weekend which you'd know if you ever left the office. After you're done with Nelson go home and get some sleep."

"I will but I'll just tie up a few things here first." Caslin hung up as he was joined by Aiden Reece.

CHAPTER TEN

"ONE OF YOUR team told me you'd most likely be here. Sarah, is it?" Reece said, pulling up a free chair from the adjoining table and sitting down.

"Am I that predictable?" Caslin asked, pushing an untouched pint towards his old friend which was gratefully received.

"Expecting me?"

Caslin smiled, "Always prepared. I used to be OTC, remember?"

Reece sat back in his chair. "Those were the days—"

"You nearly got us thrown out!" Caslin admonished him. "You remember the fireworks—"

"Now that was your idea. I'm not taking responsibility for it going pear-shaped," Reece countered with a grin. Caslin laughed, for a fleeting moment seeing the flash of youth reflected back at him.

"What are you doing here, Aiden?" Caslin asked. A question that briefly appeared to throw his friend.

"You know why I'm here, Nate," Reece replied, sipping his pint.

"No. I know what you told me," Caslin said, fixing him with a stare. "But I'm asking why you're really here?" Reece put his drink on the table, wiping foam from his mouth with the back of his hand. He met Caslin's gaze.

"Nothing gets past you does it, Nate?"

"I pulled your file."

"Ahh… I see," Reece smiled and rocked his head from side to side. "Must've made for interesting reading."

"Not really. You graduated from Hendon and you're recorded as being posted to a station in Croydon but we both know that's not true. The remainder of the file is restricted. Why would that be?"

Reece exhaled deeply, blowing out his cheeks. "By the time someone made that call, I was out. So, you're asking the wrong person. Fair to say I became somewhat of an embarrassment."

"Did you leave or were you pushed?"

Reece waved the comment away. "Ancient history, Nate. It's all under the bridge."

"What happened to you, Aiden? You were top of our class at Hendon. You passed out and were away, never to be seen or heard from again. I have to admit, I was pretty pissed off with you back then."

Reece smiled. "I assure you, the reality was far less dramatic than you're imagining," he paused, appearing thoughtful, staring off towards nothing in particular. The excited laughter of a group seated nearby carried over on the breeze. "Sometimes you take a turn in life… that you don't see coming. Plans change. That's all."

Caslin studied the man seated opposite. They were part of a close-knit group at university, all highly regarded Officer Candidates in the British Army Training Corps. Four of whom were recruited into the police together upon graduation. Only Aiden Reece had turned his back on that select unit. The one member held in such high esteem by all of the others was now someone Caslin found himself struggling to trust.

"And here you are, working for Renton Sands."

"Here I am," Reece replied, tipping his glass towards Caslin in a salutary fashion. Knowing the explanation wasn't satisfactory, he shrugged. "Renton have a substantial investment account. It's managed by—"

"None other than, Chris Fairchild. We've covered that," Caslin stated.

"Quite right," Reece confirmed. "I'm here to make sure their… interests are not under threat."

"And what are their interests? Corporate security, wasn't it?"

"As an overarching model, yes," Reece said. "Business is global and hot zones around the world are dangerous places to trade in. Danger makes for good returns." Glancing around to make sure they would not be overheard, he continued, "Renton provides contracts in Latin America but we are mostly centred on the Middle-East, Afghanistan and West Africa."

"Protection details?"

"Yes… of sorts."

"Mercenary contracts?" Caslin asked flatly.

"Private contractors," Reece said. Leaning forward and resting his elbows on the table, he continued, "IT companies, engineering firms and the like are in great demand these days. The decimation of infrastructure in some of these countries is astonishing. You don't need me to tell you, just watch the six o'clock news. All of that needs to be rebuilt and modernised and let's not forget there are others desperately trying to sabotage the process. Nothing we do is ever done without the consent of the authorities."

"The current authorities? Whoever is in the hot seat at the time," Caslin said dryly and was acknowledged with a wink. "Where does KL Global fit in to this?"

"Like I said, with investment funds," Reece said, spreading his palms in a gesture of transparency. "KL have always delivered sound returns for us. We're confident Fairchild's murder has nothing to do with our wider business operations but we'd be negligent in the extreme not to check it out."

"How confident?"

"Absolutely," Reece confirmed. "Renton is above board. Don't take my word for it, check it out yourself. I know you will."

"I will," Caslin said with a smile.

"You never trusted anyone, Nate," Reece said, returning a warm smile of his own. "Probably what makes you such a decent copper but... most likely... largely a shit husband."

"Thanks for that," Caslin replied, raising his own glass. Reece laughed aloud. "And what exactly is in your job description within this global enterprise?"

"Strictly logistics these days, Nate. On the ground, whatever needs arise. Be it equipment, training, procurement, whatever's necessary."

"So, why did they send you?"

"Ahh... this one. I told you, I requested it. It's certainly not my usual assignment but I figured it was a good opportunity to look in on you."

"How did—"

"I know you were here?" Reece asked, Caslin nodded. "I was back in London around eighteen months ago taking part in a conference and I looked you up. We were well overdue for a catch up. I went over to your place and... Karen filled me in." Caslin stared into the bottom of his glass, an unreadable expression on his face. "I was sorry to hear—"

"More of those life-changing moments coming at you unannounced," Caslin interrupted. "We tried but... well, we couldn't force it, you know?"

"I hear that," Reece replied, taking a mouthful of beer. "How are you getting on now? I gathered things weren't great back then. That's why I left it to be honest. I wasn't sure what use I would've been to you."

"No matter," Caslin dismissed the admission. "Karen's brought the kids north, so I can be more involved." Sucking air through his teeth, he continued, "Lizzie is a delight. She looks so much like her mother—"

"Lucky for her," Reece said with a cheeky wink.

"Sean, on the other hand, is..."

"A teenager?"

"Very much so," Caslin agreed, finishing his drink. "What about you? Did you ever tie the knot with... oh, heck... what was her name... you were engaged, weren't you?"

"You don't mean, Michelle?"

"Michelle," Caslin confirmed, excitedly pointing a finger across the table. "The two of you were inseparable."

"Good heavens man. No," Reece said with affirmation. "That was over within a year of leaving Hendon."

"Shame. I liked her," Caslin said. "Anyone else hit the spot?"

"Nah," Reece replied. "Career path put those plans well and truly on the back burner." Caslin detected a note of regret or a deeper feeling being downplayed but chose not to press.

"How long do you expect to be in town?" he asked, routing the subject matter back to business.

Reece shrugged. "A few days, no more than that. Unless you feel Renton is exposed in some way."

"Not as far as I know."

"Who do you think is responsible?"

Caslin shook his head and smiled. "I'm still not giving you access to the case file. Not even the random suppositions floating around in my head. Tell me, how well did you know Chris Fairchild?"

Reece blew out his cheeks. "Personally, I never had any dealings with him nor anyone else at KL. Why do you ask?"

"He had a limited client list. All were heavily invested in his funds."

"Renton must have a lot riding on his success then," Reece said thoughtfully.

"And it stands to reason he would've had a close relationship with those clients. Which of your colleagues would've dealt with him?"

"I'll find out for you. Same again?" Reece asked, rising. Caslin nodded. He watched his friend until he disappeared back inside in the direction of the bar. A sense of unease descended over him. One that he couldn't justify but was there nonetheless.

It was after midnight when Caslin fumbled with his keys, dropping them whilst trying to unlock the communal access of Kleiser's Court. Reece knelt and retrieved them as a group of weekend revellers, in celebratory mood, ambled past. Caslin braced himself against the wall, feeling lightheaded. *What was happening to him? He hadn't drunk that much.* Reece unlocked the door, pushing it open and Caslin stumbled through, his friend gripping his upper arm in an attempt to steady him. Climbing the stairs they reached the front door with Caslin slightly out of breath.

This time he bypassed the obstruction without delay. Surprisingly, the lights in the hallway were on. Furthermore, a chink of light emanated through the crack in the doorway to the living room. Suddenly alert, he indicated for Reece to wait and threw off his coat inching warily forward. The sound of the television grew as he approached. Gently easing the door open, he peered around the corner. Until that point, unaware that he'd been holding his breath, he let out a sigh of relief. Observing the still form of a person stretched out on the sofa before him, he put his head against the door jamb and shut his eyes.

Reece appeared alongside and observed the scene. Caslin entered, crossing the room and switching off the television. The sound of the band playing their gig on stage was silenced and he turned to his unexpected guest. Sean was sound asleep. Still fully clothed, he lay there, snoring. Caslin took the throw off of his armchair and laid it over his sleeping son. Beckoning Reece to join him, he walked through to the kitchen. Taking out his phone, Caslin scrolled through the contacts and selected Karen. When the call connected, he gently pushed the kitchen door to.

"He's here at my place," Caslin said to his near-frantic, ex-wife.

"You said you couldn't take him this weekend," she accused him.

"I wasn't expecting—"

"How long has he been there?" Karen asked aggressively. "Couldn't you have let me know earlier?"

"I've only just got home," Caslin countered.

"Have you been out working or only drinking?" she accused him.

Caslin found his own voice rising in reply. "You hadn't let me know he was missing. If you had—"

"Is he okay?" Karen asked, cutting him off. Her attitude softening. Caslin recognised her fear and adopted a conciliatory tone.

"He's asleep. I'll speak to him when he wakes up. Did you have words?"

"It's not my fault, Nate."

"I didn't say otherwise," he reassured her. "I'm just wondering how he's come to be sleeping on my sofa that's all."

Karen, his former wife of ten years, paused to collect her thoughts. "We did. It was nothing new. I don't care for how he's living his life."

"He's nearly fifteen, Karen. Show me a parent who thinks their child is making the right choices."

"Not like this, Nate. He's out all hours with who knows what type of people. Last night, he didn't get home until gone three—"

"He's a teenager, Karen. It's the weekend—"

"He's not old enough to be out until that time. You'd never stand for it! It's not only that, Nate, he's not paying attention at school," her tone softened a little. "Next year, he'll begin the run up to his exams—"

"All right, calm down. I said I'll speak with him and I will. Let's leave it for tonight, he can stay here and I'll bring him back in the morning." There was a moment of silence. He could hear her breathing on the line. Knowing Karen, she would want Sean back immediately but only out of concern not to score points. That wasn't her style.

"Okay. To be on time for his football coaching, he needs to leave here at a quarter-past eight," she advised. "You'll take care of him?" Caslin knew she was worried and that manifested itself into the question rather than hinting at his level of competence. He didn't take it personally.

"Of course, I will. How's Lizzie?" he asked after their daughter. She laughed, it was genuine and reminded him of happier times.

"She went to bed having told me to lighten up and that Sean would be back when he was ready."

"Did she?" Caslin asked, breaking into a laugh of his own. "Eleven going on forty."

"Isn't she," Karen agreed. "Thanks, Nathaniel. I'm glad you are there for him."

"Goodnight, Karen."

"Is she still angry?" a voice came from behind. Caslin put the phone down onto the countertop and turned to see Sean standing in the doorway. His son emitted all the attitude that teenage angst could muster borne either from fatigue or embarrassment. Caslin couldn't tell which.

"I think, perhaps, I should leave you to it," Reece offered. Caslin nodded. "I'll see myself out. Catch up with you later." Turning to Sean, he inclined his head, receiving a half-smile in return.

"She's worried about you," Caslin replied once they were alone. Filling the kettle with water he set it to boil. "Do you want something to drink? Squash or maybe a bottle of coke, I think there's one in the fridge."

"Anything else?" Sean asked nonchalantly.

"Tea, coffee?"

"I'll have a beer if you're offering?"

"Not a chance, sunshine," Caslin replied with a grin.

"Worth a try."

"What's going on with you, son? A year ago, you were well on course with your studies but now... you're skipping school, battling your mother at every opportunity and hanging around with—"

"You're starting to sound like her," Sean said with disdain, rolling his eyes.

"Maybe, not a bad thing. Your mother moved you up here to get you away from the people you were mixing with in London. Now you're taking up with similar—"

"Come on, Dad," Sean argued. "We moved up here so she could offload me onto you." Caslin drew breath as the kettle boiled. Taking two mugs out of the cupboard he set them down and turned to face his son.

"Put your mother's motivations aside for a moment because you may have a point, I don't know. Regardless, you're making life unnecessarily hard on yourself let alone those around you."

"It's my life—"

"And we're your parents. Like it or not we're responsible for you and… we care. Have you taken a look at yourself recently?"

"What's that supposed to mean?" Sean replied curtly.

"Rings under your eyes, your pupils are dilated," Caslin indicated. "What else are you taking?"

"Nothing," Sean said defiantly, looking away and shaking his head.

"Don't lie to me, son. People lie to me every day. I'm used to it. You stink of weed. What else, amphetamines?" Sean didn't answer and refused to meet his father's gaze. "You know you can talk to me, don't you? Whatever it is, I'll listen."

Sean looked up, locking eyes. "Can I come and live with you?" Caslin was caught off guard. His expression conveying precisely the wrong response. "Thanks a lot, Dad. Nice to know you care," Sean snapped, turning his back and stalking off into the living room. Caslin followed.

"It's not that I don't want you here, it's…" he floundered as words failed him.

"It's what?" Sean asked, sinking onto the sofa.

"Look around. This place is small. I only have the one bedroom—"

"So, I'll sleep here on the sofa."

"I'm not in most of the time. My job keeps me out all hours, you know that."

"I can take care of myself."

"What about your mother… and your sister for that matter? She only wants what's best for you."

Sean shot daggers in his direction. "You know she's drinking?"

Caslin took a seat opposite in the armchair. "Most of us have a drink—"

"No, I mean proper drinking. Like…" he let the thought tail off. Caslin looked down at the floor.

"Like I used to?" he asked, glancing up. Sean nodded. Caslin sighed. "All right. We're not going to solve anything tonight. Tell you what, you get your head down in my room and I'll take the sofa. We can talk about it some more in the morning."

Sean stood up and made to leave. Caslin caught his son by the arm as he passed, drawing him in. They hugged tightly, Sean putting his head into his father's chest. The moment was over in seconds and they separated without another word. The bedroom door closed and Caslin's eyes strayed to a lonely bottle of scotch sitting high upon a shelf alongside the fireplace. Shaking his head, he returned to the kitchen. Of all things that certainly wouldn't help.

CHAPTER ELEVEN

Awoken by the sound of a ringing mobile, Caslin rolled off the sofa and began rooting through his jacket. Answering before the voicemail kicked in, he found it was Hunter.

"Sir, Dr Lawton has been in touch. He has an image for us."

"Fantastic," Caslin stated, blinking at the daylight streaming through the sash windows. "What time is it?"

"Half eight, sir. Did I wake you?"

Caslin muttered something incomprehensible, getting his bearings. "No, don't worry. I'll meet you at the university in thirty minutes."

He hung up on the call, his thoughts turning to the time. Cursing, he took the shirt off that he'd slept in and called out. "Sean! We're running late."

There had been no reply by the time he reached the bedroom. Knocking didn't bring a response either and he pushed the door open. The bed was empty and there was no sign of his son. Dropping his head, he swore. At that moment his phone beeped. Glancing at it, he read a text message from Karen, *thx for getting Sean back. He's off to training x.*

Feeling guilty and relieved in equal measure, he put his phone away and hurried to his wardrobe. Dressing in a clean shirt, he grabbed his jacket and headed out. The short car journey across town took a little over twenty minutes, Sunday morning traffic was a delight compared with any other day. Meeting Hunter in the university car park, she scanned his appearance when he got out of the car throwing a couple of breath mints into his mouth as he did so.

"Rough night?" she asked.

"How can you tell?" Caslin replied, with no attempt to conceal the sarcasm. She fell into step alongside him. "Sorry I missed the briefing. How did it go?"

"Terry's working through the finances. We've got a forensic accountant on board, so results should come quicker."

"Excellent. How did Scenes of Crime get on with running back over Coughlan's room at the Lord Percy?"

"Nothing new. Whoever broke in, was a ghost. It's like they were never there. Without the cut in the glass and the broken slates we wouldn't have known."

Caslin was annoyed by that. "What did you get on Paraic Nelson?"

"He's well known to our colleagues in the PSNI, sir," she said with confidence.

"He's got form?"

"Nothing that's stuck in recent years," Hunter offered. "He has strong links to Republican paramilitaries dating back to the troubles. He was interned in the seventies and did a three year stretch for fraud, eighty to eighty-three."

"What about now? Is he still in the loop?"

"No, not anymore. By all accounts his ties were cut back in the mid-nineties and he was disavowed by the leadership in '98."

"On what grounds?"

"The file doesn't have that information. It all gets a little sketchy around 1996 and there's nothing beyond '98. Presumably, he was no longer considered a person of interest but I've put a call in to the locals and I'm waiting to hear back. It's strange though."

"It is that," Caslin agreed. "What about Hardy, how is she getting on with Foley?"

Hunter shook her head, "Nothing out of the ordinary. He's stuck to the same routine, religiously. No pun intended. The man doesn't socialise with anyone nor has he had any visitors. His house is rented and I checked with the networks, he doesn't have a broadband connection. Are you sure we're not trying to see something that just isn't there?"

"How so?"

"The connection to Foley, I mean. What if he's not involved?"

Caslin stopped, turning to face her. "She was asking about him specifically. Why else would she visit him?"

"Spiritual guidance?" Hunter suggested. Caslin responded with a dismissive gesture and they set off again, mounting the steps up to the entrance of the building. "He is a priest, sir."

"If she hadn't spoken to my source about him, I might agree," Caslin said, holding the door open for Hunter. "Let's not forget, Coughlan was drawn here for a reason and if not Foley then who or why? Tell Hardy not to get complacent. Make no mistake, he's pegged to this somehow. I want the surveillance team operating in pairs from now on. We've got Coughlan looking at Nelson and it's also possible someone else is following Coughlan's investigation independent of whoever killed her. If either of them end up at Foley's door, I want us prepared for it."

"Resources are stretched," Hunter stated, although her demeanour indicated agreement.

"Hang the resources. We'll draft some more uniform if needs be. I'll clear it with Broadfoot later. We're a DCI down, so there's money left in the budget," Caslin said, mounting the steps towards the Physics Department.

"He asked after you this morning."

"Broadfoot was in on a Sunday morning? That's a first. What did you say?"

"That you were on your way here."

"Thanks," Caslin replied. The last he needed was intrusive

scrutiny from the chief superintendent. Taking the lift to the third floor, Caslin stopped as they walked out onto the landing. He had the stirrings of a headache, no doubt a hangover, and he took a moment to steady himself.

"Sir?" Hunter asked, having realised he was no longer beside her. He waved away her concerns and caught up. Approaching Dr Lawton's office, he took several deep breaths to try and clear his head. The professor noted their arrival and beckoned them in, negating the need to knock. He was so excited to share his results that he'd barely offered them a seat before he was encouraging them around the desk to view his monitor. Within a couple of clicks, both detectives were assessing the image of their chief suspect.

"I can hardly believe how well this has come out," Lawton said, almost gleefully. "I had my doubts while working through it yesterday."

"That's a result," Hunter stated. Although the resolution still wasn't clear enough to match it to a photo identification, they had enough to be positive about. The figure was white, approximately thirty-five to forty years of age with an athletic, muscular build. Caslin reached over and pointed at something on the upper part of the left arm.

"Enlarge that for me, would you?" he said. Dr Lawton was happy to oblige and highlighted the area, enlarging it with a couple of clicks.

"Looks like a tattoo," Caslin stated openly. Although grainy, he could make out a semi-circle with five lines, spaced evenly, descending from it towards a point, where they intersected. Surrounding this were a dozen marks but they were less clear and the entire motif was encompassed by a dark blue background, in the shape of a shield.

"What do you think it is?" Hunter asked, straining her eyes to make out the detail. Caslin stepped back folding his arms.

"They're stars encircling a parachute," he said softly.

"That's quite specific. Do you recognise it?" Hunter asked, glancing back at him. "It could be military. If you're right?"

"I've seen similar," Caslin said quietly. "Dr Lawton, would you be kind enough to email this across or burn us a copy. Can you print off that still?" he asked, pointing at the monitor.

"Certainly."

"Needless to say, please keep the details of this to yourself," Caslin said firmly. The professor bobbed his head enthusiastically. Hunter glanced in his direction with a serious expression. Caslin took the printout and excused them from the office.

THE PLEASANT SUMMER was a fading memory as September dragged them towards Autumn. Leaving the building and crossing the car park, Caslin scanned the grey clouds rolling in from the west bringing the very real prospect of rain at any moment.

"Are you going to share?" Hunter asked him as they approached her car. She was visibly frustrated. He hadn't spoken a word since leaving Lawton's office.

"I'm sorry," Caslin replied, turning his back and leaning against the vehicle. "I was preoccupied. This isn't making a lot of sense."

"What isn't?"

"The tattoo. You're right, it is military," he confirmed, staring out in the direction of the city. The sound of traffic from the ring road carried to them.

"You did recognise it, didn't you?"

Caslin chuckled. "One of my father's more interesting obsessions, military insignia."

"Interesting, you say?" Hunter replied, grinning.

"It's on a par with model railways in my opinion," Caslin said with a wry smile. "When we were kids, he'd describe them to us challenging my brother and I to name them by expertise rather than their specific unit. We were children after all. You remember the significant ones. The exciting ones. This is most likely a contemporary incarnation of the one I remember."

"So? Spill it."

"It's a Paratroopers' insignia."

"Not ours?" Hunter asked. Caslin shook his head turning his gaze to her.

"German," Caslin said softly. "Elite, special forces, to be exact."

"You're right. That doesn't make a lot of sense," Hunter said, sounding perplexed.

"Let's walk it through. We figure our guy is a professional. Have a look through the database, tie up what we know about him with any other intelligence. Perhaps he's on the radar of the Organised Crime Unit already as an enforcer, hitman or such like. Run it through Europol as well. In the meantime, get this picture out," Caslin indicated the print in his hand. "Maybe we'll get lucky."

"What about the press?" Hunter asked.

"No, not yet," Caslin said thoughtfully. "I don't want to spook him. He's willing to take the risk of breaking back into a crime scene, so I don't think he'll take off unless he thinks we're onto him. Let's not tip our hand. We can always go wide at a later time if we need to."

"Understood," Hunter said, unlocking her car. "What's your next move?"

Caslin drummed his fingers on the roof of the car deep in thought. "Coughlan was digging around Paraic Nelson before she came to Foley. Someone else is doing likewise but no one's talking about it."

"Do we wait for this other person to arrive at the same conclusion as Coughlan did or shall we put some pressure on Foley?"

"I don't want to wait but without any detail if we bring Foley in we'll just be fishing. I doubt it'll get us anywhere."

"Then we need to go directly to where all this started."

"Nelson?" Caslin questioned with a flick of an eyebrow. Hunter nodded. She was right. Coughlan's investigation in Northern Ireland had uncovered something which led her to ask questions across the border about Nelson which, in turn, brought her to Foley. Hunter was right, whatever her relationship with the aging priest was still remained to be seen. If he didn't want to bring Foley in there was only one course remaining open to them and that was to put Paraic Nelson under scrutiny.

CHAPTER TWELVE

THE WATER FLOWED STEADILY PAST. Mini-torrents formed as they clashed with his legs. He should be cold but there was no such feeling, no sensation at all. As usual, the whispers carrying from the riverbank, taunted him with words he couldn't make out. The branches of the dense foliage swayed in the breeze, almost in synchrony with the current. A body drifted too close for comfort and Caslin shoved it away with as much force as he could muster. The faceless corpse turned its head to look at him as the pull of the water swept it away.

Waking with a start, he sat bolt upright, his breath coming in short, ragged gasps. Dripping with perspiration, Caslin threw off the duvet and levered himself out of bed. Far more alert than would normally be the case, he made his way to the bathroom. Turning on the shower, he stepped in before the water had a chance to reach temperature, the cold snap felt refreshing. Placing his hands and forearms on the tiled wall in front of him, Caslin bowed his head, allowing the water to cascade down the back of his head and shoulders. Steadily, the water temperature increased and he remained in that position, trying in vain to decipher what his subconscious was communicating to him.

Throwing on the first shirt he came to in his closet, Caslin left his apartment by way of the café next door to purchase a coffee and a breakfast roll. Both of which were long gone by the time he pulled into the parking area of Fulford Road. Entering through reception, Caslin acknowledged Linda's customary smile with a wave. Punching in his code, he passed through and took the elevator up to CID. Entering the squad room, he skipped the formalities. Today was going to be where they'd make some headway. Repeatedly clapping his hands together, he addressed the team.

"Everybody listen up," he called above the general noise. A silence descended on the room. "I want two teams. Team One, I want you looking into Paraic Nelson. Hunter, you've already made a start so they're yours. Emily Coughlan was digging into Nelson's interests and we don't know why. When we do, we'll have a better idea of who killed her and why. Team Two, that's yours, Terry," he said, pointing to Holt. "I want to find the guy in the CCTV from the Lord Percy. He could be our killer and we've no reason to believe he's left the city so let's find him."

"What was Coughlan's interest?" a voice asked from the back of the room. All turned to see Kyle Broadfoot entering.

"As yet, sir, we don't know," Caslin replied. "Accusations of being a slum landlord were raised in the past but nothing came of them. We speculate she may have been following that line but, in reality, we don't know. We need to get into his affairs. From what we're led to believe she was repeatedly warned off."

"How have you come across this information?" Broadfoot questioned, coming to the front of the room. Caslin glanced across at him appearing momentarily unsure.

"A journalistic source with ties to the area," he answered.

Broadfoot nodded. "A word in your office?" Caslin dismissed the team leaving Hunter to divide up their assignments and followed the DCS into his office. Closing the door behind him, he took a deep breath. "This source? It's not James Sullivan, is it?"

"As it happens, yes, it is, sir."

"He's not exactly been reliable in the past—"

"I know, sir. However, on this occasion, his strong links to the deceased and her associations could prove useful."

Broadfoot pursed his lips, appearing pensive. "It's your investigation, Nathaniel. Just make sure you treat his information with a degree of caution."

"Understood."

"Now what headway have you made with the Fairchild inquiry?"

Caslin was crestfallen. "The crime scene has offered us little. Ballistics indicate we can match a bullet to the gun it was fired from if we can locate the gun. There are no hits on the database tying it to other crimes."

"So, the weapon was clean?"

"Apparently so," Caslin stated. "No one has a bad word to say about Fairchild. Only the attitude of his employer, KL Global, has drawn attention. With the warrant we're into his accounts. I believe that's the strongest line of inquiry."

"Are they hiding something?"

"Couldn't say at this time, sir."

"I want an update on this by the end of the day, Nathaniel," Broadfoot said. "The Fairchild case appears to be stalling—"

"With respect, sir, I disagree. The most likely scenario is that his business interests played a role and until we can get through the financials—"

"Sir?" Holt said apologetically, knocking on the door and entering unbidden much to Broadfoot's frustration.

"Can it not wait, Detective Constable?" Broadfoot said aggressively.

"Sorry, sir. No, I don't think it can."

"What's up, Terry?" Caslin asked.

"We've had a tip regarding the man in the CCTV."

"Already?" Caslin was surprised.

"I know," Holt agreed, matching Caslin's reaction. "We only started circulating the screenshot around yesterday."

"Where?"

"A hotel in the city centre, the Ousebank," Holt said, his eyes flicking between the two senior officers. Broadfoot exhaled heavily.

"You best get a move on then," he stated, rising from his chair. "Update me as soon as you can."

"Will do, sir," Caslin said as Broadfoot left. "Get your coat, Terry. Let's go and kick someone's door in."

Holt smiled. "Or we could just ask the manager for a key?"

Caslin ushered him out of the office with a hand on the shoulder. "You take all the fun out of this job, Terry, you really do."

———

THE OUSEBANK HOTEL was situated alongside the river flowing through the heart of the city. A five-storey building with over two hundred rooms it could easily accommodate a guest seeking to be anonymous during their stay. Approaching the concierge, Caslin took out a copy of the printed screenshot and passed it across the reception desk whilst discreetly brandishing his warrant card. The concierge took it in his stride.

"I may have seen him but from this it's hard to say for certain," he said, passing the image back.

"Who's currently residing in room 423?" Holt asked. The concierge turned to the computer system and within a few moments found what he was searching for.

"Room 423 is occupied by Mr Schmidt," he said. "He's been with us for the last four nights."

"When is he due to check out?" Caslin asked, glancing to Terry Holt.

"One second... he's booked in until tomorrow."

"Is he here now?" Caslin asked.

"As far as I know, yes," the concierge said. "We don't require our guests to leave us their keys. Would you like me to phone through—"

"No," Caslin said, forcefully. "I'd like you to give us a key."

"I'll need to speak to the manager—"

"Please do," Caslin said quietly. The duty manager was summoned and having been advised of the situation, led the policemen upstairs. Leaving the elevator on the fourth floor the manager greeted some passing guests and waited until they were beyond earshot to raise an objection.

"I must say this is highly unusual. If Mr Schmidt is not in his room without a warrant I shouldn't really unlock the room for you."

"You don't have to," Caslin said as they walked, admiring the standard of finish in the décor, "we can always kick the door in, if you prefer." Holt resisted the urge to laugh, bearing in mind their earlier conversation. The manager grumbled under his breath but didn't voice his reservations again. "What do you make of Mr Schmidt?" Caslin asked the manager.

He shrugged. "I don't recall ever having met him. Although, I've no doubt seen him at some point."

They came to the room and Caslin noted the *Do Not Disturb Sign* hanging on the handle. Indicating for the manager to stand at a safe distance, he and Holt took a position either side of the door. Holt glanced at his boss meeting his eye.

"I'm starting to wonder whether we should have come mob-handed, sir," he said, referencing his doubts at there being just the two of them. Caslin grinned, rapping his knuckles on the door.

"Some of that fun I was telling you about," Caslin said, lowering his voice. There was no response from within, so Caslin knocked again only this time more forcefully. "Police!" he barked but again there was no reply. Beckoning the manager forward, he was passed a key card. Putting it in the slot, he caught Holt's eye, "Ready?"

"Do it," Holt answered. Caslin unlocked the door and pushed it inwards. Half expecting some movement from within both men braced themselves. They edged forwards. The initial entranceway opened out into a large suite. The double bed was set to the left, a sofa at the foot of it with another recliner underneath the window opposite them. Caslin could see a laptop computer on a desk on the far side of the room adjacent to the access to what Caslin figured was the bathroom. The door to which was cracked open. The sounds of running water from a shower came to ear and steam was drifting out into the bedroom suite. Caslin indicated for them to proceed in that direction. Holt nodded his silent acceptance.

Glancing behind him, Caslin saw the hotel manager hovering at the doorway. With a flat palm, he told him to remain where he was. Caslin scanned the desk as he came to it. There were various sections taken from newspapers alongside a folded copy of an ordnance survey map of the North York Moors. Catching Holt's attention he pointed to it and using the end of a pen he flipped the folded map over to view the reverse. The first names that leapt up at him were Ampleforth and Helmsley. A point in between those two towns was where Emily Coughlan met her death. Inclining his head back towards the bathroom, Holt joined him at the threshold. Looking down, Caslin noted the carpet here was sodden. Water was steadily seeping from the room beyond.

Gently easing the door further open, Caslin peered into the steam filled room. Stepping forward they made their way through the pooled water. No dissent was levelled at them for breaching privacy and it soon became clear as to why. Curled up, face down in the water which was cascading over the top of the bath, with the shower still running overhead, was the man they were looking for. The tattooed arm was facing him and even a cursory inspection suggested they had found who they were looking for. Holt reached up towards the shower only for Caslin to stop him.

"Prints, Terry," he reminded him. Holt nodded and looked around. The shower was electric. Pulling the cord, he cut both the power and flow of water whilst leaving any prints on the shower unit intact. Caslin took in the man under water. Undoubtedly, he was deceased but Caslin checked for a pulse anyway. Unsurprisingly, he didn't find one. The water was off colour. Blood had been flowing from a visible head wound but the red was so diluted due to the passage of water to and from the bath that it now had a brown tinge to it. The way in which he lay meant Caslin couldn't tell whether or not the drain was blocked by the body or by a foreign object.

Holt pointed towards the taps. Caslin saw the residue of blood on them and looking around, he saw no signs of a struggle present elsewhere in the room. In contrast to the size of the bedroom suite the bathroom was quite cramped hence the presence of a shower-bath rather than a standalone.

"What are you thinking?" Holt asked.

Caslin shook his head glancing around again before returning to the bedroom. Holt followed. Going over to the desk, Caslin inspected the newspapers. The first two were articles about Emily Coughlan's murder taken from copies of a local paper. The third, Caslin found incredibly curious. It was an article detailing the progress of the Fairchild murder inquiry. Both detectives donned latex gloves and began a search of the room. Caslin opened up the laptop and swiped his finger across the glidepad, bringing the machine out of hibernation. A password screen prompt came up and Caslin closed the lid back down.

Moving to the bed, he could tell it had been slept in but not made although something about the set up piqued his interest. Gently lifting the duvet and rolling it back towards the foot of the bed, he saw the mattress protector but the bedlinen was missing. Addressing the manager, rooted to the doorway and curious to know what was happening, Caslin called out.

"Have housekeeping been through here this morning?"

"No, I shouldn't have thought so, not with the signage on the door."

"You're certain?" Caslin persisted as Holt came alongside, looking over his shoulder.

"I'll have to check," the manager replied. "Is something amiss?"

Caslin ignored the question as Holt drew his attention. "Over here, sir." Holt led him across the room to the wardrobe. Holding the left-hand door open with one hand, he drew aside the clothes hanging on the rail with the other. Caslin looked where Holt directed towards the back of the wardrobe. Reaching in, Caslin withdrew a small, leather holdall. The zip was open and a semi-automatic pistol was tucked within. Caslin slid it out, finding the safety was off. Making it safe, he then moved the slide and sniffed the chamber. The smell of cleaning fluid was strong but not overly so. If the weapon had been recently fired, he was unable to tell. Releasing the magazine, he saw it was fully loaded.

"When's Iain Robertson and his CSI team getting here?" Caslin asked.

"Any moment, sir," Holt replied. Caslin put the gun back into the holdall but placed the magazine into a plastic evidence bag that Terry Holt provided him with.

"Have ballistics compare this weapon to the bullets that killed Fairchild," Caslin said quietly.

"What's the link?" Holt asked. Caslin pointed to the desk.

"So far? A newspaper clipping," he said, pursing his lips. "Terry, the tip you received…"

"Yes, sir?"

"Who called it in?"

"Didn't leave their name, sir. The Control Room tracked it back to a payphone."

"The caller said they recognised Schmidt and he was here?"

"Yes," Holt said. "They thought they'd seen the man we were looking for in and around this hotel and gave us the room number."

Caslin's brow furrowed as he looked around searching for answers. "And yet, the concierge in the lobby couldn't pick him out."

"YOU WERE GOING to find out who dealt with Fairchild's accounts, at your end."

"Yeah, I know. I'm working on it," Reece replied.

"What's to work on? It's a phone call, right?"

Reece chuckled down the phone line. "This myth of the private sector being efficient really has caught hold in society, hasn't it? I'm on it. I'll get back to you." Caslin put the phone down. He sat in silence for a few moments drumming his fingers on the desk before him, chewing his lower lip. Finding Schmidt had given them leads and simultaneously shut them down. Frustration was starting to gnaw away at him.

"Sir," Holt said, standing at the entrance to his office. He beckoned him in. "Sorry to break your train of thought."

"It's okay. What is it?"

"I've pulled some info together on Schmidt."

"Is that his real name?"

"Yes, sir. Heinrich Schmidt. The prints we took from him at the hotel match those on file with the *Bundeswehr*, the German Ministry of Defence. He was born, raised and educated near Heidelberg, took a role in the military for his national service and upon completion of that was expected to go on to university. However, he signed on rather than returning to education. I've requested his full service record but as of now, I only have the headlines. He served with distinction, several commendations for bravery and was highly regarded by his superiors. There's no criminal record in Germany or lodged with Europol."

"A first-class citizen," Caslin mused openly. "When did he leave the forces?"

"That's where it gets interesting, sir. He didn't."

"He's still serving?"

Holt shook his head, "No, sir. Heinrich Schmidt died eight years ago."

Caslin sat up in his chair. "How can that be? Where?"

"Apparently he went missing on a climb in the Alps. The weather deteriorated rapidly and avalanches were reported in the area in which he was last seen. Three members of the party didn't return to base camp. Once the weather broke a rescue team subsequently failed to locate any of them. They've been recorded as missing and presumed dead. The Germans are very keen to know just what is going on."

"They'll have to get in line. How have you got on with his computer?"

"I was into that pretty quickly, sir. There's not a great deal to tell you. Very little of the memory has been used and there's no evidence that he has a cloud storage facility. Basically, it's as if it's just been plucked off the production line."

"Anything useful at all?"

"His browser history is revealing," Holt said, despondent. Answering Caslin's raised eyebrow with a shake of his head, he continued, "Schmidt had an appetite for violent pornography. Rape-porn in particular."

"Gather as much information about him as you can, personal, intimate stuff so we can pass it on to Alison Taylor. I want definitive confirmation it's him—"

"There's going to be a delay on that," DCS Broadfoot interrupted them, entering the room. "DC Holt, can you give us the room." Body language and tone indicated it wasn't a request. He acknowledged with a bob of the head.

"Yes, sir."

"Close the door on your way out," Broadfoot stated, without looking towards him. Holt did as he was instructed on his way out.

"Is there a problem, sir?" Caslin queried.

"Dr Taylor will be unavailable for the foreseeable, she's required elsewhere. You have the remainder of the day to get whatever you might need from her."

Caslin raised his eyebrows. "Okay. One of her colleagues can step in—"

"That won't be necessary, Nathaniel. The Home Office are sending someone to cover for Dr Taylor. He'll be in place within a couple of days."

"A couple of days?" Caslin said, failing to mask his irritation.

"With respect, sir. This is a murder inquiry. I need this—"

"You have your man, Inspector, and he's already dead, so I don't think a few more days is going to put anyone at risk."

"We think we have our man but until we've proved it, I'm not ready to tie it off."

"And no-one's asking you to. All the evidence indicates—"

"Exactly!" Caslin exclaimed. "*All the evidence*. How many cases have you investigated where the suspect drops dead, leaving you everything necessary to convict him post-mortem? I'll hazard a guess at none."

"What are you suggesting?"

"That it's a little early to be closing the book on this. We still don't have motive—"

"The pornography that Holt describes demonstrates an attraction to violent sex—"

"Emily Coughlan wasn't sexually assaulted, sir. She was tortured for information and then killed."

"Speculation," Broadfoot countered. "His motivations could just as easily have been centred on power and control."

"Yes, sir. Thank you for making my point, we don't know, yet."

"All that will come out in your investigation, Nathaniel. I am sure of that. In the meantime, I suggest you get a photo line-up including Heinrich Schmidt over to Mrs Fairchild and see if she can pick out her husband's killer. Then, at least, you can be satisfied you do indeed have your man."

"Why would someone who died eight years ago travel to the UK to randomly kill a financier and a journalist who, coincidentally, happened to arrive in the country around the same time?"

"All questions for you to answer in due course," Broadfoot said, meeting Caslin's gaze but not sharing the incredulity. "I'll also need you to begin scaling back the investigation team. Beginning with your surveillance of the Catholic priest."

"What?" Caslin said forcefully. Too forcefully.

"Your suspect is dead."

"In suspicious circumstances—"

"Not according to Iain Robertson. His reading of the crime scene is that Schmidt's death was accidental. He slipped and fell, knocking himself unconscious along the way. The bulk of his frame blocked the drain and he drowned."

"Well that's bloody news to me," Caslin said, rising from his chair.

Broadfoot remained in his seat. "I had Iain report his findings directly to me."

"Is there something in the manner I'm handling this inquiry that you don't like, sir?"

"I back you, Nathaniel, because you are damn good at what you do. I wouldn't have boosted you to Acting DCI if I didn't have faith in you."

"However…"

"It doesn't matter how good you are or what you've achieved for me in the past. We all answer to somebody and you know as well as I do you receive more scrutiny than most. When you graduate from skipping out early from your sessions to blatantly failing to show up questions get asked."

"Is this what it's all about? I miss a session with my head doctor—"

"Your position here depends on boxes being ticked. It might not be how you, or I for that matter, like it but it's a fact. Without me, you'd have been gone some time ago. Get your head straight and get on with the game."

"Is that what it is to you, a game?"

"A figure of speech, Nathaniel. Speak to Nicola Fairchild and get this squared away. With a fair wind you'll be able to sign off barring all the loose ends you've mentioned. Having done all that, rearrange your session and make sure you attend," Broadfoot said, standing up and heading for the door. "Another thing."

"Sir?"

"Why did you request access to the file of Aiden Reece?"

Caslin was momentarily thrown but he hid it well. "His name came up in an inquiry, sir. Why do you ask?"

"As I'm sure you found out, Reece's file is restricted and your request was flagged. What's your interest?"

Caslin shrugged, a dismissive gesture. "It was passing. Entirely unrelated as it turns out."

"Fair enough."

"Why was the file restricted, sir?"

Broadfoot hesitated but only for a moment. "It's beyond me, Nathaniel. Just thought I'd ask."

"Fair enough," Caslin said, keeping a poker face.

Broadfoot levelled a gaze at him, lingering in silence for a few seconds. "I will expect you to provide me with something for a press conference by the close of play today."

"Yes, sir," Caslin said, almost defiantly. Broadfoot turned and left.

Hunter entered Caslin's office glancing over her shoulder at the departing DCS, noting that he was seething.

"What was all that about?"

Caslin rubbed at his face with both hands drawing them away slowly across his cheeks. "We're done here or he wants to believe so anyway. Told me to pull the surveillance on Foley."

"But sir, we don't know what—" she stopped as he raised a hand.

"I know," Caslin agreed. "Apparently, Iain Robertson sees Schmidt's demise as an accident."

"Since when?" Holt asked, joining the conversation as he entered.

"Since he spoke to the chief superintendent. I'll call him in a bit and get the full story."

"The bedlinen?" Holt persisted.

"It's on my list of questions, don't worry. For now, I'll have to pull the detail on Foley," Caslin said. Hunter was about to object further but Holt, placing a hand on her forearm, halted her protest.

"Speaking of which I've come up against something more than a little intriguing," Holt said. "What with finding that cutting about Fairchild in Schmidt's room you asked me to cross reference the two cases."

"In case we missed something, yes. Did we?" Caslin asked.

"No, is the short answer but I did find this," he stepped forward, passing Caslin a list of telephone numbers alongside dates and call lengths.

"What am I looking at here, Terry?" Caslin asked.

"That's a list of entries in the Fairchild's telephone logs. Hunter has already crossed off the mundane calls to known friends, business calls and the like but it's that one number, I marked there." Caslin looked. There were three entries struck through with a blue highlighter.

"And?"

"It's to a local church, sir," Holt stated as if it was the most obvious comment he could possibly make.

"I know that," Hunter said, sounding confused. "The Fairchilds are a religious family. It's no secret."

"Quite so. Most of the calls into and out of their residence were to members of their congregation."

"And that one is to a church—"

"Yes. A Catholic church," Holt said, grinning. "The Fairchild's were Anglicans, right?" he looked at Hunter first and then Caslin. "Why would they be calling a Catholic church?"

"I don't know, Terry," Caslin said. "Not quite the breakthrough I was look—"

"It's Callum Foley's church, sir," Holt clarified, excited at his find. Caslin sat back in his chair rereading the list in front of him and passing it to Hunter. She also pored over the detail.

"I can't believe I missed that," she said apologetically.

"Now, we don't know that it was Christopher Fairchild who called nor whether it was Foley he spoke to," Holt explained his thinking, "but there's a link for you."

"Let's keep this between us for the time being," Caslin said thoughtfully. "I don't want to pull the surveillance on Foley but I can't see the record of a few phone calls turning Broadfoot's head. We need more. The problem is our leads have a habit of dying out before we get to them. There'll be a delay on Schmidt's post-mortem. Alison Taylor will be away for a time and they're bringing someone else in. That gives us a couple of days to find a justification to keep this case fluid. You and I," he indicated Hunter, "are going to see if Nicola Fairchild can identify Schmidt as her husband's assassin. In the meantime, Terry, chase up the forensic accountants—"

"The specialists have already been pulled, sir," Holt said. "I took a call just before I came back in."

Caslin wasn't surprised. "In that case find me something in Fairchild's accounts that can keep us active. I don't want his file being passed over to the Fraud Squad or whoever else fancies benefitting from our hard graft."

"What happens if Schmidt *did* kill Fairchild?" Holt asked.

"Then Broadfoot has something to throw at the media during this evening's press conference and we are right up against it. Did we get anywhere with the access card, the one that Coughlan had on her when she died?"

Hunter shook her head. "Tech told me that they can't trace it. It's a generic type of card. Hotels usually have their data digitally stamped on them but this one has nothing, merely a serial number and another that could be a personal identifier. However, nothing that will tie it to a particular person, business or building."

"All right. Maybe we can match it to somewhere that comes up in the course of the investigation. Put together a photo line-up and I'll give the widow Fairchild a call, set up a meeting."

"That's a bit callous, sir," Hunter said.

Caslin shrugged. "She's withholding. I'm almost certain and I don't have the time for it. Not now."

CHAPTER THIRTEEN

NICOLA FAIRCHILD's expression didn't change in the slightest. The seconds developed into minutes as she stared at the photographic collage before her. Caslin waited in silence allowing as much time as necessary for her to implicate her husband's killer. When confident enough time had passed, he pressed.

"It's okay if you don't recognise the m—"

"That one," she pointed to the third from the right.

Caslin looked down at it and then back to her. "Are you certain?"

"Absolutely," she said emphatically. "That's the one."

"Have you seen him before the night he called on you and your husband?" Hunter asked. Nicola Fairchild shook her head, finally breaking off her gaze at Heinrich Schmidt's photograph. "Not in passing, in the street or supermarket perhaps?"

"No. I said I hadn't," she snapped.

"I'm sorry, Mrs Fairchild. I had to ask."

"Why?" she switched her focus to Hunter.

"We initially believed that this man was a professional but as yet we haven't found a connection to Christopher, you, or your family. In many cases, the victim knows their assailant, either well or in passing."

"I do not know this man," she repeated, tapping his picture to emphasise the point. "You said *was*. What does that mean?"

"He was found dead this morning," Caslin stated. Nicola gasped.

"How?"

"We're unsure. At this point it is becoming difficult to ascertain a motive for his actions."

She paused before looking at Caslin. "Who was he?"

"A German national by the name of Heinrich Schmidt. Does that name sound familiar? Perhaps Christopher mentioned him."

"No, I would remember if that was the case."

"There is another matter we are trying to resolve," Hunter said, changing tack. "Your faith. As a family did you share it?"

"Yes, of course," Nicola said, her eyes flitting between Hunter and her friend. "We are all part of the congregation."

"You are Anglican, is that right?" Caslin asked, she nodded. "Can you think of any reason your husband would have to be contacting a Catholic priest?" Nicola looked up in astonishment, open mouthed.

"No, I can't."

"Were his family Catholic, his parents, siblings?"

She shook her head. "Christopher's parents weren't in the least bit religious and he was an only child. Why do you ask?"

"We were going through your telephone records and there were a number of calls made recently to a local Catholic church."

Nicola shook her head. "I don't know. Maybe someone borrowed his phone—"

"The calls came from your home, Mrs Fairchild. The last was on Tuesday evening around 9 o'clock," Hunter offered.

Nicola was taken aback. "I was out last Tuesday. In fact, every Tuesday. It is the night of my ceramics class. Christopher didn't mention it though. Maybe he dialled the wrong number."

"Perhaps," Caslin said, nodding and pursing his lips, "although, in my experience calls placed to a wrong number don't last for a duration of six minutes and are seldom repeated on different occasions."

"I'm sorry, Inspector," she said, "I can't help you. Is it relevant? A phone call to a church? Please tell me your investigation doesn't hang on this."

Caslin shrugged. "Anything that seems unusual, out of character or routine, needs to be investigated. We're being thorough, that's all. What about the names Emily Coughlan or Sylvia Marshall, do they sound familiar?"

"No, I'm afraid not. Who are they?"

"Names that have come up in our inquiries that may or may not be related to the case."

"I'm sorry, I've not heard of either of these people."

Caslin locked eyes with her for a brief moment before accepting he wouldn't be learning any more from her. Smiling gently, he closed off the conversation.

"Okay, thank you for your time. If you recall any detail about this man, anything at all, please let us know," Caslin said. "We will be making a statement to the press later on this evening. I should imagine he will be named in connection with your husband's death. We will ask the journalists to respect your privacy—"

"Thank you, Inspector. You have been very kind."

"Did you notice that she couldn't take her eyes off of his picture?" Hunter asked, as they made their way out to the car.

"Yes. She clocked him straight away but didn't say so."

"Nervous?"

"Or she was surprised to see him."

"Picked up on your use of the past tense though."

"Aye, she did. She's either very sharp or the news didn't faze her at all," Caslin said, glancing back towards the house.

"Do you still think she knows more than she's letting on?"

Caslin sighed. "If Christopher was as secretive about his work as she implies then perhaps she didn't know the details. Maybe wilful ignorance is bliss?"

"She chose not to see what was going on?"

Caslin nodded. "Perhaps."

"Where to now, back to Fulford Road?"

"Not for me. Drop me off at Alison's office. I want to try and catch her before she heads off."

It was pushing half-past four by the time they pulled up. Alison Taylor was already at her car placing a briefcase and another bag in the boot as Caslin called out to her. Bidding farewell to Hunter, she drove away and he covered the short distance across the car park to the waiting pathologist. Her raincoat was slung over her forearm and she placed that onto the passenger seat along with her ID badge having removed it from around her neck.

"You'd better make it fast whatever it is, Nate. It's been a terrible Monday and I've got one hell of a drive ahead of me."

"Where are you going in such a rush?" he asked, coming alongside her and catching his breath.

"You're out of shape," she said with a smile.

"Never been fitter," he replied, knowing it to be false.

"They want me to oversee operations down in Torquay."

"What does that mean?"

"They've had a few procedural issues recently," she said with resignation. "The Home Office have asked for a senior pathologist to review their work practices."

"Short notice," Caslin said, thinking aloud. "I mean, no disrespect but it's not like lives are at risk in your field of work. Why the sense of urgency?"

Alison slammed the passenger door shut. "You're right. It's not like I have enough work to do here as it is without having to dash across the country to carry out a job that any number of others can do."

"Why did they want you?" Caslin asked, immediately realising the unintended insinuation contained within it.

"Who knows, Nate," she said, an edge to her tone. "Maybe someone values my skills and thinks I'd be rather good at it."

Caslin checked himself. "I wasn't implying otherwise. Only that it's… well… happening so fast."

Alison walked around to the other side of the car and opened the driver's door. Leaning against the roof of the vehicle, she put her palms down upon it, fixing him with a stare. "You're right. Why on earth they've requested me to do this, I don't know? Nor do I have a clue as to why it's so bloody urgent. There, happy?"

"I just… well…"

"Is there something that you needed from me before I go?" she asked, taking a deep breath.

He felt awkward. "How long will you be away?"

"A week, month. I don't know. Miss me?"

He wasn't sure what the right answer should be for that question. "Yes. Of course, I will."

"Anything else?" she said flatly, leaving him profoundly unsure of the validity of his response.

"Who is coming in to take over your caseload?"

Alison exhaled. "Buggered if I know." With that said, she got into the car and slammed the door. Caslin swore under his breath, realising he'd made a mess of that conversation. The engine fired into life and he bent down tapping the passenger window as she put the car into gear. Alison rolled her eyes, lowering the window. A withering look told him his assessment was accurate.

"I hope you're not away too long," he said. The words were feeble and they sounded so.

"Goodbye, Nathaniel," she said, depressing the accelerator and moving off. Caslin cursed again only this time aloud as he watched her pull away. Taking out his mobile, he scrolled through his contacts and dialled Iain Robertson's number. The call took a few moments to connect.

"Iain, it's Nate. What's going on with Schmidt?"

"Good afternoon to you, too, Nate," Robertson replied curtly. "I take it you're not too happy with something?"

"Many things, Iain. Many things."

"Broadfoot was pissing in your pool wasn't he?" Robertson laughed as he spoke. "He came to—"

"I get it, Iain. I know how it works. He said by your reckoning it's accidental?"

"Not quite how I put it, no. However, there isn't enough forensic evidence present for me to see it any other way. The post-mortem examination could throw something up, mind you. If not it'll be on the coroner."

Caslin thought on it for a moment, Robertson waiting patiently. "What about the missing bedlinen? Terry Holt double-checked and housekeeping didn't access the room before us."

"Aye, agreed. That's why I mentioned about there not being enough evidence *present* for me to see foul play. If I were reading the crime scene, as is my job, I would want to know why the sheets were missing or at the very least who removed them?"

"How much did you take away for analysis?"

"Not a great deal," Robertson said. "There were no significant secretions or otherwise on the mattress protector and I'd have expected far more prints to come out of a hotel room but those cleaners are either incredibly efficient or…"

"Someone swept the room beforehand," Caslin finished for him.

"Of course, that is pure conjecture. Schmidt may well have minimised his own forensic footprint. We might never know."

"Any indication of a struggle or that anyone else had been present recently?"

"None that I could see. Schmidt's fingerprints were all over the laptop. Nice, clean prints. None were overlapping."

"I know how someone might read that. Are you suggesting what I think you are?"

"I'm only stating what I found. It is a very tidy crime scene from a forensic point of view. Everything fits as it should."

Caslin let that sink in. "About Broadfoot…"

"Aye?"

"I'll be discreet… did he… press you at all?"

The Scot drew breath taking a moment to select his own words carefully in reply. "He's certainly taken an active interest over and above what I've become accustomed to expect."

"Did he mention me at all?"

"No. Why would he?"

"Just curious," Caslin replied. "Did you find a mobile phone in the room?"

"No, we didn't. He doesn't strike me as a technophobe."

"Me neither. He had a laptop so, if we follow the logic, it would be unlikely he didn't have one."

"My thoughts exactly," Robertson agreed. "That point didn't cut much ice with our boss though."

"Thanks, Iain. I'll catch up with you later." Caslin hung up and replaced the phone in his pocket. Despite the unanswered questions revolving around inside his head, he couldn't help but wonder whether the DCS was, at least in part, justified in taking the stance he had. Currently, a massive team was allocated to a manhunt that was apparently no longer required. Their quarry was dead. The remaining leads were circumstantial and every course of action within the investigation appeared only to muddy the waters further. The fear of the dark paranoia that had so plagued his past also threatened to resurface. *Why do I struggle to trust everything that comes before me* he thought to himself?

Knowing he was expected back at Fulford Road, Broadfoot wanting his moment of camera-time, Caslin set off on the short walk back to the station. En route, he puzzled over the loose connections thrown up between the key players. Foley appeared to have had contact with Coughlan and Fairchild only days before they were both killed and yet, with another body in the morgue, Caslin was left wondering whether or not the last play in this game had already been executed?

CHAPTER FOURTEEN

THE INTERCOM BUZZED BREAKING his focus. Caslin stood up placing the folder on the coffee table alongside his Macallan. Another blast came through as he reached the front door. He pressed the button.

"Hello."

"It's Aiden."

"Come on up," Caslin said, unlocking the communal access door. The sounds of both tourists and traders, out on Stonegate, carried through the system. The summer season had been good for business this year. He then unlatched the door to his apartment leaving it ajar as the sound of the outer door swinging shut and footsteps in the stairwell came to him. Caslin was already back in his seat in the living room when Reece let himself in.

"Hey, how's it going?" Reece said, entering.

"All good," Caslin replied, over his shoulder but without looking up. He had already returned to scanning his paperwork.

"I saw your boss on the TV earlier."

"Oh aye, he was as crisp as ever."

"You didn't fancy some airtime?" Reece asked with humour. Caslin scoffed.

"Do me a favour. Grab a glass," he indicated the kitchen. Reece did so returning with a tumbler moments later. He sat down as Caslin put the file back down and took the stopper from the bottle, pouring a second glass of scotch. Reece nodded his appreciation as the glass was slid across the table towards him and sat back.

"I know he didn't release everything but there looks to me as if there're a few loose ends," Reece said, inclining his head so he could scan the top sheet of Caslin's file. The latter made no attempt to stop him.

"More than a few."

"Dublin? What's that about, then?" Reece asked, gesturing to the pile of paper. Caslin had been reviewing Coughlan's notebook, trying to get to grips with her coded entries.

"Looking at travel dates, trying to tie them in with a code one of the victims appeared to document everything with. We have her entering and leaving the UK on dates that fit into the numbers."

"May I?" Reece asked. Caslin knew he shouldn't but in all honesty, he was pretty stumped having made little headway in cracking it himself. He passed the top two sheets of paper across. Reece scanned through them. "Walk me through it."

"Well, for example, we have her flying from Dublin to Manchester on the 24th of last month, hence *DM2408*."

"Straightforward enough so far."

"Correct. With help from the Border Agency I can tell where she was travelling to or from but it's what she was up to over there and while she was here that I'm struggling with. She was investigating something or someone, meticulously documenting her movements and presumably who she met."

"The problem is identifying these people?"

Caslin nodded. "You'll see there on the 27th of August she travelled to or met 'C' and on the 30th, 'F'."

"Any idea who or what those initials are?"

"We have evidence to tie her death in with another and I reckon these initials are relating to the same person, Christopher

Fairchild. She's used the initials separately in order to throw anyone who comes across it off the trail but I think it's possible."

"Reasonable assumption," Reece agreed. "Did she have known contact with him then, this woman? What was she to him?"

"I can't put them together. She was a journalist."

"Investigating what?"

"I don't know that either and I've no proof she was in actual contact with him but they had a mutual contact, so it's not beyond the realm of possibility they were three parts of the same puzzle," Caslin said, not wishing to name Father Foley.

"Right," Reece said, still reading through. "And this one here, 'RF'. Who is that, do you think?"

"No clue," Caslin said honestly. "I can't find a person, town, city or hotel within her circle that matches those initials."

"I reckon 'PN' refers to a guy in Dublin that I believe she was looking into. He's been mentioned elsewhere by another witness but as to her interest I don't know that either."

Reece flicked his eyebrows and exhaled. "You're not getting very far are you?" He passed the papers back and Caslin made to lay them atop the file. "The photo, is that your killer?"

Caslin glanced down at the picture of Schmidt, now at the top of the pile. He nodded, passing it to Reece before putting Cough-lan's papers back into the folder.

"Heinrich Schmidt, as my DCS read out at the press conference." Picking up his glass, he saw off the remainder and poured another. Reece lingered on the photo for a few seconds and then passed it back. "And you're right. No, I'm not getting very far."

"What on earth have you been doing for the past week? I remember you as being fairly bright but, I guess, that was back in the day."

Caslin laughed, sitting back and lifting his feet up onto the coffee table. "What can I do for you, Aiden?"

"I stopped by to say my farewells. There doesn't appear to be any exposure to Renton in this so I've been reassigned. We haven't noticed anything untoward in our portfolio, hack attempts or that sort of thing. They're seeing my presence as a bit of a waste of resources."

"Ahh… that private sector efficiency thing again," Caslin said dryly. "You never got back to me on Fairchild's contact with your company."

"Oh yes, well remembered," Reece said, reaching into his jacket pocket and taking out a slip of paper. He passed it across to Caslin who accepted it graciously. "I wouldn't get your hopes up though. He's a bit of an arse to deal with."

Caslin smiled unfolding the paper and noting the name and telephone number underneath. He read the name aloud, "Martin Champion. How well do you know him?"

"Well enough to not want to. Like I say, he's a dick."

"Okay, thanks for that," Caslin said, re-folding the paper and slipping it into the folder in front of him. Sitting back, he nursed his scotch as the streetlight outside the window flickered into life. "So, are you going to tell me why your file in Human Resources is restricted or not?"

Reece sucked air through his teeth, shaking his head slightly.

"Long story."

"It's also flagged you know?"

"Really?"

"Yep. My DCS wanted to know why I accessed it."

"Did he give you a reason for asking?"

"No. He was largely disinterested and asked only in passing," Caslin said, knocking back his drink. "He was lying, obviously."

"What did you say?"

"That I came across your name and you weren't relevant to either case. Now though, you're going to tell me, aren't you?" Reece met his eye. Despite being apart for many years, he knew when his old friend was demanding an answer albeit with a calm assuredness.

"It's not suspicious, not really," Reece began. "They were looking for new faces, people without baggage who could go on operations without fear of compromise. I met the criteria they were looking for and they didn't want me leaving footprints within the force. That's why I was taken off straight from Hendon... and why I couldn't tell you. It wasn't a choice... just how it had to be."

"Now that I look back, I figured it went down something like that. So, what happened?"

"I'll spare you the details but let's say I took to the life. It was exciting, emotionally crippling at times if I'm being honest but I was good at it."

"Until?"

Reece laughed, seeing off his own scotch. "Until I got in over my head."

"Sounds like you," Caslin said with a smile, pouring Reece another.

"Anyway, things came to a point and I was pulled. That bugged me, I wasn't happy about it and ran my mouth off... the end. I was considered... how did they put it? That's right, *strategically compromised* was the phrase I was quoted."

"You fucked up, then?" Caslin said with a nod.

"Thank you, yes. I fucked up," Reece confirmed. "No need to look so happy about it. I figure they don't want details of my operations to come out and that's why they placed the restriction on my file."

"Sounds like it was a bad time."

Reece agreed, "Not great but we all have them. Like I said before, ancient history. Any chance of you filling in your blanks?"

"What do you mean?"

"Karen didn't just tell me about your marriage situation."

"Unsurprising," Caslin said, staring into his glass.

"You got burned as a DCI."

Caslin nodded slowly, deliberately. "What's done is done. If you let it eat away at you, it sours your soul."

"Profound."

"I read it on a beer mat once."

"You have a grip on your excesses?"

Caslin looked up, meeting Reece's gaze, and raised his glass. "This is my only vice."

"You sure?"

"I've been to the bottom," Caslin said softly, "or pretty close to it. I looked elsewhere for a while."

"Drugs?"

"Yeah. At first it was a release, you know? Then there was an incident…"

"The shooting?"

"You're well informed," he said.

Reece shrugged. "People talk."

"Well… painkillers take the edge off."

"And now?" Reece asked, sipping his drink.

"Now?" Caslin paused, mulling over his answer. "Now, I have my moments but I've accepted my situation. My counsellor talks a lot about embracing the emotion, putting an end to deflection and distraction. That kind of shit." Reece laughed. "What's so funny?"

"Just western society and their approach to drug dependency. That's all. Did you know, during Vietnam, the amount of American G.I.s taking Class As was at epidemic levels. Pretty much out of control. I mean, they were freely available, cheap and let's face it, who could blame them. And yet, tens of thousands of soldiers came home from that war and there wasn't a corresponding spike in recorded addiction or drug-related crime."

"Your point?"

"This whole addiction argument. How come an army of addicts didn't swamp the US. There were some, perhaps many but the majority went back to their lives and got on with it. How much is physical and how much a state of mind?"

"What's your advice then, Sigmund?" Caslin asked, smiling.

"Choose."

"Choose?" Caslin repeated.

"Yes. Choose what you're going to be and be exactly that."

Now Caslin laughed. "Simple as."

"Simple as," Reece replied, nodding. He glanced at his watch. "Listen, I'd better make a move. I've got a train to catch."

"Where are you headed?"

"Straight down to Heathrow. I'm booked on a red-eye," Reece stood, downing his scotch, he placed the glass on the table and reached inside his pocket. "I've got something for you, for old time's sake." Taking out a USB memory stick, he passed it to Caslin who looked at it, slightly perplexed.

"What's this?"

Reece smiled. "You remember graduation year from Uni, we went to Kings Place for that concert?"

"Of course, I do. We saw Antonio Meneses, playing—"

"The Tchaikovsky recital that won him international plaudits, absolutely. Anyway, he still tours Europe and I was lucky enough to catch a performance in Berlin a couple of years ago. I purchased a copy on the night. It's well worth a listen."

Caslin eyed the memory stick, tossing it gently in his palm with the excitement that only someone with a love of the Cello would appreciate. Fond memories came back to him and he found a smile creeping across his face.

"Thanks, Aid. Thanks a lot."

Reece clapped him on the shoulder. "I figured you'd be pleased although, had my doubts that you might be into hip-hop, grime or something else these days. What with having kids and all that."

Caslin's smile faded. "Don't. It's hell."

Reece laughed. "It's been good catching up, Nate. Maybe next time I'm in town, I'll swing by."

"Anytime. You know that."

"Give my love to Karen when you see her," Reece said, making his way to the front door.

"I will," Caslin said. The two men shook hands and then warmly embraced before Reece departed. Caslin closed the door behind him. Returning to the living room, he fired up his laptop. The response of the SSD drive was rapid and he plugged in the memory stick. There was only the one file present and he double-clicked it. Within seconds, the sound of an expert cellist came from the speakers and Caslin sat back down. Thinking of his old friend, he couldn't help but wonder what Reece had done in the past. Unable to trust him as he once had, Caslin resolved to enjoy this moment and lose himself in a memory. It felt good.

Reopening the folder in front of him, he flicked through Emily Coughlan's code once more. *PN* was almost certainly a reference to Paraic Nelson and she had either met Nelson or followed him, on multiple occasions. Without any tangible cause to bring in Father Foley, the only lead currently unexplored, beyond a scan of the Police Service of Northern Ireland's database and a few phone calls, was Nelson. Picking up his mobile, Caslin called Jimmy Sullivan.

"Jimmy. Do you have any contacts in the Gardaí?" Caslin asked, raising his voice slightly over the top of the music.

"One or two," Sullivan replied, hesitantly. "What is it you're looking for?" Caslin paused as several notes appeared to drop out of key and, internally, he voiced his displeasure. Perhaps the performer wasn't quite what he once was or, more disappointingly, quite as good as Caslin remembered. "Nate? What is it you're after?"

Caslin refocussed on the conversation. "Sorry, Jimmy. Something distracted me. I'm going out to Dublin to see Paraic Nelson... and I'll need a little help."

"When?"

Caslin looked at the time. It was approaching eight o'clock. "Tonight, if I can get a flight."

CHAPTER FIFTEEN

THE FLIGHT out of Leeds landed in Dublin shortly before eleven o'clock. Passing through passport control with minimal delay Caslin, with only carry-on luggage, was one of the first to reach the arrivals zone of the airport. A small group of people waited patiently beyond the secure gates to welcome friends or relatives. Glancing around unsure of what he was expecting to see, certainly not a card with his name on it, he walked forward assessing the waiting figures. Scanning the overhead signage, he set off for the taxi rank. This late in the day, he'd need to find a hotel in the city having nothing arranged.

The automatic doors parted before him and he stepped out into a summer evening on the east coast of Ireland. It had been raining but for now was clear with the whiff of moisture on the warm breeze.

"Nathaniel Caslin?" a man asked, coming to stand alongside. Caslin glanced to his left taking in the newcomer. He was in his early fifties, powerfully built but more by way of natural bulk than muscle. Caslin replied, nodding.

"The very same. And you are?" he queried, offering his hand. The man took it in a brief handshake.

"Detective Hanlon. Seamus to my friends and any friend of

Jimmy Sullivan's is a friend of mine. I've got a car in the short stay," he replied, inclining his head in the direction of a multi-storey car park. "This way." They crossed the main thoroughfare under a green traffic light, causing consternation from several drivers who were forced to stop. Once into the car park, Hanlon led them up one flight and over to the bays marked for fifteen-minute waiting only. "This one," he told Caslin, pointing to a green Ford and unlocking it. Caslin placed his bag on the rear seat and got into the front. Once both were in and the engine was running Hanlon turned to him before engaging a gear. "What is it you are looking for from Paraic Nelson?"

"Jimmy didn't say?" Caslin queried.

"Only that it was part of a murder case. Nelson a suspect?"

Caslin wasn't entirely comfortable sharing information with a total stranger but he was out on a limb in this scenario and he needed help.

"I don't know how he fits in to this but the victim had a strong interest in him."

Hanlon bobbed his head and moved off. "I've booked you into a half-decent hotel in the centre of Dublin. I didn't think you'd mind."

"Not at all," Caslin said. "I appreciate it." Leaving the confines of the airport, Caslin took in the outskirts of the city as they headed in. He'd never visited before despite how quick and easy it was to get here and he felt disappointed for not having made the effort. Retail parks and industrial centres flew by on either side of them and the similarity to the UK struck him. The number of familiar business names leapt out in contrast to the altogether different signage denoting road nomenclature and destinations.

"Tell me," Hanlon asked casually, "why arrange this trip through Jimmy and not more… conventional channels?"

Caslin smiled, surprised the question had taken nearly ten minutes to be asked. "I wouldn't get clearance for it."

"Is this an old-fashioned hunch you've got going on?"

"Not so much, no," Caslin replied. "I could probably leave the threads where they are if I chose to."

"But you're going to pull on them?"

Caslin smiled again. "I've never liked leaving loose ends."

"You know," Hanlon began, taking on a more serious tone, "they say not to pull on loose threads because everything tends to unravel leaving one heck of a mess."

"True enough. Maybe I need it to," Caslin countered. They drove in silence for a few miles the city starting to build up around them.

"Nelson has an interesting background. Do you know of it?" Hanlon asked.

Caslin shrugged. "Some of it. Probably only the headlines."

"He was part of the Belfast Brigade of the IRA back in the day. Quite a senior figure I believe. Not to mention a convicted fraudster. A man with many dirty fingers in many dirty pies."

"So, I'm told," Caslin replied, glancing across. "What about now?"

"On the face of it a very successful businessman."

"And behind the façade?"

"Now that's another matter," Hanlon said, taking an exit from the main road signposted for the centre. "Are you going to make waves on this visit?"

"You worried?" Caslin asked, trying to gauge whether he would be helped by Sullivan's contact or potentially hindered. Pulling the car into a small car park located next to an imposing four-storey, period building, Hanlon stopped the car. Turning the engine off, he took a deep breath both hands locked on the steering wheel and staring straight ahead, before responding to the question.

"If I was a betting man, which I am by the way, I'd wager your impact will be minimal. You're here off the books implying you've got little or nothing to go on. You'll stoke the fire a bit see whether you can draw a flame. If not, you'll be away home by this time tomorrow."

"And if I do, Seamus, what then?" Caslin countered.

His host fixed him with a stare. "Then I'll be most interested in fanning it with you. I'll pick you up in the morning, eight o'clock, sharp."

The hotel room was pleasant. Left to his own devices, Caslin was certain he'd have checked into something a little less grand. Not that the accommodation was ostentatious, a tastefully decorated, contemporary room layout that spoke of comfort rather than grandeur. Opening the wardrobe, he located the room safe. Kneeling down, he set the six-digit pass-code and placed his case file and laptop inside. Sitting down at the foot of his bed he suddenly felt drained, physically and emotionally. Hanlon was spot on. He was here on a fishing expedition. There was nothing to implicate Paraic Nelson in the deaths of either Fairchild or Coughlan, merely hearsay nearly two decades old that spoke of his character and associations. And yet, Emily Coughlan had been drawn here in perhaps a very similar way to himself and now she was dead. The only name with any prior form for such violence circling her investigation was Nelson.

UNUSUALLY FOR CASLIN, he was up before the sunrise. Having been unable to sleep, he had avoided the hotel bar the night before and instead turned his energy into an early morning run. Leaving the cobbled streets of Temple Bar behind he ran the length of the North Quay Wall following the path of the River Liffey until it opened out towards the harbour. Turning east, he skirted Tolka Quay and Dublin Bay before heading back to the hotel.

Sweat was pouring from him as he walked into his room. His face felt hot to the touch and a brief look in the mirror told him more about his state of fitness than any personal trainer could manage in an hour. Stripping off, he stepped into a cool shower, holding his head under the water and trying to regulate his breathing. His legs wobbled, the strain on his calves and thighs were evident. Disappointed in himself, he showered and got dressed. Having put some effort into regaining some of his lost fitness over the past year he was somewhat alarmed to be heading in what could only be described as a backwards direction.

Descending to the lobby, he went in search of refreshment. Not feeling the desire for a "Full Irish" breakfast, he served himself with cereal and fruit, allowing a black coffee to be his morning vice. Barely had he finished when Seamus Hanlon appeared in the doorway making a beeline for him. A glance at the clock showed he was early.

"Good morning," he said, a grin splitting his chiselled features. "You about ready?"

"Of course," Caslin stated, rising. They were in the car and heading for Nelson's office minutes later.

"What kind of response are you expecting, from Nelson, I mean?" Hanlon asked, as he negotiated the traffic. It seemed to Caslin that, with a population of around two-million, everyone in the entire country travelled through Dublin's rush-hour. His chauffeur appeared to read Caslin's mind. "Some people travel for the better part of two hours just to work here."

"What is it about Dublin?"

Hanlon laughed. "It's where everything happens. What about Nelson?"

Caslin shrugged, accompanying it with a slight shake of the head. "I'll throw him a bone and see how he reacts."

"If so, this could be a quick meeting."

"Why?" Caslin asked.

"He's a cool bastard, Nelson," Hanlon replied. "Doesn't rattle easily."

"You know him?" Caslin asked but didn't get an articulated reply, more of a grunt.

"A bit."

"Are you aware of anyone taking an interest in his activities in the past few months?"

Hanlon shook his head. "Nothing has come my way to say so."

The remainder of the journey was largely spent in silence. They arrived at an office building on the western edge of the city. Hanlon parked the car and they made their way inside. There was a large information board at the entrance denoting which company was based where in the building alongside which set of elevators best served them.

"We're on four," Hanlon stated, indicating towards the eastern side. Caslin fell into step with the Irishman.

Leaving the elevator they entered reception on the fourth floor. The lady behind the desk greeted them with a broad smile, professional happiness, expertly presented.

"Good morning, gentlemen. Welcome to Forsythe's. How can I help you?" she asked.

Hanlon smiled his own greeting. "We would like to speak with Mr Nelson, please."

The receptionist glanced down, presumably at her diary of appointments, before responding. "I'm very sorry. Mr Nelson is in a meeting and... well, it's scheduled for most of this morning. I could look at making an app—"

"No. That won't be necessary," Hanlon interrupted her, brandishing his identification. "I think his meeting is about due a coffee break."

They lingered in the lobby of Forsythe Holdings & Investments for what seemed like an age but was more likely to have been less than fifteen minutes before they were ushered through into the offices beyond. Guided through a semi-open plan set-up, Caslin counted roughly two-dozen cubicles before they took a right into a narrow corridor that led to a small collection of offices at the far end of the fourth floor. Coming to the furthest one, they were passed over to another lady, waiting patiently behind a small desk. Caslin presumed this was Nelson's PA. Their guide departed and they were shown through.

The office was large with a seating area to the left denoted by a set of leather sofas arranged in a crescent. On the other side was an imposing desk easily seven feet wide with a man seated behind it, his back to them. He was looking out through the wall of floor-to-ceiling glazing, taking in the view towards the water in the distance.

Upon hearing their arrival, he turned the chair allowing Caslin his first view of the man he'd heard so much about. Nelson's appearance wasn't quite the presentation of an ogre that one might expect, bearing in mind the abject terror his reputation seemed to instil in most. He was in his mid-to-late fifties, once most likely of slim build but now spreading with the advent of age. Piercing green eyes, in stark contrast to his darker complexion, appeared to sparkle as he stood. A welcoming grin split his face revealing tobacco-stained teeth.

"Inspector Hanlon," he said warmly, too warmly for Caslin's liking. "What can I do for you this fine day.

"Paraic," Hanlon replied in greeting. "I have someone here, who would like to ask you a few questions if you don't mind?" He indicated to Caslin who stepped forward.

"Mr Nelson," Caslin began, taking out his warrant card. "I'm Inspector Caslin of North Yorkshire Police."

Nelson appeared genuinely thrown. "Yorkshire? What brings you to this Fair Isle?"

"Your name has come up in an inquiry and I need to ascertain how that's happened." Further conversation was halted by the outer door opening and Nelson's personal assistant reappearing with a tray bearing cups and a large cafetiere.

"Please, take a seat," Nelson offered. Both men did so. As the coffee was poured, Nelson didn't stand on ceremony. "How am I referenced in your case, Inspector?"

"It's a murder inquiry."

Nelson's assistant stopped pouring the coffee but only for a second. She finished up, Nelson helping himself to the nearest. "That's utterly ludicrous," he exclaimed. "How on earth did I get drawn into that?"

"Oh, come on, Paraic," Hanlon said softly. "It wouldn't be the first time."

Nelson smiled. "All a very, very long time ago and none of it proven as you well know."

"Does the name Coughlan mean anything to you?" Caslin asked, firmly intent on spotting any reaction, however slight. There wasn't one.

"No, should it? Who is he?"

"She," Caslin corrected.

"All right. Who is *she*?" Nelson asked.

"Emily Coughlan. A journalist, in her twenties."

"And she's dead, is she?" Nelson sought to clarify, taking a sip of his coffee and turning his attention to the plate of biscuits that accompanied the drinks. Caslin nodded. "No. Never heard of her. How is she linked to me?"

"I thought that you could tell me that," Caslin countered.

Nelson shook his head. "Sorry, can't help you."

"But you would, if you could. Right?" Hanlon asked. To Caslin it appeared to be asked with borderline sarcasm but not being familiar with Hanlon, he couldn't quite tell. The Garda detective was proving hard to read.

"Of course," Nelson replied, grinning. "Now, it's very sad that young... what was her name... *Emily*... has passed away but what does this have to do with me?"

Caslin tasted his coffee. It was far better than the one he'd had over breakfast. "She was investigating you and, or, your business affairs."

"Was she now?" Nelson said, unfazed. "What was she hoping to find?"

Caslin ignored the question. "What is your business, Mr Nelson?"

"Import, export predominantly," Nelson stated. "Ireland is perfectly placed to take advantage of Atlantic shipping. Much the same as your west coast in England. We ship a great deal of product between here, the UK and over to the continent. Dublin is a gateway of sorts."

"Which areas of the continent?" Caslin asked, making conversation.

"Ostensibly Rotterdam, Ostend, among others. What was her interest in my operations? I'd be interested to know. Is this yet another inexperienced journalist trying to find a story? Digging up the past, seeking a new angle. Seriously, everything on me has been done and dusted years ago. Ask your man here," he said, indicating Hanlon. "If there was anything to the rumours I'd have been locked up by now."

"Again," Hanlon said flatly.

"Excuse me?" Nelson asked.

"You'd be locked up again," Hanlon said, locking eyes with their host, taking a bite from a biscuit.

"That was a different life, Mr Hanlon. You're going back to my youth. The Seventies were a long time ago. I'm above board now."

"So it would appear," Hanlon replied, chewing through a mouthful of sugared oats.

"Any other questions?" Nelson asked, curtly. Hanlon looked to Caslin, who indicated that he didn't. "Then please do excuse yourselves gentlemen. Some of us have real work to do." Both men stood up. Caslin put his coffee down offering his hand. Nelson took it. Hanlon merely headed for the door without a backward glance. He opened it but paused as Caslin spoke.

"Come to think of it," he said, turning back to Nelson who had returned behind his desk, "how about Sylvia Marshall? You know her, don't you?"

Nelson stopped, fixing Caslin with a stare. "What about her?"

"Tell me about her."

"She died. A long time ago. What's she got to do with any of this?" Caslin could've been forgiven for thinking Nelson was markedly more interested than he had been previously but retained his reticence in showing it.

"Coughlan was looking into her as well."

Nelson didn't flinch, his expression unaltered but the stare remained, centred on Caslin. A moment passed between the two men, Hanlon observing from the doorway. "Let me know how that works out, for you," Nelson said softly, sitting down.

"I will," Caslin replied, turning on his heel and walking out. Hanlon followed Caslin past him with his eyes and, having glanced back towards Nelson, also departed allowing the door to swing closed.

They were in the elevator before any conversation was forthcoming from either man.

"Jimmy mentioned Coughlan but not Marshall. Who is she to you?" Hanlon asked. Caslin glanced across at him, noting his own reflection in the mirrored walls of the elevator. He felt enlivened by the meeting.

"You first, Seamus," Caslin said. "Tell me the story between you and Nelson. And don't insult me with any cack about barely knowing him. Jimmy Sullivan knew about Nelson and he put me onto you. My guess is you know more about Nelson than he does." A ping sounded indicating they'd reached the ground floor and the doors opened.

"That's a sharp spot from you, Nathaniel," Hanlon said but chose to keep his counsel until they were clear of the building and back to the car. Evidently mulling over his choice of words, he sat back in the driver's seat and looked at Caslin. "I'm guessing you and Jimmy go back a way?" Caslin nodded. It was true, to a point. "I've been looking at Paraic Nelson for a long time on and off. He's connected. Nothing I've worked on has stuck."

"Paramilitaries?" Caslin asked.

"I don't hear as much from within their ranks as I used to but it's more than that. I've got close to him on several occasions and he's always managed to be one step ahead as if he knows exactly what we have going on."

"Does your office leak?"

Hanlon frowned. "No more than any other police force. I can

assure you of that. He doesn't get to hear everything, of this I am certain."

"How do you know?"

Hanlon looked across at him. "I have someone. They're on the inside."

"Well integrated?"

"For the past eight months," Hanlon stated. "If Nelson knew, he wouldn't be there."

"Any decent intel?"

Hanlon smiled. "First, you can tell me about Marshall."

Caslin had to fold his hand there and then. "I was bluffing. Marshall was a name Coughlan checked into a hotel under. Her real name didn't garner much of a reaction, so I thought I'd chance it." Hanlon stared at him. The intensity of the gaze was unnerving.

"Well, it appeared to work. You suckered him."

"Really? I thought he remained calm."

"You're right, he did. However, that's the first time I've seen him lost for a response. You hooked him. A stunning effort seeing as you've no idea who she is," Hanlon said with a chuckle.

"Your source, can we utilise him?"

"He'll need to know what you're looking for. Otherwise it's a needle in a haystack."

"What about Sylvia Marshall?"

Hanlon shook his head. "Very unlikely."

"Why?"

"She's been dead longer than that company has been in existence."

CHAPTER SIXTEEN

"Who was she, Sylvia Marshall?" Caslin asked, intrigued.

"Linked to the *Provos* in a big way," Hanlon explained. "Officially, a part of Sinn Féin but definitely had ties to the boots on the ground. Following the Good Friday Agreement, she left, apparently putting the troubles behind her."

"And she's dead?"

Hanlon nodded. "Oh aye, yeah. Murdered. Must be coming on for nearly two decades ago now."

"Nelson?"

Hanlon shook his head, "Not as far as I'm aware, no. I don't think they got anyone for it but not my patch. You should know more about it than I do."

"How do you figure? Twenty years ago I was out getting hammered most nights, at university."

"She was killed north of the border in Belfast." Caslin thought on it for a moment. Nelson may well have known her but that didn't mean that he'd killed her. He could've merely been thrown by the mention of a name from his past.

"There has to be a link. Coughlan was looking into Nelson and used Marshall's name to check into a hotel."

"I'll make a call, try to find out whether there was any suspicion of his involvement in Marshall's death at the time," Hanlon said, before adding dryly, "It's a pity you can't do the same really."

Caslin smiled. "How come you're so knowledgeable about the internal workings of the paramilitaries and their political affiliations anyway?"

"I didn't like the nasty bastards popping south any more than your colleagues did. It won't help you regarding Paraic's business interests though. I very much doubt you'll find Sylvia Marshall's name will be mentioned anywhere."

"What do you think he's up to then?"

"Old fashioned smuggling operation and throw in some money laundering would be my guess. He's using Forsythe's as a front."

"What's he shipping?"

"That is where I'm struggling. Without more detail, I can't get the resources I need and without the resources—"

"You can't get the detail. I get it," Caslin said, falling silent while he thought. Turning to him, he said excitedly, "I need to get in there."

"Uh-uh, no way. Forget it—"

"Look," Caslin protested. "I'll know it when I see it. Your man has got to get me in."

"You must be out of your mind! You reckon I'm going to risk the best informant I have, let alone the months it's taken to cultivate—"

"Yes," Caslin said emphatically "I believe you will."

"And why would I do that?" Hanlon asked.

Caslin fixed him with a stare, his eyes gleaming with positivity.

"Because you don't like the nasty bastards any more than I do."

Hanlon sighed. "You reckon that's enough?"

"Plus, the fact you've had a guy in there for eight months and, correct me if I'm wrong here, you've got nothing."

"WHAT TIME DID you say he would meet us?" Caslin asked, feeling the familiar sense of building frustration. The rain was drumming on the roof of the car, squally showers carried in off of the Irish Sea.

"Relax. He'll be here," Hanlon said softly. He'd reclined his seat some time ago and now lay back, eyes closed, arms folded. A figure appeared from around the corner of the alleyway, making directly for them. Caslin couldn't make much out through the rain-soaked windscreen and in any event, he wore a hooded coat, leaning into the wind as he approached. Coming alongside, the man opened the rear passenger door and clambered in, shaking off the loose water as he did so. "Brendan," Hanlon said in greeting. The newcomer nodded his hello and glanced at Caslin in the front passenger seat.

"Nate Caslin," he said, offering his hand. Brendan took it.

"What is it you want from me, Seamus? My shift starts in half an hour."

"Exactly why we need to speak with you," Hanlon began. "I need you to get my friend here," he indicated to Caslin, "up onto the fourth floor."

Brendan took on a puzzled expression.

"Why?"

"Does it matter?" Caslin asked.

Brendan shook his head. "I guess not. Risky though."

"Can you do it?" Caslin asked. Brendan thought about it for a moment, looking him up and down before nodding.

"The contract cleaners are all part-time. Most of them barely know their line manager let alone each other. I give them access to their respective offices. I can slip you in around the same time as I do them."

"You'd best get going," Hanlon said. "I'll catch up with you later back at your hotel. You can let me know what you found then." Caslin agreed and, along with Brendan, got out of the car, turning the collar of his jacket up against the rain. The engine started and Caslin tapped the roof as Hanlon put the car into gear and drove away. The two set off on their short walk across the industrial estate to the offices of Forsythe Holdings.

Most of the building had long since emptied of staff by the time Brendan opened a door at the rear used as a service access. Ushering Caslin inside, he glanced around nervously before closing the door behind him. Leading them back into the building through an apparent labyrinth of corridors circumventing the plant rooms that controlled ventilation, air conditioning and the elevator housing, Caslin tried to keep up with the pace.

"I only have a twenty-minute window to get the cleaners to their respective floors. After that any access to a floor will be duly noted."

"That's tight."

"You're telling me but this building is managed by a security company that specialise in industrial sabotage prevention."

"Your company?" Caslin asked.

"No, I'm subcontracted. Basically a caretaker with a uniform," Brendan replied, taking a left and entering the stairwell. From there they ascended to the fourth floor. By which point Caslin was breathing heavily. Pulling his access card, Brendan swiped it and a green light illuminated along with an audible click, as the lock mechanism disengaged.

Entering the reception area, Caslin noted how different it looked under secondary lighting. Only every fourth ceiling-light was powered up giving rise to shadows everywhere.

"Is there anyone else on this floor?" Caslin asked as he was passed an access card.

"Not yet. The cleaning company are a few hands short today. It's not unusual. Their staff are unreliable. They're sending over some cover from another site. I reckon you have twenty-five, maybe thirty minutes before they get here. Take this," he said, offering Caslin a walkie-talkie. "I'll buzz you when they get here. At that point you'll have less than five minutes to get behind that reception desk," he indicated over his shoulder. "I'll start them off at the rear giving us enough time to get you out unseen. Understood?"

Calin nodded. "Understood. You done this before?"

Brendan grinned. "The card I've given you is the one the cleaners' share. It's generic and programmed to give access to the offices but not the elevators or stairwells."

"What do they do if there's a fire or emergency?"

"The system overrides everything unlocking all the emergency exits," he said over his shoulder, walking back to the elevators. Caslin checked the time. Thirty minutes at best. There wasn't a great deal of time. He set off tentatively swiping his access card to enter the open plan office suite. The light changed to green and he walked through. Despite knowing he was alone, he progressed as if he wasn't, peering into the gloom as he went. It was an eerie feeling being somewhere that he knew he shouldn't be. Of all things excitement wasn't what he was supposed to be getting out of this but he could feel the adrenalin starting to surge as his heartbeat increased.

Picking up the pace, he made for Nelson's office. Once again, he nervously swiped the access point half expecting it to turn red but it didn't and he was in. Not wishing to turn on the main lights, Caslin took out his pocket torch and went to Nelson's desk. Trying each drawer in turn, as expected, he found them all locked. Turning his attention to a line of filing cabinets, he crossed the room. The first was also securely locked but the next was open. Pulling out the top drawer, he shined the beam of light onto the contents. Scanning over the tabs, he looked for anything that stood out, a name that perhaps he had already come across. There was nothing.

One by one he opened the drawers below. He found bills of lading, tracking consignments in and out of the country, contacts for various offices in multiple destination ports around the globe but nothing that struck him as unusual. By the time he reached the end of the second cabinet, Caslin had used up most of his patience and almost all of his time. It dawned on him that a company operating as a front would, if run correctly, have everything above board at least at a glance. It would take far greater knowledge of their operations than he currently had in order to expose them.

Unwilling to give up just yet, he moved to the next cabinet. Caslin hovered, considering where his time was best spent. Brendan's insight into how this office building was managed had piqued his interest. Could such a level of security be achieved without knowing what else was going on in this company? His radio unit burst into life. Picking it up from atop the cabinet, he answered with a single click of the receiver.

"You're going to have company," Brendan's disembodied voice crackled through.

"How soon?" he whispered unsure as to why he did so. There was silence. Caslin waited. Figuring he still had a minute or two, he put the radio down and returned to the folders before him. Holding the torch between his teeth, he flicked through the folders at a greater speed until coming across one entitled *Security Services*. It wasn't anything incredibly illustrative, merely a collection of time-codes registered alongside professional services from the previous quarter but the name of the provider jumped off the paper. It was none other than *Renton Sands*. Finding no further reference to the company in that file, he moved on to the last cabinet but, much to his frustration, found it locked. Redoubling his efforts, he started back through the unlocked cabinets specifically looking for references to that company. His progress was interrupted once again by the crackle of the radio.

"You'd better be out," an anxious voice hissed at him grabbing Caslin's attention. He scooped up the unit.

"Not yet, why?" he asked, dreading the forthcoming response.

"They're in the elevator on their way up."

"The cleaners?"

"No. Paraic bloody Nelson!" Caslin's heart ran cold. He had only minutes. Shoving the filing cabinets shut, he lingered on the one file denoting Renton's name. Putting it down on the top of the cabinet, he took a picture of the header with his mobile phone via torchlight before replacing it where he found it. Closing that drawer also, he glanced around, checking to see that he'd not left an impression of his presence. Confident he was all right, he made to leave the office. Opening the door the unmistakable sound of approaching people caused him to close it again. A flash of panic struck him but he looked around for another way out. There were double doors beyond the casual seating area and he ran to them testing the handle gently in case someone was the other side. The room was shrouded in darkness and he slipped through pulling the doors to behind him.

Before turning off his torch, he realised he was in an adjoining conference room. There was a huge oval table in the centre with multiple chairs set around it. Eyeing another door on the far side, he judged that to be his best exit route but resisted the urge to take flight. Curious as to what Nelson was doing in the office at this time of the night, he resolved to take the gamble and wait. Something niggled him but he couldn't put his finger on what but as soon as he heard the party entering the office on the other side of the door it hit him. *The radio.* It was where he'd left it on top of the filing cabinet. Cursing himself for being such an idiot, he rolled scenarios over in his mind in quick succession. None of them ended well.

Dismissing it as something he could no longer control he tried to listen as best he could. Nelson's voice was easily distinguishable. As far as he could make out there were two others, perhaps three, but only one appeared to be in conversation with Nelson. The accent was heavy but Caslin judged it was most likely eastern European but any more than that, he couldn't tell. What he rapidly concluded was they were certainly talking about him. Clearly their visit that afternoon had caused some consternation.

"… but what was he doing here?" the voice said, stress evident in the tone.

"How should I know?" Nelson replied calmly. "He doesn't know anything."

"How can you be sure?"

"Because I would know," Nelson replied confidently. "I will accept, interest from across the water is… unexpected… at this point and how the hell he's onto us is beyond me, truly. But I assure you our timetable remains unchanged."

"We must assume they are—" conversation stopped at that moment, prematurely in Caslin's mind. Looking around, he wondered if he should run for the door or hide. He picked the former and ran as quickly as he dared around the conference table slowing as he reached the exit. Cracking the door ajar, he checked that the corridor beyond was clear and slipped out back into the sanctity of the secondary lighting. Managing to close the door behind him momentarily before the double doors flew open from Nelson's office, he paused, waiting for the alarm to be raised but the shout didn't come. Aware that, potentially, he barely had moments, he sprinted down the corridor. Reaching a junction, he took the path left colliding with a man operating a floor polisher who was sent sprawling to the ground. Using headphones, he'd been completely blindsided.

Considering that he was now, most likely, either being pursued or was about to be Caslin ran through his options as he picked himself up and took off down the corridor. If Brendan had contacted him on the radio they'd know he was still around. Had they only found the unit by itself they may assume his presence but might not initiate a full lockdown. On the other hand, to use his access card now to escape, would tip them off as to how he had gotten in in the first place.

Stopping at the next bend, in order to catch his breath, he listened out but heard no signs of pursuit. Conscious that they could be searching for him, he realised the first he might know about it could be when they were upon him.

Turning the access card over and over between his fingers a thought struck him. It was quite obvious to him as he stood there but why he hadn't picked up on it before irritated him. Pushing the thoughts aside, he knew he would return to the idea when he got home. For now, he had more pressing problems.

In the corner of his eye, he noticed a sign, suspended from the ceiling. The familiar symbol of a stick-man, running on a green background indicated the nearest fire exit. Looking to his left, he found what he was looking for. Running over, he used his elbow to strike the fire-alarm box, breaking the glass and initiating the system. Emergency floor-lighting kicked in and he took off, towards the stairs. Muttering a silent prayer of thanks towards Brendan, he was out and into the stairwell moments later. Charging downwards, he took them as fast as he could, nearly losing his balance on several occasions.

Upon reaching the ground floor, he didn't stop but took the nearest path to the outside. Once there, he hugged the building, running towards the rear, safe in the knowledge that his departure from that side wouldn't be visible from anyone in Nelson's office. Assuming of course that they were still there. Turning the corner, he glanced back to observe figures leaving via the main entrance. Various perplexed looking individuals were gathering in the car park, Brendan being among them, corralling them into a roll call. It was a short sprint up an embankment to get clear of the building, dropping down the other side into the adjacent building's car park. From here, Caslin sought cover and put as much distance between himself and his would-be pursuers as he could.

The moment he felt safe enough to do so, he took up a position out of sight from the main thoroughfares and sank down onto his haunches to catch his breath. Far from the evidence of a smoking gun, at least he'd uncovered another connection, albeit one about as tenuous as it comes. The triangle of Coughlan, Fairchild and Nelson, although further reinforced, still remained shrouded in darkness.

CHAPTER SEVENTEEN

WALKING through the lobby of his hotel, Caslin was still buzzing with the surge of adrenalin generated by the evening's events. The reference to *Renton Sands* wouldn't be strong enough to progress the investigation in itself notably because he had no legal recourse to have come by the information the way he had. Taking out his mobile, he opened his contacts list scanning down the list for Reece's number. A voice called out to him. It was the night porter behind reception.

"Mr Caslin," he said, beckoning him over. "Your colleague was here asking after you."

"What did he say?" Caslin asked, walking towards him and glancing up from his phone.

"I'm sorry, he didn't leave a message."

"That's okay, thanks," Caslin assured him. "I'll catch up with him later."

Turning away, he dialled Reece's mobile and headed across the lobby. The call struggled to connect. Reaching the elevator, Caslin summoned it before glancing at his screen to check the call progress. Hanging up, he redialled. This time he was redirected straight to an automated message, *the number you have dialled has not been recognised, please check and...* Caslin hung up.

The doors parted and he stepped in. Gently tapping his phone against his lips, he considered whether it was a network issue or…

"Please hold the lift," a man called, trotting across from the lounge bar at pace. Caslin pressed the hold button allowing the newcomer to ease off. Stepping in, he nodded his appreciation as the doors came together.

"What floor?" Caslin asked, pressing the third for himself.

"Three is good, thanks," he replied. Caslin put his phone back into his pocket resolving to try Reece again later. The elevator lurched to a halt accompanied by the notification they had reached the third floor. Caslin allowed the other passenger out first who turned to the left. Caslin went right towards his room. Upon reaching his door, he wondered why Hanlon had come looking for him at the hotel when they'd agreed he would contact him once clear of Nelson's office. Perhaps they'd misunderstood each other's intentions. Dipping his key-card into the lock, he opened the door and stepped through.

The door swung closed behind him and Caslin was greeted by three men in his room. Two were standing at either end of the room, another was sitting on the end of his bed. The surprise was momentary as all three looked towards him.

"Good evening, Inspector Caslin," the seated man said, politely.

"I think there's been a mistake," Caslin replied. "I didn't order room service." He spun on his heel making for the door. Unsure of whether the three were moving after him, he assumed the worst. Dragging the door open he glanced over his shoulder. A fateful misjudgement as he missed the man in the corridor, landing a blow to his midriff. Air exploded from his lungs and he crumpled to the floor. Bent double, on his knees, struggling for breath, Caslin felt like his chest was on fire and his eyes were about to pop out. Strong hands took a hold of his jacket heaving him up off the floor whether he was willing or not.

Unceremoniously dumped back inside his hotel room, he fell

against the wall. Seconds later he was able to draw breath albeit with sharp pain accompanying every inhalation.

"As I was saying," the seated man said. "Good evening, Inspector Caslin."

"Fuck off," Caslin replied, bitterly. Glancing over his shoulder, he recognised the man from the elevator. Steadying himself by bracing against the wall, he stood, assessing the group. Two of the three were evidently the muscle. Their attentive nature, physique, coupled with their general stance defined them as such as they stood silently awaiting instructions from their senior. A third was of slender build and seemed far more interested in the contents of the room than in Caslin. The leader had a somewhat ascetic demeanour about him. The others hung on his every signal, be it even the slightest of intimations. They were well drilled.

"Your phone, if you please?" he said. Caslin locked eyes with him, defiance burning brightly. The man looked away, bobbing his head. Caslin felt another blow, this time to his left side, a forceful kidney punch. He dropped once again. Without waiting for permission, he was roughly shoved against the wall, enabling better access to his pockets. The briefest of searches returned his phone. A quick review of the handset then took place. The finger-print scanner was noted and another silent instruction was given. Caslin felt someone grip his hand. Struggling, he managed to pull his arm free. Two swift kicks to his chest and stomach followed, all resistance evaporating as he coughed uncontrollably, spitting bile. His limp hand was used to unlock the phone before it was passed over. The man on the far side of the room came to collect the handset. He was young, possibly in his early twenties. Using another phone, he connected the two devices and began tapping away at one of the screens.

Taking everything in from his position on the floor, Caslin now realised they had already opened the safe. The contents of his case file were strewn across the desk alongside his laptop. They'd hardwired it to another, presumably to bypass the security and download the data from the drive.

"Is violence always necessary, Nathaniel? You could have saved yourself the pain and just given me the phone." Caslin looked up, eyeing the man warily. He wasn't Irish nor was the man from the elevator. With hindsight, he should've clocked that something was up when the porter spoke to him.

"Forgive me. My brother always said I was never good at sharing," Caslin replied, levering himself up into a kneeling position. "Who did you say you are?"

The man grinned without any genuine humour. "What is it you hope to achieve by coming here to Ireland, Inspector?"

"See the sights, drink the Guinness," Caslin replied with intended sarcasm. The man to his left tensed and he braced himself for another onslaught but was relieved when restraint was indicated.

"How are you coming with the phone," he asked over his shoulder.

"I'm in. I'll just need a minute to transfer everything over."

"Good."

"Who the hell are you people?" Caslin asked. The man on the bed stood up, facing him.

"You're in way over your head, Inspector Caslin," he said in a casual manner. "From this moment on Forsythe Holdings, Paraic Nelson and any other interest you hold in his business ventures are off limits to you permanently. Do you understand?"

"You don't work for Nelson, do you?" Caslin asked, standing up whilst gingerly touching his side.

The man shook his head. "Certainly not. I serve a far higher authority."

"And who might that be…" Caslin questioned drawing yet another, enigmatic smile. "SIS, DIA… Special Branch?"

"You're booked on the first flight out of Dublin back to Leeds tomorrow morning. Your ticket is there," the man indicated an envelope on the desk. "Be on it," he added in a forceful tone, walking past Caslin to the door which was duly opened for him. Across the room, the technical work was complete. Caslin's phone was tossed onto the bed and his laptop was disconnected from the other.

"And if I'm not?" he asked, without turning.

"Your superiors are expecting you. I would strongly advise, for your own sake that you don't disappoint them... or me... for that matter."

With that, he was gone. The remaining members of the team filed past him and out into the corridor. As the door was slammed shut by the auto-close mechanism, Caslin hurried over, flicking the latch to secure it. Knowing they were unlikely to come back he still sought that reassurance. Only then did he breathe a sigh of relief.

"AND YOU RECKON they were your intelligence services?" Hanlon queried. Caslin nodded. Every passing step made him wince. The bruising to his rib-cage was already starting to show. "Fair to say we're not the only ones investigating Nelson then." Caslin snorted cynically, stopping to lean on the railings. They were on the quay-side overlooking Dublin Port with the contemporary Samuel Beckett Bridge in the foreground lit in a stunning fashion by night, only slightly less impressive by day.

"You have more faith in our agencies than I do, my friend," Caslin said quietly.

"You think they're not?"

Caslin shrugged. "Maybe. They might be using him or his operation. He could be unaware but—"

"But?"

"You said it yourself," Caslin glanced over, flicking an inquisitive eyebrow. "Nelson always seems to be one step ahead. You ever wondered how he manages it?"

Hanlon's expression changed. "Well, they don't have authority over me."

"See what happens if... when... you get close enough to

damage him. From what he was saying in that meeting the other night, he isn't worried about the police in the slightest."

"Throws up another scenario for you," Hanlon went on. Caslin encouraged him. "If Coughlan was getting close to exposing Nelson it might not be him she should've been wary of."

"Now that's something I hadn't considered," Caslin agreed. His thoughts shifted to Broadfoot and the indirect order to shut down his investigation. He chose not to share. "For a moment, I wondered how they got onto me so fast?"

"And you thought of me?"

"Only for a moment," Caslin replied, honestly.

"You didn't like how Paraic and I were with each other, did you?"

"At first. You play a role well, Seamus."

"It's cat and mouse between the two of us."

"Which is which?" Caslin asked, grinning. Hanlon returned it with one of his own before glancing at the waves lapping against the quayside below them. "Have you spoken to Brendan?"

"Briefly. He's on edge but he's a decent guy, used to be military until he had an accident and they invalided him out. I'll keep an eye out for him. What are you going to do now?"

"You mean other than go home?"

Hanlon chuckled. "I know you're not going to let this lie. For men like you it's not in your nature."

Caslin smiled but said nothing.

CHAPTER EIGHTEEN

"WHAT THE BLOODY hell do you think you were doing over there?" Broadfoot was yelling. Caslin sat in silence feeling very much the schoolboy in the headmaster's office. "You had no clearance—"

"I didn't know I needed it, sir," Caslin countered. "I'm heading up this investigation—"

"No, you're not," Broadfoot stated, calming himself down and pulling up a chair. "Not anymore."

Caslin seethed. "You're taking me off the case? On what grounds?"

"How about breaking and entering for starters?" Caslin sank back in his chair. The dossier on him was clearly substantial. "It's lucky for you that we don't want to turn this fiasco into an international incident. I expect the Irish would have a field day with this if they chose to."

"But they're not?" Caslin asked, hope edging into his voice.

"No but I've had to do some serious arse kissing. Not just to them but to the chief—"

"Probably going to mess with your promotion prospects—"

"Whatever were you thinking?" Broadfoot hissed.

"Sir," Caslin began, "there's more going on here than just Schmidt. Paraic Nelson has ties to both our victims. Coughlan was either on to something with Nelson or he was feeding her information. Wilfully or not I can't say. Likewise with Fairchild. He had links to the same firm as Nelson. There's a circle here but I don't know what's at the centre of it. I know Dublin was a risky move but we needed to explore it and you wouldn't have given permission, let alon—"

"You're damn right I wouldn't have. Not with what you have, it's circumstantial at best."

"We can't just look the other way."

"I've told you once before we all have our masters, Nathaniel."

"None of whom outrank the oath we both took when we signed on. Or have you forgotten that?" Caslin asked forcefully.

"Get out of my sight," Broadfoot said in an understated manner. "I don't want to see you back in this station before the end of the week."

Caslin stood, taking a deep breath as he did so. "Am I on suspension, sir?"

Broadfoot stared at him, red-faced. "If the Irish government wanted to take issue with your actions you wouldn't be on a suspension. You'd be out of a job."

"Annual leave?" Caslin asked, slightly mocking and most certainly pushing his luck.

"Out," the DCS muttered.

The door to Broadfoot's office clicked as the latch dropped into place. Caslin exhaled setting off for CID. He planned to make two stops before leaving. Entering the squad room, several faces acknowledged his arrival but few appeared willing to talk. News had spread and everyone waited on tenterhooks to gauge the reaction to his dressing down. Caslin wasn't bothered. It had happened before and he was confident it would certainly happen again. Entering his office, he began flicking through the various messages left on post-its, stuck to his desk. Nothing was of significance.

"Sir, got a sec?" Holt asked, standing at the doorway looking nervous.

Caslin glanced over. "Of course, Terry. That's about all I have, mind you. What can I do for you?" Holt hovered at the door, reluctant to enter. Caslin beckoned him in. "Come on, Terry. Spit it out."

Holt entered, glancing over his shoulder as he did so, "Thing is—" Another knock at the door saw Hunter walk in, Caslin greeted her with a wave.

"Sorry, Terry. I didn't mean to interrupt," she said.

"Ah… no, it's all right," Holt mumbled. "It's nothing, really. A personal matter that's all."

"Can it wait five days?" Caslin asked. "I'll be back on Monday, Terry."

"Absolutely."

Holt left, shooting a nervous smile towards Hunter as he passed her. She returned the smile shifting it to a frown once he was out of her sightline.

"What was that about, do you reckon?" she asked.

Caslin shook his head. "No idea. What can I do for you? You have one minute and then I am out of here."

"Going anywhere nice?"

"There's a bottle of Macallan with my name on it somewhere. I expect I'll come across it on the way home," he replied with a wry grin.

"Nice," Hunter said, "particularly at lunchtime."

"Time on my hands, Sarah. Time on my hands," he replied. "What do you need?"

"A couple of things. The temporary pathologist has ruled Schmidt's death as accidental. He's referred it to the coroner but sees no reason to investigate further."

"That's not a shock," Caslin said. "Who is he? Anyone we know?"

Hunter shook her head. "Never come across him before. I think he's on a secondment from the Ministry of Defence."

Caslin looked at her chewing his lower lip. "That's interesting."

"What do you make of it?"

He shrugged. "Probably for the best if I make as little of it as possible. Did you get to the bottom of the missing bedsheets?"

Hunter shook her head. "No. That's bugging me."

"But no-one else evidently," Caslin said rhetorically. "What's the other thing?"

"Sir?"

"You said you had two things?"

"Oh, yes. Broadfoot called down. He says I'm to take the team for the remainder of the week. Presumably this is what's prompted your plans for the day?"

"For the week, my dear Hunter," he said. "If you need me, you know where I'll be. You'll do just fine."

Leaving his office before Hunter had a chance to, he clapped her lightly on the shoulder as he passed. The sanguine demeanour left her visibly confused. Departing CID, Caslin took the stairs down but rather than make for the exit via the lobby, he took a left heading towards the evidence archive. Signing himself in, he went in search of both Emily Coughlan's personal effects, such as they were, along with those of Fairchild. Once he had both boxes, he donned latex gloves and began rummaging through their contents until he found what he was looking for.

Holding the transparent evidence bags up alongside each other, he silently chastised himself. Here he was, now able to confirm what had struck him whilst on the run from Nelson's office in Dublin. Having tried to match Coughlan's key-card to a hotel room they had wasted days in a fruitless search. Fairchild's security pass for KL Global had been right there all along. The two cards were identical. Coughlan knew Fairchild and both knew Foley. The question now foremost in his mind was the dynamic in which their relationship took. Was Fairchild a willing communicator or was she blackmailing him. The latter seemed unlikely. By all accounts, Coughlan was still pretty green when it came to this level of investigative journalism.

Upon hearing someone else entering the archive room, Caslin

quickly secreted the two cards inside his jacket. Replacing the lids on the evidence boxes, he returned them to their respective shelves. Signing himself out, he returned to the ground floor and this time left the building through the main entrance. Crossing the car park, he glanced around as if unsure as to whether he was being followed. Unlocking his car, he drove out of Fulford Road keeping a watchful eye in the rear-view mirror.

The first stop he made was at a supermarket. Withdrawing cash from the ATM, he put it into his wallet and passed through the entrance. Once inside, Caslin went directly to the tech section seeking out the mobile phones they had for sale. A member of staff approached him.

"Can I help you with anything?"

"I want your cheapest pay as you go phone," Caslin replied, scanning the shelves.

"We have some excellent contract options. Even for occasional use they're far cheaper than you think—"

Caslin looked at the assistant, barely older than his son, Sean.

"Non-contract."

"Okay, we have these—"

"That one," Caslin stated, indicating the cheapest, "and one of those," he added, pointing to an in-car charger.

Having parted with nearly fifty-pounds in cash, Caslin returned to the car park. Not wasting any time, he unpacked the phone on his way out discarding the packaging into a waste bin at the entrance doors. Getting into his car, he plugged the charger into the auxiliary point of the central console and connected the phone. The screen lit up. Caslin started the car and set off for the city centre. Turning onto the ring road, he skirted the city and headed west. Rush hour was building and whereas it would usually frustrate, today it signalled he was on time.

A little after six o'clock, he pulled off the main road bringing the car to a halt. The spaces were already numerous but many staff hadn't left for the day and so Caslin took up a position away from the offices shrouded under the overhang of sprawling vegetation, strategically planted to improve the aesthetics of the car park. Lifting his recent purchase, he dialled Reece's number only to be advised, once again, that the number was unobtainable. Looking up his new contact at Renton Sands, Caslin called it. After a few rings, the call connected.

"Martin Champion," a polished voice said, answering.

"Mr Champion. It's Detective Inspector Caslin from North Yorkshire Police. I'm sorry to trouble you this late in the day."

"Not at all, Inspector," he replied. "Forgive me for interrupting but… is everything okay?"

Caslin was slightly taken aback. "Regarding what, sir?"

"Well, you're phoning. Is my wife—"

"Oh, no… please, everything is fine, I'm sure," Caslin assured him. "I'm calling you regarding the Fairchild case." There was a pause at the end of the line.

"Fairchild case?"

"Yes. The death of Christopher Fairchild. I'm the investigating officer in his murder inquiry. I understand that you're Mr Fairchild's contact at Renton Sands."

"I see. Yes, that's true. What do you require from me?"

"I'm trying to get in touch with one of your colleagues. He's left town and I wanted to check a few things with him but can't raise his mobile. I was wondering whether you would be able to point me in his direction."

"I'll see what I can do. What's his name?"

"Aiden Reece."

There was silence apart from the telltale sound of keys being tapped on a keyboard.

"That's not one I recognise, Inspector. One moment." Caslin waited while the search was returned. "Do you have the correct name?"

"Of course," Caslin said.

"Not on my system," Champion said. "Who did you say he worked for?"

"Renton, the same as you."

"Not according to our records. You say he was working with us?"

"No. *For you*. He has been for years."

"I'm sorry, Inspector. Your information must be incorrect. Can I help you with anything else?"

Caslin's mind was racing. "How well did you know Christopher Fairchild?"

"Hardly at all. We traded emails. I'm over here in Singapore and spend little time in the UK. We would have the occasional conversation regarding investment structures but other than that, very little contact. I have a note here to say his company have already been in touch. Our account will be administered by one of the senior partners in future."

"Which one? If you don't mind me asking?"

"Not at all. Tobias Eldridge."

"And you're no longer worried about Renton's exposure."

"Exposure to what?"

"Never mind," Caslin said. "Thank you for your time."

"Not at all, Inspector," Champion replied before hanging up.

Caslin set the phone back down. The exodus of people from the nearby office buildings was slowing to a trickle. Fewer vehicles remained. Another thirty minutes and he would be set. Thoughts drifted over the conversation with Champion. Alarm bells were sounding but as to what they were advising him, he was less certain. The notion of being played kept revisiting him no matter how hard he tried to push it away. The puzzling question was by whom? Realising there might be a few stragglers putting in some extra time at the end of their work day, Caslin reclined his seat. Lying back, he closed his eyes, seeking a level of clarity that thus far had escaped him.

Awaking to find himself in darkness with only the overhead lighting illuminating the car park, Caslin sat up. Glancing at the dashboard, he saw the clock read 22:35. Looking around, there were barely a handful of cars nearby. Reasonably certain that he could safely expect the offices to be empty, he got out of the car.

The distant hum of the city carried on the breeze as he crossed towards the entrance.

Approaching the building, he saw no movement within which was a good sign. The main doors were locked as expected. Reaching into an inside pocket, he took out Fairchild's access card. Caslin was hopeful that no-one had yet seen fit to revoke his clearance. Removing it from the evidence bag, he eyed the card for a magnetic strip but there wasn't one, only a small chip embedded in the rear. Laying the card flat to the pad, he touched it. The light changed from red to green and a reassuring click greeted his ear. Caslin walked into KL Global.

Making his way through the lobby he walked with purpose as if he belonged there. That was a trick he'd learned long ago at boarding school. With no father to teach him and only his peers to learn from, Caslin adopted what he saw as the best attributes others had on show. Personal confidence, natural charm and how to come across as the one guy in the room everyone wanted to know helped mask his frailties with a cloak of invincibility. All traits he was happy to use when it suited. In this case, looking like he had every right to be somewhere when he most certainly didn't.

Taking the stairs in order to avoid the attention of anyone who might be present, he reached his intended floor after a somewhat grinding ascent. Heading directly to Fairchild's office the access card breached every security barrier he came to. As it turned out, there wasn't a soul present and judging by the levels of presentation the cleaners had been and gone. Coming to stand before the door to the office, Caslin paused as a thought crossed his mind. Swapping Fairchild's card for the other in his possession, he hesitated for a moment considering whether he'd read this whole situation wrong. Pushing the thought aside, he pressed the card against the access pad. The light turned green and he was in. Exhaling deeply, as another piece of the jigsaw fell into place, Caslin closed the door behind him.

Emily Coughlan had been here before.

CHAPTER NINETEEN

WITH THE PRIMARY purpose of his visit proving successful, Caslin set about Fairchild's files by torchlight. The team had been sifting through the financials for days, so he knew not to waste time looking for the obvious. The motivation here was to join the dots and nothing more. Doing so would give him leverage to keep the investigation alive. It didn't take long before Forsythe Holdings and Investments came into view. A quick scan revealed nothing referencing Paraic Nelson directly but the significance of joining three players in this case, Forsythe's, Renton Sands and KL Global, buoyed Caslin's optimism.

"How did you know what to look for?" Caslin said under his breath, Emily Coughlan foremost in his mind. Other company names came and went and frustratingly, Caslin felt some of them were no doubt relevant but without a reference point he was scrabbling around in the dark. Closing the folder in his hand, Caslin placed it onto the top of the open drawer. Glancing around at the number of filing cabinets along with the multitude of lever-arch files adorning bookcases around the room it dawned on him. He'd got as much as he would from this venture. "You knew where to look, you must have," Caslin said softly, thinking out loud.

Replacing the folder back where he had found it, Caslin pushed the drawer closed. As expected there wasn't a smoking gun. However, the companies were linked via business, the victims knew each other and someone, somewhere was very keen to ensure the details never reached the light of day. Crossing the office he cast an eye across Fairchild's desk. Trying the drawers he found them to be secured. Realising that he wasn't going to get anything else useful, Caslin resolved to call it a day. First checking the corridor beyond was clear he slipped out closing the door behind him. As before when he had arrived he descended via the stairs and passed through the lobby without incident. Having not triggered any alarms, he figured no-one would bother to review the surveillance recordings from the security cameras. The impromptu search would in all likelihood pass unnoticed.

Picking up the pace, he trotted back to his car. Setting off for home, Caslin considered what his next move should be. The friction with Broadfoot was going to cause a problem. Even if the DCS could be brought onside who above him in the chain would also need convincing? Leaving the office buildings behind him and pulling out onto the main road another car moved off behind him. Caslin noticed the vehicle's lights coming on shortly after it set off. Paying attention to the car in his mirrors, he watched as it took a left and disappeared from view shortly after following his course. Taking a few unnecessary turns to satisfy his paranoia, Caslin relaxed as the vehicle didn't reappear.

Leaving his car in one of the city-centre car parks, he entered the cobbled pedestrian zone of the old town. The Shambles were quiet what with the time approaching midnight on a week day. Every bar and restaurant were long since closed. Despite this, Caslin found his senses piqued as he picked his way through the narrow streets, back to his flat in Kleiser's Court. The sound of footfalls nearby came to his ear but when he glanced over his shoulder no-one else was present. Likewise a shadow would flash across the corner of his vision but under scrutiny there was nothing to note out of the ordinary. Caslin was on edge and he knew it.

Coming to the communal access to Kleiser's Court, he stopped a few feet from the door. Looking in both directions of Stonegate, nothing stood out as unusual. The lights illuminating the nearby Minster and the myriad of independent artisan shop windows were all that drew his attention. Taking out his keys, he stepped forward and unlocked the door. There was that sound again. Footfalls on stone. Caslin slipped into the passageway gently pushing the outer door to but not closed. Edging back into the shadows he waited. A hand grasped the edge of the door stopping it from closing.

Caslin drew a deep breath and set himself. As soon as he recognised inwards movement he charged forward, throwing his entire body weight against the door. The solid hardwood construction of the door elicited a deep thud, followed immediately by a groan from the other side. Whoever sought to enter released their grip. Caslin took advantage of the surprise pulling the door open and lunging forward, aiming a punch at the man now stumbling backwards. At the last moment, he managed to pull the force of the blow. Not quickly enough for Terry Holt, already clutching the side of his face, who took yet another whack for good measure. A strange sound emitted from within him, like that of a mortally wounded animal, as he dropped to his haunches with one hand held aloft in protest. A flash of anger and relief came over Caslin at the same moment.

"Terry!" he exclaimed, curbing the adrenalin rush as best he could. "What are you doing here?"

"Sorry, sir," Holt replied, looking up. "Any chance I can have that word?"

"You couldn't have phoned?"

CASLIN PASSED OVER A DAMP HAND-TOWEL, ice cubes packed tightly within. Holt accepted it applying the compress to the side of his face. Caslin wondered whether in daylight he'd be able to make out the grain of the timber on Holt's skin.

"What's on your mind, Terry?"

"The financials, sir," Holt said, removing the compress. His skin was reddening and looked tender to the touch. It was likely to bruise. "I haven't managed to get entirely to the bottom of it. There's too much to go through."

"Give me the headlines."

"The financial accountant we got over from the Serious Fraud Office uncovered an abnormal pattern of trades. KL, or Fairchild I should say, was adopting positions on the markets that didn't seem to make sense at first. Subsequently though they turned out to be advantageous to certain clients."

"That winning streak you were talking about before?" Caslin clarified.

"Bigger than I had found though. We only had access to the accounts administered by Fairchild but the number of companies that benefitted—"

"All of his, right?"

Holt nodded. "Every one."

"Would this stand out within the company itself?"

"There's no way that only Fairchild would see this. The senior management must have been aware."

"They were probably benefitting their own client-lists at the same time."

"There's more. The clients appear to have been communicating with each other. On the surface it's all legit but once you delve deeper looking into subsidiaries, who owns what, it all starts to become clearer. It's an operation involving multiple shell companies registered around the globe. Contracts are being awarded to other companies on KL's client list just prior to trades being logged on their future performance."

"Insider dealing?" Caslin asked.

"Exactly," Holt confirmed, "with Fairchild, for example, arranging shorts on particular stocks as and when required. However, thinking we know and being able to prove it are entirely different matters. The SFO want the case. To be fair, they have the software capable of tracking this kind of thing. We've got no chance unless someone in the know starts singing."

Caslin sat upright. "What was that?"

"What?"

"What did you just say?"

"That we've got no chance—"

"No, after that."

"Unless someone in the know feels like telling us how they're doing it. We'll struggle to prove what is—"

"Someone on the inside," Caslin said quietly, almost to himself.

"Yes, someone on the inside with intimate knowledge of how they go about it."

"Someone like Chris Fairchild," Caslin stated.

"I guess so, yes," Holt agreed. "What are you thinking?"

"Two dead, an investigative journalist and someone who may have been singing."

"Fairchild would've burned himself at the same time."

"He was dying, Terry. With only a few months to live what did he have to lose? The next question is why would he throw it all out there?" Both men sat in silence for a few minutes, Holt returning the ice to his battered face. "What did you find on the NGOs that Fairchild was working on?"

"Nothing untoward there, sir. Why?"

"It strikes me as an intriguing mix of clients that he took on."

"Smokescreen for the illegal trades?" Holt suggested.

"Or a salve for the conscience," Caslin replied. "Why didn't you bring this up earlier in the office rather than creeping around outside here?"

Holt shook his head. "I don't want to speak out of turn."

"Bit late for that."

Holt agreed. "Probably. Ever since I started looking at those financials and in particular when the guy from the SFO came in on it… it hasn't felt right. It's been different, you know?"

"Not really, Terry, no," Caslin said flatly.

"I got the impression… that the SFO were ahead of the game."

"In what way?"

"They covered a lot of ground very quickly, tracing ownerships titles and global bank accounts with an impressive level of speed."

"So?"

"Sir. Government departments aren't that fast… ever. They had to know, then…"

"Then?"

"I know compartmentalising when I see it. Information flowing in my direction started to dry up and was rerouted."

"Where to?"

Holt took the towel away, glancing nervously at Caslin. "Upstairs."

"Broadfoot?"

"I reckon. Maybe higher. Attitudes started to change from professional to overly friendly. Almost as if I was being put off guard, to keep me onside whilst treating me like a mushroom. You know, keeping me in the dark and feeding me on shit."

"Illustrative," Caslin said, exhaling deeply.

"The point is, they're side lining our investigation. Everything had become vague and nondescript… unprovable. Despite this, they've made moves to transfer the case and files to them."

"Has it been done?"

"Not yet but it'll be a matter of days now that it's being shut down at our end."

"What did the Germans bring back on Schmidt?"

"When he died they had him fronting as an unofficial agent for an arms manufacturer but selling illegally on the black market. By all accounts, he was a significant asset, well established."

"He'd have made a lot of connections along the way," Caslin said thoughtfully.

"True, the Germans are bricking it that he may have been playing them all along."

"There's a lot of it around," Caslin mused openly. "Nothing is quite what it seems." He stood up, crossing to the window and looking down into Stonegate. Putting his hands in his pockets, his fingers brushed against the memory stick that Reece had given him. Taking it out, he rolled it in the palm of his hand. "Nothing is quite what it seems," he repeated.

"Sir?" Holt asked in response to a perceived question.

"This," Caslin said, holding up the memory stick. Throwing it to Holt who deftly caught it one handed, he pointed at it. "Have a look, would you?" Holt examined it with a cursory inspection.

"May I?" he indicated Caslin's laptop. Powering it up, Holt plugged the drive in and waited a few moments. Right-clicking he went through the properties before opening the file. Seconds later music began to play. Holt glanced at Caslin, slightly perplexed. "Not my style."

"Anything about the file?" Caslin queried.

Holt returned his attention to the computer shaking his head. "No. Nothing. Why, what are you expecting?"

Caslin shook his head just as the maligned notes played out. He took on a pained expression. "No idea. It was just a thought."

"You don't like it either?" Holt asked.

"I do, very much. A friend gave it to me. He's peripherally linked to the case and I was hoping he'd thrown me a bone. The sound recording's either got an error in it somewhere or the cellist wasn't very good. The latter, I would argue, is impossible. Perhaps it's my machine or—"

"Hang on," Holt said, returning his focus to the file. He paused the playback and busily set about pressing keys.

"What are you doing?" Caslin asked. Walking over, he could see Holt had connected to the internet and was accessing a site he didn't recognise. "What's that?"

"One second," was the only reply which turned out to be five minutes. An excited Terry Holt voiced his satisfaction at an achievement. "Got it."

"Got what?" Caslin asked. Holt looked at him.

"It wasn't an error in the recording. It was deliberate," Holt said with a smile, angling the screen in his direction. Caslin came to look over his shoulder, unsure of what he was seeing. An image was gradually revealing itself, one line at a time from the top to the bottom.

"What am I looking at, Terry?"

"Someone embedded an image into the file then altered it so you'd notice."

"Altered it how?"

"The notes that you didn't like. They were deliberate, manipulated after the recording. Presumably, your friend expected you to find it. Now it's just a case of decoding the data."

"He expected much," Caslin said, focussing on the download in progress. They waited patiently. The following minutes felt like hours. The image was a photograph, apparently taken in a bar some years previously. Clearly visible, seated in a booth in the foreground was a young Aiden Reece, beer in hand, grinning with his other arm draped across the shoulder of an attractive woman. Caslin didn't recognise her nor the man sitting awkwardly to her right. However, standing behind the couple, leaning over with hands on their shoulders, smiling for the shot was none other than Paraic Nelson.

CHAPTER TWENTY

"Do you know them?" Holt asked, glancing over his shoulder. Caslin blew out his cheeks. Pointing at the image, he nodded.

"That one there, standing at the back, is Paraic Nelson. A younger version anyway."

"The others?"

"We'll have to find out," Caslin stated. Holt's expression didn't change, his gaze lingering on his boss for a moment before he turned back to the screen. Caslin's mobile phone vibrated on the coffee table indicating he'd received a text. His eyes flicked towards it and then to the clock on the wall. Picking up the phone, he saw it was from an unknown number and opened it. The message was simple, *Meet 6 A.M. York Racecourse.* Pressing the home key, he stared at the phone for a second.

"Would your friend know?" Holt asked. Caslin looked at him quizzically.

"Know what?"

"Who they are?" he said, pointing at the image on the screen.

"Probably. Listen, Terry, let's keep this to ourselves for the time being. We need to identify these others. Can you take a copy and run it through Nelson's known associates?"

"First thing," Holt said, standing up. Stifling a yawn, he

touched the side of his face, evidently still sore. "I'll see myself out."

"Terry," Caslin called after him, "be careful. None of this ended with Schmidt's death." Holt, having stopped in the doorway, bobbed his head in agreement and left without another word.

Caslin reread the text message. The feeling that to attend would be dangerous was tough to ignore but by the same token a little voice at the back of his mind suggested he might get some answers if he did.

CASLIN PASSED through the village having left the A64 and picked up the Bishopthorpe Road, taking him to the racecourse at York. There was very little traffic on the minor roads, early morning commuters sticking to their usual faster routes. Pulling into the public car-park, he found he was alone. Not knowing where the meeting was set to take place, Caslin drove along the access road, lined with barriers, towards the stands. Off to each side were parking areas stretching several hundred metres in every direction, predominantly flat and laid to grass, separating the racecourse from the highway. Even at this time, the sounds of nearby construction machinery moving on the site of the old chocolate factory, adjacent to the racecourse, could be heard.

The night had passed slowly due, in the main, to an inability to get any sleep. Resisting the urge to contact the sender of the mysterious text, Caslin had denied himself the possibility of satisfying that particular curiosity, at least in part. If they'd wanted to say more they would have. Coming to a stop alongside the entrance to the stands, he got out of the car drawing his coat about him. The mornings were turning fresher by the day. The midday temperatures may still be pushing towards eighteen degrees but at dawn, despite the blue skies and the promise of warmth, they were more commonly in single figures. An early morning mist had also descended into the Vale of York overnight, the moisture in the air adding to the sense of the coming autumn. Reaching back into the car, he took out two coffees that he'd purchased on his way.

Sipping at one of the brews, he placed the other on the roof of the car and looked around. The only movement he could see came from the traffic on the nearby dual carriageway barely visible through the mist. With no race meeting planned for the weekend there was little reason for anyone to be here at the crack of dawn on a Thursday. Caslin pondered his vulnerability. Having confided in no-one about the meeting and with no knowledge of who would show up being here was very much an act of faith. He wasn't overly concerned. Instinct told him on this occasion there was little to fear. Glancing at the time it was already 6:15. The turnstiles were closed, the entrances barred. Caslin turned his back to them and waited.

Five minutes later another car arrived driving slowly into the car park and taking a circuitous route before joining the arterial access road towards him. Caslin watched, still drinking his coffee, as the newcomer carried out what he considered to be a sweep of the area. Only a single occupant was visible inside. Apparently satisfied that Caslin was alone the car stopped barely fifty feet from him. The driver's door opened and a man stepped out. Dressed for the weather, he wore a bulky overcoat with the collars turned up and sported a dark woollen hat.

"I figured as much," Caslin called out, offering up the spare cup. Aiden Reece approached, shoulders hunched and hands pressed into warm pockets. Accepting the coffee gratefully, he offered a greeting.

"Hello Nate," he said, almost apologetically.

"Old habits dying hard are they?" Caslin asked but no reply was forthcoming. It was obvious that he wasn't the only one who'd had a rough night. Reece appeared pale and gaunt in comparison to how he'd been the other night back at his flat in Kleiser's Court.

"They're watching you. You know that, don't you?"

Caslin glanced around them. "Aye, guessed as much. I'm being careful."

"You lost your tail," Reece said, drinking his coffee. "Impressive."

Caslin looked him in the eye. If he was being followed, he hadn't noticed but the experience in his hotel room in Dublin made him suspect he'd be under someone's watchful eye. Multiple, unnecessary deviations on his journey had brought him to the racecourse just in case. Likewise the assumption his mobile was compromised inspired the purchase of the burn phone. The realisation he'd failed to spot someone shadowing his drive to the racecourse despite a heightened state of awareness was, however, unnerving to say the least.

"You were following them, following me?"

Reece grinned. "I learned from the best."

"And they were?" Caslin asked but Reece looked away. "Never mind," he said, swilling the remnants of his latte at the bottom of the cup and finishing it off. "Do you feel like telling me who's doing the watching? I'm assuming you know."

Reece laughed. "You're captivating these days, drawing a lot of people to you."

"Let's start with yours then. Renton Sands. Provided you do work for them of course. Which I have a hard time believing seeing as they've never heard of you."

"That doesn't surprise me," Reece said, perching himself atop a half wall behind him. "There're a couple of reasons for that."

"Care to explain?"

"Plausible deniability," Reece stated as a matter-of-fact. "I'll bet they don't have my name on record anywhere. Besides, I can hardly lodge my real name with them under the circumstances. Neither will you find mention of Heinrich by the way."

Caslin's eyes flicked across at him, instantly alert. "You recognised his picture the other night in my case file, didn't you?" Reece inclined his head slightly, indicating so. "Why didn't you say?"

"You're a good man, Nate. You don't know what it is you're getting close to."

"Well then, it's about time you told me," Caslin bit back, angrily. "What's Heinrich Schmidt to you?"

"Former special forces, German Intelligence. Was working in the private sector as a high-level fixer for Renton."

"What exactly did he fix for them?"

Reece shrugged. "Whatever was required. Men like that... they don't have a conscience."

"Men like you?" Caslin asked, drawing a stern look from his friend.

"Heinrich was on another level."

"And you? What is it that you do for a living?"

Reece ignored the question. "You have them worried, Nate. That fact alone should worry you."

"I got turned over in Dublin," Caslin said defiantly. Reece seemed surprised at least momentarily.

"I doubt that was Renton. It's not their style."

"You knew?"

"No," Reece said, with a shake of his head. "It wouldn't be beyond them to approach you abroad, mind you. Had anyone paid you a visit from the company we wouldn't be talking."

"Why not?"

Reece fixed him with a cold stare. "Because you'd have turned up floating in Dublin Harbour the next day or not at all, which is more probable. Your death abroad would muddy the waters of any subsequent investigation."

"I pegged them as working for an intelligence agency to be honest. Mi6, Special Branch, or someone else you most likely know. Correct me if I'm wrong but you knew I'd reach for Nelson eventually."

"I expected you to. If you were even half the policeman I thought you'd make, back at Hendon."

"Your past with Nelson," Caslin said, "why not just tell me?"

"I didn't know how compromised you were," Reece replied.

"Compromised?"

"Yeah. They're all over your investigation. You must have them spooked if they made contact with you in Dublin. For them to risk breaking cover like that—"

"What the fuck is going on?" Caslin said, cutting him off. "Why are the Secret Service protecting Nelson?"

"Protecting... using..."

"You're really pushing the limits of friendship, you know. What the hell are you now, Aiden?"

"I'm trying to find out what's going on. The same as you," Reece said flatly. "I've not figured it out yet."

"You've been following on behind Emily Coughlan, haven't you?"

Reece nodded. "Yes, piecing together all that she did... or at least, I'm trying to." He drained the last of his coffee, tossing the cup aside. "Before I left Hendon, I was approached."

"By whom?"

Reece smiled. "They didn't tell me. Apparently, my psyche profile fit the parameters of... how should I put it... a certain, moral flexibility. That, plus my background, second-generation Irish immigrant tallied with what they were looking for. Ulster was well down the road to peace, Sinn Féin were in the driving seat with the IRA but not everyone was happy about it, you know? The paramilitaries were splintering right before our eyes. Whereas before, in the main, the IRA leadership were the focus. Suddenly we were facing several militant factions opposed to the peace process and hell bent on bringing it down at any cost. The scramble to identify these guys, their networks and plans became the priority or risk it all unravelling. It was bordering on chaos for a time."

"They sent you in?"

"That's why I left as I did. I was fresh faced, unknown. I knew the country, I knew the people. I wouldn't stand out. To be honest, it was an awesome opportunity. Do you remember how excited we all were to be on the verge of hitting the streets?"

Caslin smiled. "We were a lot younger back then."

"Imagine being selected for this. It was like Christmas to a five-year-old. Not to mention my career path was set. I was adamant that assignment would make me."

"I sense a hefty *but* coming?"

Reece laughed, without real humour and tinged with a bitter edge. "Man, I was naïve. I figured, once I was done, I'd go back to my normal life."

"How did it play out?"

"I was good, Nate. Damn good. Far better than my handlers had hoped for let alone expected. I got myself tight in with one of the splinter groups, a breakaway from the Belfast Brigade of the Provisionals. That's where I first came into Nelson's circle."

"What did he do?"

"Nelson?" Reece asked, Caslin nodded. "He headed up their internal security, or as they liked to call it, the *Nutting Squad*. A proper bunch of lunatics. Most of the Provos ran a mile from that duty but not Nelson, he was well up for it. They took the lead in interrogating informers, suspected infiltrators but also got to debrief anyone who'd been picked up either side of the border. A group with almost absolute power. They assessed how much information was given up and if they considered it too much, you were done for."

"I've heard the horror stories," Caslin said.

"Believe them," Reece replied. "Then expect the reality to be far worse. Even the faintest whiff of you crossing the line put you up for a kicking at best but, more often than not, you'd see a bullet before sunrise and they'd find you on some waste ground next to a primary school."

"Nelson?"

"He loved it, absolutely loved it. You know, one time, a guy was suspected of giving information to the Garda. Nelson was a childhood friend of his. The two families would hang out together, best men at weddings and the like. They sent Nelson round to bring him out for a beer. Broke his legs and caved his head in with a hammer. His kids found him hanging from their climbing frame, in the morning."

Caslin stared off into the distance. "Was he guilty?"

Reece shrugged. "No-one knew. He denied it as did the family. I doubt Nelson cared either way. As I understand it, he was either responsible for or played a part in the killings of multiple British agents. Perhaps fifteen to twenty over the years. Some were snitches but many were active agents."

"Like you?"

"Just like me."

"Who were you working for?"

"The lines get blurred, Nate," Reece said, appearing thought-ful. "When it started out the group were an offshoot of the military called the FRU, the *Force Research Unit*. By the time I was in we were integrated with the intelligence agencies, Special Branch and the Counter Terrorism Special Forces. Who you'd find at the top of the pyramid I have no idea."

"You're out, now?"

"Very much so."

"What happened? You said you got in too deep or was that more dazzling bullshit?" Reece stared straight ahead. His demeanour visibly shifting to one of melancholy.

"The woman in the picture."

"You were close?"

"Yes," Reece stated, his voice cracking. He cleared his throat. "She was another way in. Well regarded. Well loved. Once I was able to get close to her, I was closer to them."

"Who?"

"The leadership. It was the only way to find out what they had planned. I'd already positioned myself alongside Nelson and she became the next target for me to acquire."

"You didn't bank on falling for her though. Did you?" Caslin asked. Reece looked to the floor.

"And I did. In a big way," he said, taking off his hat and running a hand through his hair. "I shouldn't have let it happen.

Geez… she was a fucking Provo. One hell of a wildcat but… something about her was…," his voice tailed off as he looked skyward, drawing a deep breath. "She didn't want to kill people. I truly believe the violence troubled her more than most. She was an idealist, a reluctant revolutionary."

"Often they're the most dedicated."

"Not wrong," Reece agreed.

"Where is she now?"

"She's dead, Nate. Sylvia's dead."

CHAPTER TWENTY-ONE

"NELSON WAS A TWISTED BASTARD," Reece said, with a faraway look, "but effective. The man had gravitas. One look into his eyes and you knew how dangerous he... or rather how much trouble you were in."

"I had the same feeling," Caslin agreed.

"Always on a hair-trigger and with freedom to act, whatever took his fancy was fair game," Reece said. "And when he turns his attention to you..."

"Is that what happened? He saw through you?"

Reece rocked his head from side-to-side. "I got the impression he was looking at me. Maybe he suspected, maybe he was casting the net more in hope than expectation. I don't know. I was uncomfortable, I'll say that."

"What could've put him on to you?"

Reece shrugged. "There were a few high-profile takedowns that shook the foundations a bit."

"Your intel?"

"No, not mine," Reece said. "If I had offered up everything that came my way, I wouldn't have lasted a week. There was one time where I thought I'd blown it. They'd abducted one of the

RUC. That guy was knocking on Heaven's door, he probably had less than an hour to live before the rescue team got him back."

"You?"

"That time I could get the word out but it could've burned me. Should have to be fair."

"How come you got away with it?"

"It was levelled at someone else," Reece said, reliving the moment etched upon his face. "You can hear your heart thudding against your ribcage, believing everyone in the room knows it was you and then someone else gets fingered. One hell of a relief, I can tell you."

"Who was it?"

"I don't recall. Doesn't matter anyway. He was dead five minutes later."

"Then what was it?"

"Nelson was getting paranoid, slinging accusations all over the place. Looking back, I reckon it was getting to him. The power, the demand for results, either went to his head or set him off, I don't know. Personally, I figured I could ride it out but my handlers were getting edgy. The word came through to pull me out."

"You left?"

"I should have," Reece said quietly.

"You refused?"

"Point blank. I was spinning a lot of plates and was probably overly ambitious in my ability to keep them up. Plus, I had other reasons to stay."

"Sylvia Marshall?"

"Yeah," Reece said, his eyes glazing over. "Bottom line, if I left, I would never get to see her again. I wasn't prepared for that. I mean, it was always the plan, so I knew the day would come but..."

"How did your handlers take it?"

"As you'd expect. It wasn't a request. They pushed it again at the next meet but I wasn't having it, concocted some bull about an imminent attack to buy some time. It worked for a while."

"And then?"

"Like I said. It wasn't a request."

"They pulled you anyway?"

"They tried, I resisted. Cutting a long story short, I guess they started to question my loyalties. If I wouldn't come willingly the decision was taken somewhere by someone to put me down," Reece said, relaying a story he hadn't shared with anyone previously. It showed.

"They tried to kill you?" Caslin asked, struggling to believe what he was hearing.

Reece shook his head. "Not directly. That would've made it clear what I was. No, they commissioned one of the Unionist Paramilitaries to do it for them such was the way of things back then. That way it looks like a tit-for-tat shooting. Common enough over the years."

"They missed," Caslin stated.

"I told you," Reece grinned, "I'm damn good at what I do. End result was the same. I had to leave. They'd have kept on trying and it only takes one mistake. Sooner or later they'd get lucky."

"Sylvia?"

Reece dragged a palm across his face. "I couldn't tell her what was going on, who or what I was. Nor could I come home. My only option was to disappear. I left her thinking I was on a Loyalist hitlist… running, like I'm some kind of hero in hiding."

Caslin processed the information whilst taking a measure of his friend. The grief appeared real enough. "Tell me about how you ended up at Renton."

Reece sighed. "I drifted around. Abroad for the most part. My skill set pays well and people don't ask a lot of questions. Well enough to keep myself low, out of sight. I worked on a contract in North Africa a few years ago and Nelson's name came up. I was surprised. That's when I started a little digging."

"Why?"

"Curiosity, at first," Reece said. "Then I got to wondering how he was so high up with this firm."

"Renton Sands?" Caslin sought to clarify. Reece nodded. "Why, was that in some way strange?"

"I couldn't work out how he got there. They employ a lot of ex-military types, senior officers as well as former squaddies and a large portion of their legitimate business revolves around government contracts. It just struck me as an odd place for him to be. As you say, old habits die hard."

"Find any answers?"

"Not yet. I came across Emily Coughlan's investigation. I wondered what she managed to turn up. I was hoping to follow the breadcrumbs but her death seems to have lit a fire under everyone concerned."

"You think Nelson put Schmidt onto Coughlan?"

"I wouldn't be surprised."

"I was warned Nelson was a cool character, not easily ruffled."

"True, in the main," Reece agreed.

"He flinched when I dropped Sylvia's name though. Why might that be?"

Reece thought on it for a moment. "Well, he certainly knew her. We were a close group."

"Could he have been involved in her death?"

Reece tensed. "Not as far as I know. Why do you ask?"

"She's dead. You've spoken of your feelings for her and you knew of her passing. I can't believe you haven't looked into it."

"I did…a while ago but don't forget, I could hardly go around asking questions."

"Who do you think killed her?"

"I put it down as a Unionist reprisal, at the time. An occupational hazard bearing in mind the company she kept. Grudges can last generations north of the border. Do you know otherwise?"

"Not at all. Mention of her caught him off guard. Maybe it was just the blast from the past," Caslin said with a shake of his head. "My guess is Coughlan was being fed information by Fairchild."

Reece considered that notion. "It would explain how she got from Nelson to KL Global or the other way around. She was almost certainly on to both companies. Which came first, I don't know. She was taking risks. Brave girl."

"Not the only one," Caslin said. "What about you?"

Reece laughed. "I can't be running all the time."

"You said I should worry."

"The guys working for Renton… are organised, well financed. All are SCARS trained. They're dangerous and I mean lethal. If you come up against them, run. Don't expect your warrant card to cut any ice."

"You make them sound like super soldiers or something—"

"I'm serious, Nate," Reece talked over him. "At least spooks have some degree of oversight to rein them in. Renton are answerable to their balance sheet and nothing else."

"I'll keep that in mind," Caslin said. For a moment, he considered dropping Father Foley's name into the mix but chose not to. Everything being discussed sounded plausible and yet, Caslin couldn't quell the feeling his friend was still withholding. For a brief but disconcerting moment the thought that Reece had killed Emily Coughlan flashed through his mind. Dismissing the notion as too unlikely, it lingered and was difficult to shake off. Reece openly admitted to shadowing her and he certainly had the skills to enter her hotel room after it had been sealed. Familiar with forensic and investigative protocols of the police in any other inquiry Reece would undoubtedly be a suspect. Caslin remembered an old saying that his father used to utter at the height of the cold war. Somehow, the phrase seemed just as valid in the modern age, *once intelligence, always intelligence.*

"Penny for them?" Reece asked, snapping him out of his thought process.

"Sorry," Caslin said, glancing across. "I was just mapping it out, in my head. Tell me, who was the other person in the photograph? You, Sylvia, Nelson and one other. What was he to this?"

"Dylan," Reece said. "That was Dylan McArthur. Another of our team."

"And where can I find him?"

Reece shrugged. "Still around, as far as I know. One that fits into the category of a *true believer*. Not sociopathic like Nelson. Dylan wanted a united Ireland and would've given his life for the cause so to speak. I don't recall him being particularly fond of Nelson. Not that many of us were."

"Would he have an insight on all of this?"

"Perhaps he could shed some light on how Nelson got where he is. Dylan was well in the frame when I left."

"Can you find him?"

"You're the bloody detective—"

Caslin laughed, countering. "Yeah and extremist Irish Nationalists are keen to speak to the British police aren't they?"

Reece grinned. "Always a hospitable welcome. I can ask around for you."

"Cheers. How can I reach you?"

"You can't."

"What about the number you gave me last night?"

"I'll call you," Reece said, standing. Caslin offered his hand, his friend took it. "I don't like lying to you, Nate."

"I don't much care for it either," Caslin replied.

"Be careful," Reece said before heading back to his car. Caslin watched him walk over and get in, the same doubts swirling around in his mind. He wanted to trust him, to believe this was the same calibre of man he remembered Aiden Reece to be. The problem was, he couldn't be certain. Such clarity, in this case, was proving elusive.

Caslin acknowledged Reece's departure with a flick of his hand. Unable to maintain the level of faith in Reece that he desired, Caslin resolved to let the situation play out to the end. Watching the car approach the junction, Reece turned left and disappeared from view behind the hedgerow lining the main road. Walking back to his own car, Caslin had the expectation that somewhere along the line the pieces would come together and make some degree of sense. The hope that Reece was not beyond redemption paramount in his mind.

The pressure change in the air surrounding him accompanied by the sound of the explosion caused Caslin to drop and brace. A moment later, he was up and running in the direction of the plume of black smoke. Upon reaching the hedgerow, separating the racecourse from the road, he clambered up the fence to see beyond. The fireball engulfed what remained of Reece's car. Debris, scattered in every direction, was alight as were the nearby trees and bushes, ignited by the blast. The breeze carried a thick cloud of acrid smoke in his direction requiring him to cover his mouth and nose with his sleeve. Multiple alarms could be heard in the distance emanating from the nearby residences such was the ferocity of the explosion.

Climbing to the top of the fence, Caslin leapt off it, clearing the hedged boundary and landing unceremoniously at the side of the road. Approaching warily, he was forced to use his jacket to shield his face from the heat. The cabin of the vehicle had practically disintegrated. The roof was non-existent and the sides bore a resemblance to little more than twisted metal rather than a car. Even the chassis was visibly bent by the detonation. Caslin backed away. There was nothing to be done.

Once at a respectable distance, he dropped to his haunches. With his heartrate racing and ragged breathing, he reached for his phone. A van pulled up in the middle of the road behind him. Glancing around, he saw two occupants get out. Both were thick set and heavily tattooed. The first reached into his jacket. A wave of momentary panic washed over him only to dissipate as the man produced a phone telling his friend he'd call the police. The second approached, placing a supportive hand on Caslin's shoulder.

"You all right, mate?" he asked. Caslin could only manage a brief nod of the head, sitting down on the tarmac with assistance from the newcomer. He felt numb. Dropping his phone into his lap he stared at the flames dancing on the breeze. The flash of intensity in the blaze was fading but the generated heat still felt uncomfortable on the skin. However, the smoke belched high into the air as those constituent parts of the car, fashioned from rubber and plastic, gave off their toxic fumes.

Caslin felt tears come to his eyes but he fought them away, brushing the reverse of his hand across his face.

CHAPTER TWENTY-TWO

THE PARAMEDIC CONCLUDED Caslin had suffered no discernible effects from the incident. Despite his protestations of being well clear of the blast, Broadfoot was insistent. Removing the blood pressure monitor she stepped down. Caslin was sitting on the back step of the ambulance.

"Your numbers are elevated but that's unsurprising judging by what you've just seen. I think we should still get you thoroughly checked out back at the hos—"

"That's not necessary," Caslin told her, eyeing the approach of the detective chief superintendent.

"Will he survive?" Broadfoot asked, an attempt at humour to lighten the mood.

"I'm fine," Caslin stated, before the medic was able to reply. Broadfoot smiled at her, inclining his head slightly. She understood the request and departed, leaving them alone. Once she was clear, Broadfoot's demeanour shifted back to his more detached, unemotional norm.

"Can you tell me who was in the car?"

Caslin blew out his cheeks, eyeing Hunter picking through the debris as the fire crews worked around her. "Aiden Reece."

Broadfoot was taken aback. "The man whose name came up but was irrelevant? That Aiden Reece."

"The very same," Caslin replied flatly, looking beyond his boss at the smouldering wreckage of the vehicle. The crews of two appliances, dispatched from York, now had the fire under control. "Looks like he was relevant after all."

"You're telling me," Broadfoot said, eyes flicking towards the scene. "What was his involvement here?"

Caslin shrugged. "Looking for answers. The same as us."

"Please don't insult my intelligence. You have more than that."

"Reece was linked to Paraic Nelson in the past," Caslin said, looking to Broadfoot. "That man you told me to leave alone remember?"

"What links?" Broadfoot asked, choosing to ignore Caslin's venom.

"You'll know more than me, sir. Reece's file was restricted. I expect your clearance is higher than mine—"

"Bloody hell, Nathaniel. Stop pissing about," Broadfoot hissed, glancing around to ensure he wasn't overheard.

"Far from it, sir," Caslin retorted. "Aiden was a friend of mine so I'll do anything *but* piss about and bearing in mind that anyone who knows anything about this case winds up dead shortly after, perhaps you don't want to know." Both men fell silent as the Brigade's Scene Commander approached them. Acknowledging Caslin with a nod of the head, he addressed Broadfoot.

"The fire's out. The vehicle is safe. My team will secure the scene if yours can set the cordon?"

"I'll take care of it," Broadfoot said.

"The investigators are here, they'll get started immediately alongside your CSI team."

"Thank you," Broadfoot replied. Waiting until they were alone, he looked to Caslin. "What do you reckon?"

"That this isn't over, no matter who wants it to be."

"What's that supposed to mean?"

"Whoever is pushing you to tie this off... their agenda is different to mine—"

"Ours," Broadfoot corrected him. Caslin glanced away. Double checking they were not within earshot of anyone else, the DCS continued, keeping his voice low. "What is it you need?"

Caslin met his eye. "A few days grace."

Broadfoot said nothing for a moment contemplating the request. "You were off for the remainder of the week in any event. I have your preliminary statement so, under the circumstances, a period of convalescence is probably advisable."

"I agree, sir," Caslin said, standing. "I do have a bit of a headache."

"Two things, Nathaniel."

"Sir?"

"Firstly, don't fuck this up," Broadfoot said quietly.

"And second?"

Broadfoot pulled himself upright, drawing a deep breath through his nose. "Stay alive. It costs a lot of money to develop good detectives. I'd hate to have to replace you."

Caslin's eyes followed him as he walked away. "I'll endeavour to do just that," he said to himself under his breath. Hunter came bounding up to him.

"Sir, are you okay?" she asked, with a concerned expression.

"Yes, of course," he replied. "Nothing a few day's rest won't cure."

"Whose car was it?"

"You'll need to have a chat with Broadfoot," he replied. "My head's feeling a bit funny. I'm off home."

"Sir?" Hunter asked.

"I'm sure you'll manage," he told her.

"You're not seriously—"

"You're always saying you want a chance to prove yourself. Here it is," he said, setting off back towards the racecourse to collect his car. Hunter threw her arms in the air in exasperation. Caslin took out his mobile. Scrolling through the small number of entries in his new phone, he found the number he wanted and dialled it. The call was quickly answered.

"Ahh… Nathaniel," the voice said warmly at the other end. "I didn't expect to hear from you so soon. What can I do for you?"

"Good morning, Seamus," he replied, in kind. "I need to find someone and I think your people are going to be more helpful than mine."

"Okay. Who's the lucky fella?"

"Dylan McArthur."

THE LIGHTS of the harbour at Rosslare and those of the town beyond were a welcome sight. Despite the gruelling six-hour drive from York to Fishguard at the tip of South-Western Wales, and the ensuing four-hour ferry journey, Caslin had been unable to sleep. His mind churning over the facts and supposition of the case refused to allow it. The inherent fatigue held back by pure determination. The public address system crackled into life announcing their imminent arrival along with the current time, a little after four in the morning. The bracing wind of the Irish Sea buffeted him as he stood on the deck watching the Republic of Ireland drawing ever closer.

The mobile phone in his pocket started to vibrate and he re-entered the interior of the ship to take the call. It was Seamus Hanlon.

"I see you're docking soon. You couldn't have got an earlier sailing could you?"

"Keeping you on your toes," Caslin replied, safe in the knowledge the Irishman was joking. With only two sailings later in the day he'd never have made the early afternoon crossing between Wales and County Wexford. Bypassing Dublin entirely in the hope of drawing less attention to himself this location also brought him in line with Hanlon's information as to where he'd find McArthur.

The ship docked soon afterwards, Caslin disembarking along-side the other foot passengers not that there were many. Seamus was waiting for him offering a firm handshake.

"Good to see you again," Hanlon said before adding, "in one piece, I might add."

Caslin laughed. "For now. Did you find him?"

Hanlon affirmed that he had. "Not far from here. A small place, along the coast near to Fethard. I've hired you a car and I've even programmed the sat nav for you."

"You're not coming?" Caslin asked, surprised.

Hanlon shook his head. "I'm not here, Nathaniel. It's for the best that you haven't even seen me. Not that I won't be all ears should you turn up something useful."

"Understood," Caslin said as Hanlon passed him the car keys and a folded map of the local area, indicating a blue Ford parked nearby. "The map's for when your signal drops from the car."

"Is that likely?"

"Down there it's a given," Hanlon replied. "You need to watch yourself around McArthur. I'm led to believe he's not all there if you know what I mean?"

Caslin acknowledged the point. "What do we know about where he's living?"

"Oh, it's a lovely area. It's where we all go on holiday. A bit quiet out of season and the summer's coming to an end so fewer people are around. The sort of place you can disappear to if you feel the need."

"McArthur, is he still connected?"

"Limited information on that, sorry. We've no mention of him for a long time but that won't be the whole story. I'm afraid you're going to have to wing it."

"I've made a career of it," Caslin joked. "Thanks again, Seamus. I'll let you know how I get on." Unlocking the door, Caslin opened the driver's side and slipped into the seat.

"Make sure you don't scratch the car," Hanlon said, casually waving him off. "I've enough paperwork to do already."

The horizon was lightening as the black of night shifted into the slate grey of pre-dawn. Following the route programmed into the navigation system, Caslin picked his way across County Wexford, the roads bringing him intermittently alongside the coast before frequently cutting inland. The towns and villages he passed through were sparsely populated. The area was predominantly farmland interspersed with hamlets consisting of detached buildings set back off the main roads. The roads themselves were narrow, the infrastructure of large cities having no place here.

The R734 took him through the main street of Fethard. The proximity to the coast and a number of beaches, the area was a favourite amongst tourists, judging by the number of holiday parks and accommodation on offer. Passing beyond in a matter of minutes, he progressed through Yoletown before the road cut right and he pushed straight on towards Baginbun. The display indicated he'd reached his destination and Caslin pulled the car to a stop. The road bore a left directly towards the sea. Presumably that was where he'd find the beach signposted ahead. Opposite him was an un-adopted road, little more than a farm track lined with hardcore. It was also gated.

Consulting the map Hanlon had given him, Caslin found where he had stopped and saw a property circled a short distance away. Figuring the road to be significantly quiet enough he could abandon the car, he stepped out and took his bearings. Ahead of him the land rose away in a shallow incline. Over the wide ridge in front of him it dropped away again down to the sea forming a small peninsula. It was here where Hanlon indicated he'd find McArthur. Glancing behind him in the direction of Fethard, he saw there was only one road in to this point. Carnivan Bay was to the right and Baginbun to his left.

Tucking the map into his back pocket he went to the gate. It was secured with a hefty padlock and chain neither of which appeared to have moved in quite some time. Caslin cleared the gate with ease and set off up the track. Reaching the ridgeline after walking a hundred metres he stopped alongside a small copse of trees as the Irish Sea came into view. The sun had risen, burning away the coastal fog in no time at all. From where he stood the panoramic view from west to east was awe-inspiring.

"Not a bad place to drop out for a while," Caslin said to himself. Looking down the track and off to the left, he noted a small single-storey cottage nestling amongst a collection of trees offering some protection from the elements. No vehicle was parked outside providing justification for the state of the padlock nor was there any evidence to suggest the cottage was occupied.

Descending towards it, Caslin heeded Hanlon's advice and kept his wits about him. Approaching, it was clear the gardens were barely tended with not even a cursory attempt at cultivation. The building itself had missing slates, rotting window frames and the front door was peeling its outer layers of paint. Doubting the accuracy of the Gardaí's intelligence gathering, Caslin made it to within thirty feet of the building before the sound of a shotgun blast came to ear. A tree two metres to his right took the brunt of the damage showering branch and bark into the air. Caslin dived to his left rolling on his shoulder before throwing himself flat to the ground.

"Hold your fire!" he screamed in a mixture of authority and sheer terror. Daring not to move, he tilted his head in the direction of the house but all he could see through the long grass and bushes was the roofline.

"Who are you? What do you want?" a voice barked at him. Caslin was unable to see from who or where it originated.

"I'm looking to talk to Dylan McArthur..." Caslin shouted back in a strained voice, threatening to crack, "just to talk... that's all." Silence followed. Caslin's eyes furtively flicked from left to right vainly trying to judge whether he was more likely to be shot if he made a run for it or if he remained where he was. "You don't need your gun. I'm unarmed." Again, there was silence. Taking a deep breath, Caslin slowly raised himself up into a kneeling position. Not easy to do with both hands raised in the air in supplication.

"Who are you?" the voice came again, only this time Caslin could see a figure stepping out from behind the rear of the building to his left.

"I'm here to talk," Caslin repeated, noting the shotgun still levelled at him as McArthur approached. He was limping as if his knee was put out, the bodyweight borne only by the right leg. "I'm not a threat."

"You're English," McArthur stated.

"On my father's side, yes," Caslin acknowledged. "Would you believe Lithuanian on my mother's?"

"What do you want?"

"Ten minutes of your time," Caslin said slowly. "May I?" he indicated towards the inner pockets of his jacket. McArthur nodded but as soon as Caslin moved, he visibly tightened his grip on the double-barrelled shotgun. Caslin carefully took out a folded piece of paper and using exaggerated movements to reassure his captor opened up the photo Reece had left him. Holding it out in front, he said, "Ten minutes. Then I'm gone."

"What *do* you want?" McArthur asked again, only this time less aggressive in tone as he scanned the photograph.

"Someone's taking out your friends, Dylan, and I want to know why?"

CHAPTER TWENTY-THREE

CASLIN ENTERED FIRST, unsettling, bearing in mind a loaded shotgun was brandished towards his back along with an apparent willingness to discharge it. The inside of the cottage was as well kept as the exterior. The small windows protected the house from losing heat in the winter but let little light in for the entire year. Looking around, McArthur seemed to understand.

"Don't be looking for the light switch. I don't have any power," he said, limping past and seating himself at a dining table, resting the butt of the weapon on the floor and cradling it between his legs. They were in one room which collectively made up a living, dining and cooking area. A large Rayburn stove stood near to McArthur, presumably servicing all heating and cooking requirements. Another door, set over on the far side, Caslin presumed gave access to a bedroom and a bathroom. The accommodation was dilapidated, cramped but suitable for someone living alone albeit with fewer of the comforts the modern world had to offer. McArthur stretched out his left leg bringing forth a grimace as he did so.

"Hurt your leg?" Caslin asked, eyeing the shotgun. McArthur noticed.

"A long time ago. Don't worry. If I was going to shoot you, I'd have done it outside. I wouldn't want to mess up my house."

Caslin glanced around spotting another chair nearby. "May I?" His host indicated he could. Caslin pulled it over and seated himself a few feet away.

"What brings you here...?" McArthur said. "What did you say your name was?"

"Caslin," he said, "and I'm trying to find out about the people in this picture." He passed it across to allow him a closer look. "I'm police but I'm not here to make trouble for you. Everything in the past can stay there. I know Sylvia is dead and to be honest I'm interested in Paraic Nelson in particular."

"Ahh... Sylvia..." McArthur whispered under his breath. "Yeah, I miss her very much."

"Do you know how she died?" Caslin asked, McArthur shot him a look.

"What's it to you?"

"Just piecing things together. People coming across Nelson often turn up dead sooner or later."

McArthur locked eyes with him. "I take it this isn't an official visit?" Caslin shook his head.

"I know you're not a fan of the British," Caslin replied. "Especially the police but I had the thought that, regarding Nelson, you might feel like talking."

"And what gave you that idea?" McArthur said scornfully.

"He did," Caslin stated, jabbing a finger against Reece's image. McArthur looked first at the picture then back at Caslin.

"I've not seen him in years—"

"No, because he's been in hiding."

"I figured he was a goner," McArthur said. "Buried in a field someplace or weighted down at the bottom of the Irish Sea. The Orangemen were after him."

"They didn't get him," Caslin said, "but I reckon Paraic Nelson did." At the mention of that, McArthur bristled but didn't speak.

However, Caslin sensed he was itching to. "He came across Nelson again recently. He's doing well for himself, a senior executive with what is to all intents and purposes a mercenary enterprise."

"Doesn't surprise me."

"There's also some evidence to suggest that Nelson was involved in Sylvia Marshall's murder," Caslin lied, necessitated by his need to loosen up McArthur's memory. The way his gaze lingered on Sylvia's picture suggested a fondness one doesn't lose despite the passage of time.

"That was pinned on the loyalists," McArthur argued unconvincingly.

"It doesn't seem like it to me. Your friend here wasn't so sure," Caslin countered, pointing to the picture still in McArthur's hands.

"It was sad what happened to Sylvia, what with the baby and all."

"Baby?" Caslin asked.

"Yeah, she got herself out for the sake of the kid. Then to go as she did and leave it to be brought up in care... was tough on her, what with Conor leaving and all. Conor didn't trust Nelson either."

"Conor?" Caslin asked, immediately regretting it.

"Yeah, her boyfriend," McArthur stated, eyeing Caslin with a suspicious look. "Why, is that not his name?"

Caslin thought fast. "He was living under the radar, wouldn't give me his name. I've come to understand why. I didn't know Sylvia had a child." He was left unsure whether or not the recovery was convincing enough.

"Yeah, little girl. Poor cow," McArthur continued, breaking the eye contact. "To think, being brought up not knowing who murdered your mother and thinking your father abandoned you?"

"Conor was her father?"

"Aye, don't your eyes work, man," McArthur said, passing the picture back. "She's pregnant in the bloody photograph." Caslin looked and cursed himself for missing it. Sylvia was probably four months gone.

"Conor knew?"

"Don't see how he couldn't, do you?"

"I reckon Nelson killed Conor, probably for talking to me."

"That'd be rich, Nelson taking someone out for being a grass."

"Why do you say that? It's what he was tasked with after all."

McArthur sat back in his chair taking the picture back and tossing it onto the table beside him. "Once, yes but people talk, you know?" Caslin forced himself to relax a little, remaining silent in the hope his patience would encourage further elaboration. As it happened no encouragement was necessary. "He pointed the finger at me one time."

"Who, Nelson?"

"Yeah. Singled me out when an op went bad. The fucker. I knew then there was something wrong with that guy. I threw myself out of a second storey window to get away from that bastard. Smashed my knee to pieces in the process," he said, rubbing absently at his leg for emphasis. "I swear it was only because it was a Saturday night in the middle of Belfast that I managed to crawl away from there. Made it over to..." he paused, remembering who he was talking to, "... managed to plead my case."

"How'd it go?"

"I'm still alive," he stated with bitter regret.

"You don't sound like that was much of a result."

"They already had their doubts," McArthur went on. "About Nelson, I mean. Many of us thought that he wasn't really one of us."

"Meaning?"

"His heart wasn't in the cause," McArthur said, leaning forward. "He was never a true Republican. Don't get me wrong, he loved the action, the violence... thrived on it even... but his cause was his own, not ours."

"What did he want?"

"Power, money... notoriety... all of the above," McArthur said. "I reckon he was skimming, so did the leadership."

"Why did they take his word over—"

"They didn't!" he snapped back. "Some of us suspected what had, until that point, been unthinkable."

"Which was?"

"That Nelson was working for you," he said, the cold stare of a focussed man turning on Caslin.

"The British?" Caslin queried, raising his eyebrows in surprise. "That's news to me."

"Yeah, you can deny it all you want but I'm not the only one who thought so. Sylvia agreed. First, Nelson suspected Conor, then me..."

"You took it to the leadership?"

"Of course, I did. By that point my life depended on it. Turns out they already knew. Not that they'd tell me so."

"What happened?"

The indignation was written across McArthur's face as he replied. "I was *granted* a stay of execution, just enough time to pack a bag and leave on the proviso I never came back."

"And Nelson? If what you say is true why isn't he dead?"

"Oh, man. How could they? It was the same reason they wanted me gone. Burning him would've exposed themselves."

"How do you mean?"

"They'd have to admit they'd put a British agent in charge of internal security for the entire Belfast Brigade. Think about it. That's knowledge of all our operations, our membership, the vetting of new members. No... they'd have been finished. Without trust we'd be looking at each other, our friends, our neighbours. One wrong word here, a sideways glance we didn't like the look of... there'd be blood on the streets within weeks. Our blood. They needed unity to deliver the peace. Better that those in the know play the game, keeping the rest in the dark. They struck a deal with him."

"Who, Nelson?" Caslin asked.

McArthur nodded. "Must have. A neat contract of silence. Nelson leaves, no-one openly discusses it. The problem goes away. Despite what they want us to believe, Mr Caslin, there's a phrase we have in Belfast. *The dogs in the street know.* Trust me, they knew... like I knew."

"What of Callum Foley?" Caslin asked, chancing it.

"The Reverend Father?" McArthur replied. "Now there's an unholy alliance between the almighty and a hypocrite if ever I saw one."

"Sorry, what did you call him?" Caslin pounced, in case he'd misheard.

"*The Reverend Father.* That's how he was known to us ever since we were children."

"*R F,*" Caslin muttered. "Of course."

"What's that you say?"

"Foley," Caslin pressed, "what was his role in everything?"

McArthur fixed him with another cold, hard stare but after a moment he relented. "I guess it doesn't matter. It's history now. The war's over."

"Not for everyone," Caslin said. "Foley?"

"What better cover to have than in the house of the Lord."

"Foley was in the IRA?"

"Not officially but many weren't. There were a lot of people who didn't actively participate but heeded the call in other ways."

"Sympathisers?"

"Exactly right," McArthur confirmed. "The Reverend Father allowed us to use his churches as rallying points, safe spaces for meetings and the like. I seem to recall we had weapons stashed under the floorboards of several churches at one point."

"The Lord works in mysterious ways," Caslin said softly.

"Not ours to judge," McArthur added. "Father Foley will stand before the gates for his reckoning the same as the rest of us."

"Do you know what happened to Conor and Sylvia's child?" Caslin asked.

"As I said, the last I knew she went into care."

"How old do you think she would be now?"

McArthur looked to the ceiling calculating in his head. "Early twenties I should figure. Why?"

"Early twenties," Caslin said softly, unable to shake the feeling he'd found yet another piece of the puzzle but couldn't quite slot it into place. Standing up, he glanced down towards Dylan McArthur, mumbling. "It's time I...."

"What is it?"

"I have to go," Caslin said, walking to the front door. Stopping as he opened it, he glanced back over his shoulder. "Thank you."

Once outside, Caslin started the short walk back the way he'd come. Taking out his phone he cursed at the lack of signal. Picking up the pace, he trotted up the incline to the top of the ridge holding his phone aloft. Managing to locate a solitary bar, he put in a call back to the UK. Muttering under his breath, he encouraged the recipient to pick up.

"Hello."

"Jimmy. You told me Emily Coughlan's mother died in a car accident on her way to work."

"She did, yes," Sullivan replied.

"How old was Emily?"

"Oh... five, maybe six... why?"

"You were her Godfather, right? Talk to me about her parents, you didn't really mention them."

"I was at school with her father. Where are you going with this?"

"Emily was their daughter?"

"Yes."

"Their daughter... *their biological* daughter?"

"Well, no. Jacob and Bernadette couldn't have children. Emily was orphaned as a wean and they adopt—"

"Fuck, Jimmy!" Caslin said, hanging up. Breaking into a run, he picked his way down the track back to the car nearly losing his footing on the loose stones several times. Clambering in, he started the car slamming it into reverse and accelerating back to the junction. Tyres squealing, he turned the car and took off, heading for Rosslare. With a bit of luck, he could still make the 9:15 crossing back to the UK.

CHAPTER TWENTY-FOUR

APPROACHING the small detached cottage Caslin's footfalls crunched on the gravel lining the driveway. The nine-hour journey did little to curb his determination to uncover what he saw as the final deceits in this case. Reaching to knock on the door, a muted whistle came from behind, an attempt to draw his attention. Caslin turned to find Hunter jogging towards him, a silhouette before the setting sun. Easing her pace as she came to him, he read her mixed expression of confusion and anger.

"Sir. What are you doing here?" she hissed at him under her breath.

"I could ask you the same thing," he replied, refraining from lowering his own voice.

"Broadfoot said—" she stopped as the front door opened. Father Foley stood in the hallway of his home, a bemused look on his face.

"You both may as well come in rather than argue on my doorstep," he said, breaking into a grin. "Would you care for some tea?"

Caslin allowed Hunter to enter and then he followed. By the time they were shown into the sitting room irritation replaced her anger but Hunter held off on further conversation until the priest departed for the kitchen. Moving closer she spoke barely above a whisper.

"Don't take this the wrong way, sir, but you look like shit," Hunter said.

Caslin could imagine. He hadn't slept since the few hours he got on the Wednesday night nearly two days prior. Ignoring her comment, he asked, "Why are you here?"

"Broadfoot put me back onto Foley."

"Why?" Caslin asked, lowering his voice to match hers.

"He didn't say. I imagine it had something to do with you. It was after you left the scene of the car bomb—"

"The kettle's on," Foley said, returning to the room. "Forgive me, was I interrupting something?" Caslin shook his head, stepping forward with the picture Reece had supplied him with. Foley took it unfolding the paper without breaking eye contact. He scanned the figures and flicked his eyes back at Caslin. "Should these people mean something to me?" he asked, passing it back.

"A little late in the day for the lies, Father," Caslin said. "I met with Dylan this morning."

"Ahh... Dylan," Foley said, taking a step back and seating himself in an armchair. Letting out a deep sigh, he appeared thoughtful rubbing a hand across his chin. "I see. How is he?"

"Older than his years," Caslin stated. "Broken and bitter... but certainly talkative when it came to Paraic Nelson anyway." Hunter was utterly lost in the conversation but maintained her composure trying to figure out what was going on. For his part, Foley merely bobbed his head in a knowing way.

"Dylan was dealt a poor hand, I'll say that."

"Whereas Nelson held all the cards, I understand," Caslin added.

"I suppose it was going to come out sooner or later," Foley said. "Regrettable as it is."

"There are people doing their best to ensure it doesn't," Caslin stated. "Now I know you were associated with Sylvia Marshall, so you knew full well who Emily Coughlan was when I first came to you."

Foley nodded. "That's true. She told me the second time I met her. Little Emily. She had come a long way to find her answers."

"She found out who her biological mother was and eventually that brought her to you. What was she looking into first, Sylvia's death or Nelson?"

Foley fixed him with a stare as the kettle clicked off in the background. "I'm guessing you're not bothered about the tea." Caslin shook his head. "The truth is both. Emily found out about her mother and tracked back. Nelson dropped easily onto her radar, the person he was with the profile he had."

"She thought he was involved in her death?"

"Not at first but later, yes," Foley explained. "The more she found out about Nelson and his current business partners the more she suspected."

"Dylan told me what many people suspected about Nelson. That he was working for the British." Hunter flinched, it was involuntary. "So she looked further which brought her to you and to Fairchild."

"Resourceful young lady," Foley said, admiring her. "Much like her father."

"Her father?" Hunter asked.

"Conor McVeigh," Foley clarified, "sitting with Sylvia in the picture," he indicated towards the paper in Caslin's hands. He passed it over to her. Hunter glanced at the picture and immediately to him. Caslin knew she'd recognised Aiden Reece but she didn't let on.

"Conor's dead, too," Caslin said flatly. "He was killed in an explosion yesterday."

"Out by the racecourse?" Foley enquired. Caslin confirmed it. "I never thought they would get him when he left. As I said, a very resourceful man."

"You gave Emily what she wanted didn't you?"

"I'm old, Inspector. I'm sure this hasn't escaped your notice. I spent many years… many years on a path unsuited for me. Call me young, naïve… foolish even. Tell me, does a lifetime of good works undo the sin that one also accumulates over the years?"

"We are all sinners, Father, but I'm not here to ease your conscience," Caslin countered. "I'm planning to bring Nelson down along with all those aiding him. That's my sole motivation."

Foley laughed with genuine humour. "Do you really believe you can achieve that? Look at what he is capable of, who protects him."

"You need to tell me what you know—"

"Like Christopher did?" Foley argued. "Another man on the path to redemption. Not for himself but for his legacy in the memory of his children. Doing what's right isn't easy and certainly didn't turn out well for him."

"We can protect you," Caslin assured him, sitting down in the chair alongside Foley. "If you come in with us we can ensure your safety."

"Inspector, please," Foley said quietly looking every bit as dejected as his tone indicated. "The only reason I am still alive is so they can assess who I've spoken to. Once they'd uncovered Emily's investigation and her links to Christopher Fairchild it was only a matter of time until they came for me. Believe me, if you've figured it out, it won't be long until they come calling."

"Who are *they*?" Hunter asked. Foley glanced at her.

"Be careful of what you ask, my dear. Sadly, anyone who knows the answer to that question tends not to live for very long."

Hunter rolled her eyes. "I'm calling it in," she said, taking out her radio.

"Sarah, hold on a second," Caslin pleaded, with a raised finger but she'd already pressed the button to transmit. "Acting DI Hunter to control," she said but there was no response.

"Father, please," Caslin implored him, "Sylvia, Conor, their daughter and countless others have all died because of this. You have to help me. If you truly care about redemption or even care about those people please help me."

"Do you remember Omagh, Inspector?" Foley asked.

"Of course. It was shocking."

"Twenty-nine dead, hundreds injured. Children. Parents. That was the moment for me," Foley said, the remorse written across his face. He appeared forlorn, the weight of guilt pressing upon him. "It was then I realised the way forward had to be one of peace. A future where children could grow without the violence and hatred passed on from father to son."

"Then help me to end this," Caslin said, leaning forward in towards Foley who was now looking at the floor. "There's been enough killing."

"It's not working," Hunter muttered, fiddling with the dials on the radio unit but to no avail.

"Battery?" Caslin asked.

"Fully charged," she said, putting the handset down and taking out her phone to call Fulford Road. Glancing at the mobile screen, she looked puzzled.

"Problem?"

"No service," Hunter said with a frown.

Caslin took out his own mobile and met her unasked question. "Mine, too." Standing, he walked to the front window moving a curtain aside in order to see out. "Use the landline," he said absently, his eyes scanning the road beyond the driveway. Everything was clear, nothing moved. Hunter crossed the room back into the hallway picking up the telephone. Repeatedly depressing the switch hook with the handset to her ear, she shook her head. Caslin cursed.

"What is it?" Foley asked.

"I'll check out back," Caslin said, heading for the kitchen. Hunter took his position at the window observing the outside. "Stay there," he indicated to Foley as he passed. Reaching the back door out to the garden, he flicked off the interior light.

Caslin paused and took a deep breath, fingers curling around the handle. Turning the key, he unlocked the door and cracked it just enough to peer out. Nothing out of the ordinary could be seen or heard. Gently easing the door open, he stepped into the darkness. There was silence as he waited patiently for his eyes to adjust. The garden was mature with trees and bushes all of which offered potential cover to him as well as anyone else, lying in wait. Listening intently, he stood still. The sound of his own, rapidly increasing heartbeat thudding inside his chest all that he could find to focus on. The sound of a car pulling up in the road out front saw him dash back inside.

"Sir," Hunter called as he reached the threshold of the sitting room. "I think we have company."

Caslin ran over turning out the lights on the way throwing the room into darkness. Coming alongside Hunter, he looked in the direction she was indicating. A black SUV had pulled up further along the street. They couldn't see movement from within it due to the privacy glass.

"Anyone get out?" Caslin asked.

Hunter shook her head, speaking quietly. "Not yet. They pulled up without their lights on."

"Yeah, you're right. We have company. I wouldn't be surprised if it's a Renton team or…" he left the thought unfinished just as all the doors opened and four men got out. At the other end of the street a Range Rover rounded the corner and came to a stop. Like the previous car this one also approached without its lights on.

"Or?" Hunter queried.

"Trust me the alternative option isn't favourable either," Caslin said, stepping away from the window. "It would appear someone has been watching you, Father. Besides us."

"I think we have a problem," Hunter whispered, glancing nervously towards him. "How do you want to play it?"

Caslin looked around. "Father, what will we find at the back of your house?" Even with the lack of light, he could sense the anxiety manifesting in the priest.

"The back… only the woods," he replied, nerves threatening to get the better of him. Caslin thought on it.

"That's our best shot. We have to move," he said as Hunter

noted another three men getting out of the Range Rover. Illuminated from the orange glow of the streetlights they were all well armed.

"Run?" Foley asked, his voice wavering, "but you're the police."

"We still have to run," Caslin said, cutting him off. Gripping Foley by the forearm, he helped the older man to his feet.

"I don't wish to disappoint you, Inspector but I'm not really one for running," Foley said with more than a hint of sarcasm. Caslin hustled him out into the kitchen, Hunter a step behind.

"We'll head to the back of the garden it's roughly fifty-feet and then break into the woods. We can cut left and try to double back to the car."

"They'll be expecting that, sir," Hunter said. Caslin knew she was right.

"There's a small bridge across the river set back into the trees. If you don't know it's there you'll struggle to find it in the dark," Foley offered.

"How far away?" Caslin asked.

"Oh, I don't know. Perhaps a quarter of a mile. Maybe a bit less. There's a path but it's rarely used so is very much overgrown."

Caslin looked at Hunter who nodded her agreement.

"Okay. We'll head for the crossing. Once we're on the other side we can use the river as a barrier and head to the nearest house to call the cavalry."

"What if they also find the bridge or reach us before we make it for that matter?" Hunter asked. Caslin looked away choosing not to answer.

Turning his focus to the door attempting to use his mind's eye to see what was waiting beyond it, Caslin set himself. Once again, he eased the door open and happy they were alone he led them out.

CHAPTER TWENTY-FIVE

FOLEY'S DESCRIPTION of a path was accurate. The reality of how dense the foliage was, however, turned out less so. With clouds obscuring the moonlight and being far from the streets they stumbled along. Every third step found them brushing against brambles or striking the branch of a tree. Caslin found himself inwardly cursing as he slipped on an incline causing him to fall. Tentatively, he got up finding his feet in the pitch black. Using the variation in the ground beneath him to denote the route of the path, he set off again, Hunter in tow aiding the priest. The going was slow and the sounds of pursuit carried towards them.

Stepping to the side of the path allowing the others to squeeze past, Caslin stopped to listen. Eyes trained on the path behind them, he stared into the gloom. Momentarily a beam of torchlight flickered through the trees. They were close. Confident their course still offered them an advantage, he moved off catching up soon enough. Hunter stopped. Foley was struggling with his breathing, the physical exertion too much for him to manage. Helping him to kneel down and get his breath, Caslin led Hunter a few steps away.

"They're too close. I don't think the three of us will make it."

"What do we do?" Hunter whispered, glancing at Foley. Caslin could read the concern in her tone.

"Find somewhere to hole up for a bit," he said, looking her in the eye. "I'll lead them off, down to the bridge—"

"Nathaniel, that's too dangerous. We should stay together. They'll have to see you for it to work—"

"It's the only way," he stated as a matter of fact. "If we all stay, they'll find us and you know it." Hunter didn't disagree. "Once they pass by make your way back but not to the house. Skirt along the edge of the woods until you're pretty sure you're clear and then go for help. Don't trust your phone."

Hunter nodded. "What about you?"

Caslin smiled. "I'll see you back at Fulford Road."

They walked back to Foley and helped him to his feet. Caslin used the bulk of his frame to ease some brush aside just far enough for Hunter to get the two of them off the path. At that point something akin to a birdcall carried to him on the light breeze. Despite being a city boy, Caslin knew what that meant. They'd found the path and most likely he had only moments before they were upon him. Releasing the brush to spring back into place he set off. This time with less concern about creating noise or the surety of his footing. Within a few minutes the track opened up a little and Caslin picked up the pace further. Glancing behind him there were now several beams of light arcing through the trees as the two teams descended on his position.

Fear gripped him bordering on panic. Breaking into a run he pushed himself seeking to put as much distance between them as he could. It wasn't long before his legs began to stiffen slowing his pace. With each stride becoming shorter and less controlled his feet felt numb. Forcing himself onward, Caslin's lungs burned and his breath came to him in short, ragged bursts. His cheeks felt flush as if they were on fire and moments later lights were dancing before his eyes like fireflies. The sound of the surging river could be heard up ahead the thought of reaching the bridge barely registering as

Caslin faltered. His vision swam and he stumbled losing his footing and pitching him sideways into the undergrowth. Rolling head first through the darkness something struck his back be it a rock or a tree root he didn't know which and he let out a primordial scream. Tumbling into the unknown, Caslin eventually found his descent slowing before coming to a stop. Then there was only darkness.

———

THE ROAR WAS CONSTANT. The sound battling the subconscious desire to sleep. His eyes flickered open. The moon was high, visible through the canopy of the trees above and casting silver shafts of light down around him. Caslin's left arm was numb, his fingers pricked by stabbing pains. Lying on his back, he watched the branches swaying in the breeze. The sound of whispers came to him and for a moment, Caslin considered whether or not he was conscious. A familiar tightness came to his chest. A sense of fear gripping him. Angling his head to the side, he observed the flow of the water half expecting to see the river of the dead that so vividly haunted his dreams. There was nothing. Only silence.

The realisation that his arm was in the water brought him back to reality. Rolling over and bringing it out of the river he hoisted himself upright and began massaging the feeling back into the muscles. How long he had lain there he didn't know. Thoughts turned to Hunter and he attempted to stand but his vision swam once again as before and he dropped to his haunches. Clenching his eyes tightly shut, he rode the wave of nausea that followed. Moments later it passed and he tried again. This time he was able to stand and look around seeking in vain to get his bearings. Rummaging through his pockets he cursed as he couldn't find his phone. Scanning the surrounding ground he failed to locate it. No doubt he had lost it when he fell.

With the aid of the clearing skies, Caslin picked his way back up the slope using whatever vegetation he could find to assist him. Progress was slow. The presence of his pursuers couldn't be dislodged from his mind and should they still be searching for him the last he wanted was to alert them to his location. Finding the path he tacked back with the river behind him. The more distance he put between himself and the river the sound decreased to be replaced by an eerie silence. Soon all that could be heard was that of the wind gently passing through the branches overhead the voices still taunting him as he went in search of Hunter and Foley.

The path narrowed and the brush increased. Aware that this was where they'd separated, Caslin stopped to catch his breath. The going was tough much to his surprise. What with the pounding in his head he wondered if he'd been struck unconscious by the fall. Brushing the pain aside he pushed his way through the undergrowth. There were no signs of Hunter not that he had an idea of what he was expecting to see. Deciding to head back towards Foley's house, Caslin returned to the path. With a bit of luck their plan had worked. Doubt crept in. If Hunter had made it to safety where were the back-up units?

Approaching Foley's cottage, Caslin crouched at the side of the path using the brush for cover. No lights were visible inside the house in complete darkness. The moon was obscured by clouds once more. Remembering their discussion, Caslin slipped past hugging the treeline in an attempt to avoid observation. Barely had he made it twenty yards before he stopped. A figure lay ahead slumped in the undergrowth. Even with the lack of light he knew who it was. His heart leapt and he rushed forward throwing caution to the wind. Kneeling alongside Hunter, he tentatively reached forward seeking a pulse. Finding one his excitement turned to fear as he realised how faint it was.

Unable to find any evidence of injury, Caslin sought to lever her up and over into a recovery position but strained to do so. His arms were weak and the exertion brought on wave after wave of dizziness. Shutting his eyes to try and avert the worst of the sensations the pulses of pain in his head grew in their intensity. He knew what was coming and searched through Hunter's pockets to find her radio. Locating it inside her coat, Caslin withdrew it only to watch the unit agonisingly slip from his grasp and into the bushes. Frantically scrabbling around in the darkness, Caslin sensed the periphery of his vision clouding over. His fingers touched against plastic and grasping it he pulled his hand back. The forest floor was spinning towards him and, unable to check whether he had the ability to transmit, he managed to press the panic button before passing out.

THE BRIGHTNESS of the room was in stark contrast to his last memory. A moment of confusion passed as he realised he was safe. Movement to his left made him look. A nurse entered the room.

"Good, you're awake," she said warmly, breaking into a smile. Caslin intended to respond but was thrown by the wires and tubes he found himself wrapped up in. The nurse checked the machine he was linked to and gave him a reassuring smile. "The doctor will be in to see you soon."

She left and Caslin took a measure of his surroundings. The tubes, providing air to his nose, felt awkward and unnecessary so he pulled them away from his face. Equipment monitoring his heart rate was clipped to his index finger and a nutrient drip was attached to the back of his right hand. Looking beyond the door, out into the corridor he saw an armed police officer at the entrance to his room with his back to him.

The beep of the monitor caught his attention. Focussing on the medical apparatus around him, Caslin judged it to be overkill but resisted the urge to begin disconnections. He felt perfectly normal if only just shy of exhausted. His thoughts drifted to Hunter and her wellbeing. She was alive when he found her, that, he remembered with clarity. A doctor approached, a large envelope in one hand. The constable opened the door for him followed closely by Terry Holt. The latter, very pleased to see Caslin conscious.

"I'm Doctor Theaker. How are you feeling, Mr Caslin?"

"I feel fine," Caslin replied honestly. "Is all of this really necessary?"

"I'm afraid so," the doctor replied.

"Where's Sarah? Is she okay?" Caslin asked, looking past the doctor towards Holt.

"She'll be all right, sir," Holt reassured him. "They hit her with a taser. Judging by her reaction to it they may have zapped her twice."

"That could've killed her," Caslin said. Holt nodded.

"She's doing okay, sir."

"Foley?"

Holt shook his head looking down. "No sign. Hunter doesn't know what happened to him. She didn't even catch sight of them before they took her out."

Caslin closed his eyes putting his head back against the pillow. "They were good."

"Who were they, sir?" Holt asked.

Caslin shook his head. "Right now, I don't know who they were working for but I could probably narrow it down," he said, unwilling to offer details. "Has Broadfoot been here?"

"Aye. He left a little while ago after speaking to Hunter. I'm to call him as soon as you are awake but I haven't yet. We're looking for Foley. Nothing so far."

"Any chance you can give work a rest for the time being?" Dr Theaker said politely, scanning Caslin's medical notes and flitting his eyes between the two men. "Your colleague is recovering and I would like to focus on you if that's okay?" Holt indicated an apology, crossing the room to look out of the window down into the hospital's car park. Turning to Caslin the doctor continued, "Any feelings of dizziness, nausea, shortness of breath…"

"Since I woke up?"

"Yes."

"No," Caslin said, "I feel perfectly fine."

"And before?"

"All of the above," Caslin stated.

"Often?"

"Fairly," Caslin replied. "What's going on with me?"

The doctor opened the envelope taking out an x-ray. Crossing the room he clipped the first onto a light box mounted on the wall. Flicking the switch, Caslin's chest x-ray was illuminated. Doctor Theaker used a pencil to indicate Caslin's heart.

"Can you see this?" he asked, holding the end of the pen at a specific point. Caslin could make out a dark object alongside a narrow sliver depicted as white.

"What am I looking at?" Caslin asked. There was a knock on the door and it opened. Caslin glanced to see the arrival of Karen, his ex-wife. She entered, shock etched on her face. Caslin felt a pang in his chest. The reaction surprised him. He and Karen barely spoke outside of matters regarding the children.

"I'm sorry. I had to come when I heard," she said, sounding flustered. Caslin smiled. He was pleased to see her. She approached the bedside and he reached out. Karen took his hand gripping it tightly. Turning back to the doctor, Caslin indicated for him to continue.

"I am afraid this is left over from a few years ago," Dr Theaker said. "Three years ago you experienced a severe trauma when you were shot."

"How could I forget?" Caslin said under his breath. Karen squeezed his hand.

"As you'll remember the bullet glanced off your ribcage, ricocheting around your abdomen before exiting to the rear. Now, Lady Luck was shining on you that day the bullet missing your vital organs, it did, however, shatter one of your ribs. Fragments of which were removed at the time apart from those—"

"That were considered too close to my heart," Caslin finished. The doctor nodded.

"And therein lies your problem," he continued, putting up a second image, only this time an enlargement of the first. "A sliver of bone has been on the move along with a fragment of the aforementioned bullet. They've managed to work themselves into a position where pressure is being exerted on your heart between your left atrium and the murmor. This is causing erratic movement in your aortic valve thereby intermittently restricting blood flow. This is why you've been experiencing the issues that you have."

Caslin took it in. "What does this mean?"

"You need surgery."

"Can it wait?"

Doctor Theaker shook his head. "I wouldn't advise it. Should you over exert yourself physically or come up against a particularly stressful situation there is every chance you could face a rupture. You would bleed out, internally, in a matter of minutes."

Caslin sighed. "That doesn't sound good."

"I must advise you that with any surgery there is an inherent risk attached, arguably more so now than three years ago. To be honest it's lucky that we found out ahead of time. A rupture could occur at any moment. At least now we can do something about it," Dr Theaker said. "We'll schedule the operation to begin as soon as the team is assembled. Provided you have no objection?"

Caslin shook his head slowly, meeting Karen's eye. She appeared on the verge of tears. He squeezed her hand gently. "It'll be okay," he said with as much confidence as he could muster. The doctor excused himself and Terry Holt also headed for the door.

"I'll give you two some space," Holt said awkwardly. Caslin smiled as he watched the DC leave.

"Well," he said, blowing out his cheeks. "I can't say I saw that coming. Listen, Karen... thanks for—"

"Nate," Karen said, cutting him off. Nervously looking over her shoulder towards the door, she struggled to remove something from her coat pocket. "When I got home tonight I found this," she said, putting a mobile phone on the bed next to him. "It had a note taped to it with your name on telling me to bring it here. Nathaniel, it was on the breakfast bar... in the kitchen. At first, I couldn't see how it got there but then..."

"Then what?" Caslin asked, sensing Karen's nerves stemmed from something far greater. She met his gaze. A solitary tear rolled down her cheek and she quickly brushed it aside as if it would reveal something precious buried deep within her.

"Nate, I don't know where Sean is."

Caslin felt his chest tighten. "It's Friday night, he's probably playing computer games at a friend's house."

"No, no, that's not it," she said, desperately trying to control her emotions. "I picked him up from school. He was at home. I left to take Lizzie to Claire's for a sleepover. I hadn't seen her mum for a while and... we had a glass of wine and... got talking. Sean's mobile was still in his room when I got back. He never goes anywhere without it. Sean must have let them in. Nate, what if—"

"Calm down," Caslin said, reassuring her. Glancing towards the door himself, he could see they weren't about to be interrupted and so he turned to the mobile Karen brought with her. Picking it up, he gave it a cursory examination. Powering up the phone it came out of hibernation. Opening the contacts list there was only one number programmed in. No name was attached but the number was of UK origin. Taking a deep breath, he met Karen's eye and dialled it. The call connected and after two rings another voice came on at the other end.

"Inspector. I have to admit I thought you would've called sooner," the voice said.

"I was sleeping," Caslin replied. "Who is this?"

"If it matters to you, to have a name, you can call me... Will. I won't beat around the bush, Nathaniel. There's something we need from you."

"And what might that be?"

"Emily Coughlan's notes. Everything she had that documented her investigation."

"You think I'm going to give that to you?"

"I believe so, yes," Will said, with confidence.

Caslin smiled. "Even if I was to do so. How would that help you? Now we know what it means—"

"Except you haven't had much of a chance to pass your information onto anyone else have you? You only figured it out today."

"You sound sure. What makes you think that?"

"Your visit to see Callum this evening. Had you been fully aware of his participation you'd have most certainly done more than just watch him. No, Inspector. The knowledge is in your head and yours alone. We want the hard evidence."

"What use is it to you? Everyone's already dead."

"We will ensure that's the case."

"It all seems academic now though. Why not come down to Fulford Road and we could have a chat about it?" Caslin said.

"Amusing, Inspector. I had another meeting place in mind but don't worry I'll give you enough time to get dressed and get yourself there."

"Bringing me back to *why* you think I'm going to help you?"

"There's someone here wishing to speak to you," Will said. There was an audible transfer of the handset. Caslin's blood ran cold as he heard the next voice speak.

"Dad..." Sean said, his voice cracking immediately as he burst into tears.

"Sean!" Caslin replied, his own voice wavering. "Sean... it's going to be—"

"Now you see from where my confidence stems," Will replied, taking control of the call once again. "By now, I'm sure you understand the level of resource we have at our disposal having experienced it yourself this evening. Open the satellite navigation app on your phone and you'll see directions to our meeting point along with a route for you to follow. You have one hour to obtain what we want and get there. If you do not arrive at the requested time make no mistake I will kill your son." Caslin glanced to Karen, sitting alongside him with tears streaming down her face. "If you do not follow the assigned route or if there is any indication that you are not alone I will kill your son. Needless to say should you show up without what I have asked you for I *will kill your son.*"

"If you hurt him, I will fucking kill—"

Will laughed. "No hollow threats, please, Inspector Caslin. I'm not a monster. This isn't personal, it's business. That said, I'd advise you not to underestimate our resolve. If you don't fulfil your end of this I might just start mailing your son back to his mother one piece at a time."

The line went dead as the call dropped. Caslin closed his eyes moving the handset up and touching it to his forehead not wanting to meet Karen's expectant look.

"Nate," she said quietly, "I don't care what you have to do but promise me…. promise me, you're going to get our boy back. Even if you don't believe it I need you to say the words."

He looked into her eyes. "I'll get him back. I promise."

CHAPTER TWENTY-SIX

KAREN OPENED the door and attracted the attention of the officer on guard. He followed her back inside acknowledging Caslin lying in bed.

"Sir?" he asked.

"Do me a favour and get a hold of DC Holt for me. I lost my phone this evening." Caslin asked, smiling.

"I'm not to leave you, sir," the officer replied.

Caslin dismissed the concern with a flick of his hand. "That's okay. I think I'll be all right for a couple of minutes. Terry's probably gone for something to eat." The protection officer was nonplussed but reluctantly agreed. As he stepped from the room, Karen drew the blinds across to the window facing into the corridor. The door was barely closed before Caslin was on his feet.

"Where did you park your car?" he asked Karen, shutting down the heart monitor and shaking off the finger clip before removing the drip feed from his other hand.

"It's out front in the car park," she said, passing him her keys. Pulling on his trousers he dropped them into his pocket as she passed him a shirt.

"You have to leave at the same time or they'll put pressure on you to know where I am. Think of somewhere to go where they won't look for you."

"I'll go to Claire's, be with Lizzie," Karen said. Caslin put on his jacket crossing to the window and moving the blinds aside to see into the corridor. It was clear. "Nate," she said as he reached for the door. Turning, he looked back at her. "What the doctor said. This could—"

"I'll be fine," he reassured her. "Doctors always err on the side of caution you know that. Besides this is Sean. I'll call you when it's over."

"Be careful," Karen said. Caslin read the expression on her face. It was as if she didn't expect to see him again. He cracked open the door glancing out into the corridor.

"They just want what I have that's all. As long as I give it to them—"

"But what about Sarah?"

"They didn't kill her," Caslin countered. "They could've done, quite easily, but they didn't. They know what kind of a storm they'd bring down on them if they killed a police officer... let alone..." he paused, considering whether or not to finish the statement, "let alone a kid."

"Okay," she said, wiping away tears.

"Are you ready?" he asked and she nodded fervently. "Let's go," he said, opening the door and moving into the corridor. Karen followed and taking her hand, he led her down the corridor to the ward's exit. Stopping before they reached the nurse's station, Caslin checked around the corner. The area was unattended. Being the early hours of the morning there was only a skeleton crew on the nightshift. They hurried to the exit, Caslin eyeing the security screen set high above the nurse's desk depicting the corridor beyond as they passed. Their path was clear and, releasing the magnetic lock they were off the ward.

The stairwell was ahead of them signage indicated the elevators were off to the right. Caslin pointed Karen in that direction.

"I'll take the stairs," he said. "Switch off your phone and only turn it back on in an hour. That way they probably won't be able to track you."

"I love you," she told him. Leaning in, he kissed her passionately for the briefest of moments and then he was off onto the stairs without looking back.

———

ARRIVING AT FULFORD ROAD, a little after 2 A.M., Caslin slipped through the custody suite unnoticed. Two men, arrested for a drunken brawl in one of the city-centre pubs, were causing havoc as the nightshift tried to incarcerate them in their cells. The sense of guilt gnawed away at him as he descended towards the evidence storage rooms in the bowels of the station. All his training encouraged him to go straight for DCS Broadfoot while experience told him that to do so would mean he might never see Sean again. Shoving the thoughts aside, he arrived at the storage rooms. Punching in his access code, Caslin walked through flicking on the lights. The fluorescent tubes flickered into life and he found the archive box relating to the Coughlan case.

Lifting it off the shelf, he put it down on the floor and took off the lid. The notebook came out first and he stashed it in his jacket pocket followed closely by her mobile phone. The access card he'd used in Dublin came next and then he replaced the lid returning the box to its rightful place. Pushing it back from the edge, Caslin stopped and stared at it. Lying to Karen had been easy but he couldn't deceive himself. In no doubt they wanted the physical evidence of Coughlan's investigation, he was far less confident regarding the assurances he was given.

Copies of the codes were taken but, judging by Nelson's potential connections within British Intelligence, they could always disappear at a later date particularly if the case was closed down. Caslin, they assumed, had cracked it or at the very least had pieced enough together to warrant kidnapping his son in order to bring him under control. The rationale behind leaving

Hunter alive was debatable. Had they killed her their credibility with regard to bargaining would've been shot. Would they allow someone with his knowledge to walk away? If so what of his son? Without answers to comfort him, Caslin left the evidence room turning out the lights and heading back upstairs.

The Duty Sergeant was standing in the rear office with a colleague both with their backs to the door. Entering the reception area the shouts from the cells echoed down to him as the detained competed to make the most noise voicing questions of the officers' parentage among other things. Not wishing to face any awkward questions, Caslin trotted across to the exit door. Passing through whilst glancing behind him, he nearly collided with two officers returning to the station for their meal break. Apologising they stepped aside and he walked on with the briefest of acknowledgments. If they were remotely suspicious they didn't offer any indication as they continued inside.

Once back to Karen's car, he turned the key in the ignition. Placing the phone next to him on the central console he activated the sat nav. The drive was scheduled to take an hour and three-quarters. Caslin was confident he could do it faster but the route was planned and his instructions were to follow it. Heading in a northerly direction, he would reach the edge of the North York Moors within an hour. From there he was to approach Helmsley, from the west before cutting north once again driving towards Helmsley Moor. His destination point was a small church once servicing the rural farmland community but now, like many of these remote locations, only occupied on festive occasions. A quick mental calculation told him he would arrive shortly after dawn.

Throughout his journey, Caslin paid close attention to vehicles that appeared in his mirrors or those he passed that were stationary hoping to catch sight of anyone he conceived might be keeping track of him. No suspects came into view. In all likelihood they were tracking the phone to ensure he didn't deviate from the agreed course. Upon reaching the outskirts of Helmsley, Caslin took the left turn signposted towards the moor. The phone pinged and glancing down, he saw he'd received a text message. Arriving at the church, he pulled up. There was no car park so remote was the site and in the slate grey light of the breaking day, he saw no-one around to greet him.

Getting out of the car, he closed the door whilst scanning the surrounding area. All was quiet. Bringing up the home screen on the phone, Caslin noted that he no longer had a signal, unsurprisingly, bearing in mind where he was. Opening the text message it simply read *Walk north*. With a fleeting glance behind, Caslin did as instructed. The path took him down the side of the church which opened up onto the moor itself.

The immediate landscape featured rolling heathland, purple heather almost as far as the eye could see. The Vale of Pickering lay to the right cutting its own path northwards into the national park. Sitting at a higher elevation in front of him were the Cleveland Hills, beautiful in its own, rugged way. The ground underfoot was muddy beneath the thick shroud of the heather. Walking upwards, Caslin kept his senses alert and he didn't have long to wait. Approaching the next crest the rotors of a helicopter came into view. Before he was able to fully process the scene two figures rose from the ground within thirty feet of him, one to his left another to the right. They didn't speak merely cradled assault rifles in their arms and looked on watching him intently. Ignoring them, he stayed on a course towards the helicopter. It was a private vehicle, black, with no identification markings that he could make out.

Ahead the side door to the helicopter slid open and three figures jumped out onto the moor. Caslin picked out one more remaining inside in the pilot's seat. Of those alighting two spaced themselves evenly apart to either side of the other. Again these men were heavily armed. Caslin pegged them as former military judging by how they moved, alert and keenly aware of their surroundings. The central figure stood casually, hands clasped behind his back eyeing the approaching Caslin. Walking to within twenty feet, he stopped.

"Inspector Caslin," the man said. "Thank you for coming. Do you have what I asked you for?"

"Who are you? Are you Will?" Caslin asked.

"If you like. Does it matter?" the man said, with a shrug. Caslin assumed this was the "Will" he'd spoken to on the phone.

"You work for Renton Sands?"

Will laughed in reply. "Still the detective, even now."

"I want to see my son," Caslin said forcefully.

"This is not a negotiation," Will said, looking to his right and inclining his head slightly. "Tony, if you wouldn't mind."

"Sir," the man closest to him said slinging his rifle across his shoulder and walking back to the helicopter. Opening the door, he reached in and manhandled a dishevelled looking Callum Foley out from the interior. Dragged across the short distance between them and unceremoniously dumped on the ground, Foley received a kick to the lower back for good measure. The aging priest let out a muted scream of pain. Reaching down and grasping a fistful of hair, Tony pulled him upright onto his knees.

Caslin felt a surge of anger course through him. The old man groaned, his head lolling to one side. There was no indication of recognition from him, he appeared barely cognisant. Foley was pale and had taken some manner of a beating for his face was bruised and swollen with what looked like dried blood mixed in amongst the matted hair.

"Did you bring it?" Caslin was asked again.

"Where is my son," he replied, only this time shouting. Will stepped forward bringing forth his right hand from behind his back. Caslin registered the pistol just as the barrel was placed against the back of Foley's head. A solitary shot passed through the priest's skull exiting just below the left eye taking much of his nose and cheek with it. Caslin jumped in shock, not even registering the sound of the gunshot. Callum Foley's lifeless body slumped forward into the heather.

"Did you bring it?" Will shouted back. Caslin, open mouthed, could only nod in response. "Show me," he instructed. Caslin reached into his pocket but found his hands trembling. Trying to steady himself, he fumbled for the notebook and finally managed to free it from the lining of his jacket. Lifting it so as it was more visible, he held it aloft, his hand still shaking. Tony came over to him. Caslin offered up the notebook. It was snatched away from him with a look of contempt. Taking a blow to the stomach, Caslin was winded, doubling over.

"Give me my son," he asked, struggling to speak. He looked towards the helicopter as Sean was beckoned out. The relief at seeing him alive and well passed in a fraction of a second replaced by rising panic as he watched his son brought directly before the one calling the shots. Still bearing a pistol in his hand, Will placed an affectionate arm around Sean's shoulder. The latter had clearly been crying, red-eyed with dry tears lining his cheeks.

"A good looking kid you have here," Will said, smiling and running the end of the barrel through Sean's mop of brown hair. Caslin tensed. Applying some pressure, Sean was lowered to his knees. The boy couldn't help but look at Foley's corpse lying next to where he knelt. The horrific sight was mirrored in his expression.

"It'll be all right, Sean. Trust me," Caslin called out but the words sounded hollow even to him.

"Who knows about Coughlan's investigation?" Will asked.

"I cracked the code and like you said I haven't had a chance to tell anyone else."

"You expect me to believe that?"

Caslin held his hands up in supplication, palms wide, "I haven't told a soul, I swear—"

"On your son's life?" Will asked, pointing the pistol at Sean. Caslin gasped, heart pounding.

"I haven't told anyone," he said. "Please… don't hurt my son."

"Who else knows?" Will barked, lodging the barrel firmly against Sean's head forcing him to lean forward. Caslin watched his son screw his eyes shut, mouth contorted through fear with spittle running free. Sean began to sob uncontrollably.

"Please!" Caslin implored him, involuntarily dropping to his knees. "Please..." he begged, tears now running freely down his face.

The gun was withdrawn but Sean remained where he was, his body racked in distress. Indicating for Tony to assume control over the boy, Will came to stand before Caslin. He lowered himself onto his haunches cupping the pistol casually in both hands.

"Get up, Inspector," he whispered, leaning in. Glancing towards Sean. He continued, "Seriously, your son's watching. It's embarrassing." Caslin stood up but on unsteady legs. They felt numb. He was powerless. Any thoughts of a last ditch attempt to seize a weapon were dismissed at the sight of a rifle being aimed at Sean's back. His son was staring at the ground, openly weeping. "You know what?" Will said, patting Caslin's cheek with a gloved hand, "I believe you. You haven't told anyone else."

"I haven't," Caslin said quietly.

"That was foolish. I had you down as smarter than that. Now you have nothing to trade for your lives," he said grinning. Caslin's heart sank and he met Sean's eye seeing nothing but despair and abject terror.

"Who are you?" Caslin said, barely audible.

"The last person you will ever see," Will replied with cold malice. Caslin glanced at him steeling himself for what was coming.

"Sean knows nothing. He's just a kid."

"Don't be too hard on yourself, Nathaniel. Once we took your boy you were shit out of options. For what it's worth if I was you, I probably would've done the same." He glanced towards Tony and inclined his head.

"No!" Caslin screamed.

A fountain of red spray exploded from the side of Tony's head, at the same time half of it disappeared. A fraction of a second later the sound of a gunshot carried to them. Caslin launched himself at Will knocking him off balance and managing to stop the pistol being brought to bear. A single round was discharged, high into the air. Wrestling for control of the weapon, Caslin threw his head forward headbutting Will and knocking him backwards. Locked together in a battle for supremacy they stumbled in the brush and fell to the ground.

Unbeknownst to Caslin, the Renton team, battle-hardened, flew into action and returned fire whilst searching for cover but there was little to be had. Another rifle shot carried forth. The round struck another man, knelt in a combat pose, high in the chest. Punched from his feet, he fell to the ground with the briefest of grunts, a significant portion of his upper torso missing.

Caslin was losing his personal battle. His opponent was too strong, too able. Unable to gain the upper hand no matter what he tried the angle of the barrel edged closer towards his face as the moments passed. The exertion of the struggle took its toll and Caslin's energy ebbed away. Resolve turned to fear and the thought of submission filled his mind only to do so meant death. Suddenly releasing the pressure on his opponent's wrist the gun lurched closer and Caslin clamped his teeth onto the base of his attacker's thumb, biting down with all his might. A scream ensued and, losing his grip, Caslin saw the gun topple away into the brush.

Rolling his body in line with the slope of the terrain, Caslin flipped his opponent away and they untangled from one other. Coming to his knees, Caslin scanned the heather for the gun but he couldn't see it. Looking up he barely managed to brace himself as a booted foot was driven into his ribs. Howling with pain, he fell to the side rolling and came back to his feet. They squared up to each other. Catching sight of Sean in the corner of his eye he yelled out.

"Run, Sean!" Not knowing if his instruction was heeded, Caslin was forced to defend himself against an attack. Another rifle shot echoed through the hills this time answered by sporadic bursts of automatic weapons fire nearby. The Renton team were returning fire. A fist connected with Caslin's cheek, knocking him backwards. A combination of blows rained down upon him, leaving him flat on his back, unsure of how he got there. Then came his attacker, towering over him, armed with a serrated blade. Caslin kicked out but the move didn't slow the attack in the slightest. Another shot. Caslin could almost feel the change in pressure along with the accompanying fizz as the round split the air between them.

Breaking off the assault, Will was off and running for the helicopter. The pre-flight start-up was underway the rotors beginning to turn. A figure was crouched next to the left skid sending two-second bursts of fire towards the south. A round came in reply narrowly missing its target and glancing off the fuselage of the helicopter. The mercenary recoiled before reacquiring his target and sending another volley in return.

Caslin searched for Sean but couldn't see him anywhere. Panicking, he looked to the helicopter but still couldn't recognise his son as one of the three figures in sight. Rooting through the undergrowth he located the pistol.

More shots came from his left one of the sentries that had secreted themselves before his arrival was targeting the sniper. With two concentrating their fire, Caslin felt the element of surprise was now lost. The distance the rounds were travelling before the sound wave caught up indicated the shooter wasn't far away, well within range of the Renton guns. There was a choice for him to make and a split second to make it. The whine from the helicopter signalled its intent to lift off. Caslin levelled the pistol at the man on the crest of the hill. Dropping to one knee, he steadied himself. Forcibly controlling his breathing, Caslin took aim loosing off a single round followed quickly by another. Both shots passed to the right of target but drew the gunman's attention. He turned but not quickly enough. Caslin's third shot took him in the chest, he fell without a sound.

A bullet whistled past him from the direction of the helicopter.

Caslin threw himself to the ground just as the downdraught from the rotors whipped up a storm of dust and debris. The roar of the engine increased as the helicopter took off deafening him but he found himself calling for Sean despite the futility of the gesture. Rounds struck the earth around him as Will, perched on one of the helicopter's skids, opened fire on him. Caslin rolled onto his back screaming incomprehensibly as he unleashed the remaining rounds towards the helicopter climbing away above him.

Momentarily the helicopter appeared to jolt first to the left and then the nose dipped the ascent stalling. Black smoke began billowing from the engine housing and the machine lurched to the right. The slide locked back on Caslin's weapon signifying he'd spent his last round and was powerless to act further watching the pilot wrestling with the controls. The helicopter spun ninety degrees turning to face him approximately a hundred feet off the deck. At that moment part of the canopy shattered and the pilot's body slumped to one side. Immediately the helicopter began to fall into a tailspin gaining momentum as the speed of the descent rapidly increased. A figure was flung into the air from within arms and legs flailing right up until the point he impacted the ground.

Caslin covered his head with his arms and tried to become one with the earth. He didn't see the helicopter crash but the ground shook and the rumble from the explosion and subsequent shockwave were intense. The rotors shredded upon striking the moor and flew off in every direction, shards of razor sharp metal travelling at hundreds of miles per hour.

Silence descended. Caslin's heart was racing as he took his hands away from cradling his head. Tentatively raising himself up onto his elbows, he scanned the scene. The wreckage was further down the hillside, a little over a hundred yards from his position. A plume of thick smoke swirled up into the sky. He could hear the crackling of the flames consuming anything combustible. Two small explosions in quick succession resonated from the crash site. Wary of the presence of the sniper and their motivations, Caslin was reluctant to stand. Shifting onto his haunches, he dropped one knee and looked around for signs of movement. There were none.

"Sean!" he called, his voice wavering. The sound carried but no answer came back. "Sean, are you there?" he yelled again, fearing the worst. This time, he caught sight of movement a little way off. Watching intently, he waited daring not to believe and then a figure stood. Caslin forgot about the threat from the sniper and was up and running. Covering the sixty yards through the heather at breakneck speed and embracing his son, Caslin held him with an iron grip. Both of them wept openly. Stepping back and gently placing his hands against Sean's face, he looked him up and down.

"Are you hurt? Any holes in you or—"

"I'm okay, Dad," Sean replied. Caslin pulled him back in again and his son buried his head into his father's chest hugging him fiercely.

"We're going home," Caslin said, turning and looking over his shoulder. At the crest of the hill some three-hundred yards distant a lone figure stood observing them. Without the aid of the backdrop of the hills beyond to skyline him, Caslin would never have spotted the gunman. Dressed all in black, including face paint and cap, he stood there brandishing a high-calibre rifle. A handgun was strapped to his thigh although his stance was non-threatening. Hefting the rifle up against his shoulder, he turned to walk away. Caslin released his grip on Sean stepping forward and shouting, "Hey!"

The man stopped, looking back on the half-turn. Even as the sun rose to break above the horizon, bathing them in bright sunlight, Caslin could barely make out the man who'd saved their lives.

"Thank you!" he called out. The words sounded lame and woefully inadequate under the circumstances. The figure stood and stared at them for a moment longer before he raised his free hand in a simple gesture of acknowledgement and with that, he was gone. Sean came to stand alongside his father.

"Who was that?" he asked.

"A friend," Caslin replied, placing a reassuring arm around Sean's shoulder.

"Are you going to stop him?"

"No. Not this time," he said, pulling his son close. "For once, I don't care."

CHAPTER TWENTY-SEVEN

THERE WAS a knock on the door and it opened. Kyle Broadfoot entered stopping as he saw Karen, Sean and Lizzie at Caslin's bedside.

"Forgive me," he said. "I can come back another time."

Karen stood, waving her hand to dismiss the suggestion.

"No, please. It's time I got the kids home for their dinner anyway."

Broadfoot smiled awkwardly as the family gathered their coats and filed past him, Lizzie the last to leave after flinging herself at her father for a farewell hug. Caslin winced but didn't allow her to see his pain turning it into a big smile to see her off.

"How is your son..." Broadfoot paused, searching his mind for the name.

"Sean," Caslin offered.

"Yes, sorry. How is he?"

"Remarkably well," Caslin said. "He's resilient but... well, we've arranged some counselling for him. One step at a time."

"Good to hear," Broadfoot responded. "And your surgery. How did that go?"

"The prognosis is good, sir. Thank you." It was evident from his demeanour that Broadfoot wanted to move the conversation on to a business footing. There followed a brief period of silence between them the minimum length of time to remain respectful.

"There isn't an easy way to tell you this, Nathaniel," Broadfoot began, "your request to issue a European Arrest Warrant for Paraic Nelson has been declined."

Caslin put his head back against his pillow. "I guess I shouldn't be surprised."

"The evidence against him is largely circumstantial—"

"So he walks away from trying to kill me, my family?"

"You can't prove he was behind Sean's abduction nor any instruction to have you killed either. Did anyone implicate Nelson directly?" Broadfoot asked, pulling aside the chair vacated by Karen and sitting down.

"No-one left alive, no, sir," Caslin replied. As much as he hated to admit it the DCS was right. Knowing and proving were very different things.

"The Civil Aviation Authority is trying to track down the origins of the helicopter but none of the nomenclature is on file. It never existed. Nothing matching it is recorded taking off from any airfield within a hundred miles. The body count you left on the moor, significant as it was, has led us nowhere. None of them appear to have been carrying identification and their prints are not on file."

"How can that be possible?" Caslin asked.

Broadfoot shook his head. "Based on Heinrich Schmidt's background I wouldn't be surprised if we're being stonewalled by other agencies. Speaking of which your mystery saviour has vanished into thin air. That strikes me as more than a little suspicious. Are you sure you didn't recognise him?"

Caslin shook his head. "No, sir. I wish I had."

"Bottom line," Broadfoot continued, "the investigation is to be handed over to the Serious Fraud Office. They, along with the NCA, will examine any role that Christopher Fairchild had in any insider dealing and act accordingly. I know it's not the outcome you were after and, for what it's worth, I'm sorry.

You lost a lot in this case... your friend... very nearly your son."

"Thank you, sir," Caslin replied, lying back and closing his eyes.

"Speaking of which," Broadfoot continued, in an amenable tone unusual for him and one he was ill at ease with, "Aiden Reece's funeral will take place in two days' time. He wasn't survived by any family and judging by his chequered past it will be a low key affair. I thought you would want to attend."

"Not really, sir," Caslin replied. "I appreciate you thinking of me but I don't feel the need."

"As you wish," Broadfoot said with a raised eyebrow. "Several points of admin for you to be aware of, Nathaniel."

"Sir?"

"Fulford Road will have a new DCI by the end of the month. You knew your appointment was only temporary but you acquitted yourself admirably." Caslin smiled in appreciation, however, much to his own surprise, he was disheartened by the news. "Lastly my confirmation has come through. I'll be taking up the lead role in Yorkshire's Crime Directorate from the beginning of November."

"Congratulations, sir," Caslin replied, eyeing movement in the corridor beyond as a figure approached the door only to veer off at the last moment.

"We don't have the luxuries of the Metropolitan Police. Here in Yorkshire resources are being centralised, Nathaniel. We have to be far more adaptable to the requirements of modern policing. I intend to restructure, build a new team. One with the ability to deploy at a moment's notice... and I want you to run it for me."

"Me?" Caslin said with genuine surprise.

"Your approach may be unorthodox but you know how to get results and that's the important thing."

"I'm not sure I agree," Caslin replied.

"You're wasted at Fulford Road, Nathaniel. You're going nowhere—"

"Thanks for the vote of confidence, sir," Caslin cut in without masking the sarcasm.

"It's a clean slate, Nathaniel," Broadfoot said, standing and making to leave. "Think about it."

Broadfoot excused himself, leaving the room and closing the door behind him. Instinctively, Caslin felt he should remain where he was at Fulford Road but with so much change afoot perhaps it was time to consider moving on. Moments later the door reopened and Jimmy Sullivan entered glancing behind him at the departing form of the DCS.

"He doesn't bite, Jimmy," Caslin said grinning. The journalist shrugged.

"Senior ranks don't take to me," Jimmy said in justification.

"I know the feeling. Thanks for paying me a visit, Jimmy but there's no need. I'll be home soon."

"Aye, I thought I'd bring you some bits and pieces. You know? Seeing as hospital food is as it is."

Caslin eyed his empty hands. "And?"

Sullivan stared blankly at him before registering the unasked question.

"Oh, right. Then, Karen told me you'd had a heart op so I thought chocolate, scotch and stuff wouldn't be good for you—"

"I didn't have a heart attack... never mind," Caslin said, shaking his head. "So why are you here?"

Sullivan glanced over his shoulder as if worried someone would overhear. "To thank you, firstly."

"For what?"

"Going as far as you did for Emily. It means a lot to me," Sullivan said, before continuing, "and also, to let you know I took a call earlier from a mutual friend."

"Who?"

"Seamus Hanlon," Sullivan said, referencing the Gardaí detective with another nervous glance towards the door. "He sends you his best. Also, he wanted to give us the heads up before it becomes common knowledge."

"What's that?"

"They found Paraic Nelson this morning at the bottom of a multi-storey car park. Looks like he took a dive off the roof sometime in the early hours. He made quite a mess by all accounts."

Caslin exhaled slowly. "You think his conscience got the better of him?"

Sullivan stifled a guttural laugh of contempt. "You reckon he ever had one?"

"He had to move fast before Nelson had a chance to react," Caslin said aloud.

"What's that you say?" Sullivan queried with a puzzled look.

"The dead don't seek justice. That's for the living to do on their behalf," Caslin said quietly, his thoughts turning to Aiden Reece.

FREE BOOK GIVEAWAY

Visit the author's website at **www.jmdalgliesh.com** and sign up to the VIP Club and be first to receive news and previews of forthcoming works.

Here you can download a FREE eBook novella exclusive to club members;

Life & Death - A Hidden Norfolk novella

———————

Never miss a new release.

No spam, ever, guaranteed. You can unsubscribe at any time.

BLOOD MONEY - PREVIEW
DARK YORKSHIRE - BOOK 4

THE AMERICANO WAS DRINKABLE NOW. Sitting in the café, having watched the world go by for the past thirty minutes, had given the liquid a chance to cool. Putting the last piece of his meatball panini into his mouth, he wiped his fingers, then his lips, with a paper napkin, before scrunching it into a ball and tossing it onto the empty plate. The mad rush of custom at this time of the day was easing off.

The establishment was still full. There were several families corralling their children in the narrow passages between tables. Presumably they were off school this week. Others, out for a dose of retail therapy, compared their purchases and discussed their next port-of-call. The general noise level meant voices were often raised to be heard above the sound of the coffee grinder and steam wands. He didn't care. His mind was a picture of calm, weeding out the unnecessary and focussing on the task at hand.

The day was overcast, the lack of direct sunlight meant the room was darker than usual. The entrance door opened as three people came in. The first held the door for the others, allowing an unwelcome blast of cold air. Some glanced in the direction of the newcomers, conveying unspoken displeasure at the draught. The street beyond the full-height window he was sitting next to was remarkably busy for a week day.

The sound of a beating drum turned his head. A throng of people were approaching from the east .

They stood out as they navigated York's pedestrianised zone. Whistles blew and those seated around him also looked out. Men and women of all ages and colours marched past. Those at the head of the column were clutching a banner. The ones who followed, brandished placards or blew into whistles with fervour.

His phone on the table vibrated. Glancing down as the text message flashed up, he shot a brief look across the street beyond the demonstrators and towards the figure directly opposite him, standing in the recess of a shop entrance. They made eye contact and he nodded, almost imperceptibly. The movement was acknowledged and the man casually set off. The attention span of those within the café was limited. The notion came to him that these people cared little for the demonstration passing by outside. They had better things to be doing: shopping, eating and chatting. *If only they knew,* he thought to himself, standing. Their lives were so simple, so superficial... so boring.

Leaving the half-cup of coffee on the table, he slipped his phone into his pocket and picked his way through the people seated around him. Wrapping his scarf around his neck, he buttoned up his overcoat in preparation for the temperature drop as he went outside. Brushing against one woman, he uttered an apology but she didn't hear it nor did she flinch, too engrossed in her conversation.

Stepping out into the street, he thrust his hands into his coat pockets. The weather had taken a turn for the worse. The brief spell of clement weather, the incredibly delayed Indian summer, someone he'd overheard call it, was now a distant memory. More rain threatened. This reminded him of home, although it was still warmer. At least *that* was his recollection.

Two police officers strolled past, accompanying the stragglers waving their placards in the air, their breath sending clouds of vapour around them as they walked. No doubt, the higher concentration of resources would be found at the counter protest, that engineered by the nationalists across the city. He admired the provocative nature of launching an anti-immigrant rally in a city with few migrants along with a high concentration of students. It was sure to draw attention which, of course, was the intention.

Setting off in the opposite direction, he felt his phone vibrate again. Taking it out of his pocket he registered the text and increased his pace. The last time he had walked the route it took him twelve minutes but today he had some ground to make up so would be quicker. Central York had an abundance of cut-throughs and passages that could assist in traversing the city, if you knew where they led and how to find them. Another message came through. This one brought a smile to his face. They had stopped briefly, either distracted or their presence had been noted. No matter. Everything was well in hand.

Leaving the hub of the merchant's quarter behind, he had to step from the narrow pavement into oncoming traffic to navigate a gaggle of window shoppers. Eyeing a break, he sprinted across the road, raising a hand in thanks to the nearest driver.

Taking a right onto Fossgate, he headed further out of the centre. The crowds rapidly thinned, as popular shops were replaced with niche establishments once he crossed the river. Fossgate became Walmgate and business premises intermingled with small, modern residential blocks.

Upon reaching his destination, he stopped, eyeing the communal entrances to each block. No one was coming or going, so the opportunity to slip through was unavailable. Knowing the security doors were not fit for purpose for someone of his skill set, he acknowledged they were merely time consuming. Of an evening, it would certainly be workable to enter that way but in broad daylight, a little too brazen even for him.

Further along were the gated entrances, giving access to the gardens at the rear. He found them to be locked. They were of metal construction, six feet high, and cast with spikes at the top.

Decorative but not effective against anything but an opportunist. A quick glance around to ensure he would pass unnoticed, and within seconds he had scaled the railings, hoisted himself over the top and dropped unobserved to the other side. Casually walking to the rear, he cut to his left and found himself in a grassed court-yard area overlooked only by the residential flats of the block. Nothing stirred. The uniform small, square windows of every flat had net curtains or dropped blinds. People here valued their privacy, even if it came at the cost of natural light. Moving with purpose, he walked to the fourth window along on the ground floor.

One last look around and he withdrew a metal strip, concealed within his coat. An inch wide, smooth and incredibly slim, he slipped it between window and frame, jockeying it into position. Once happy, he thrust it upwards and felt the reassuring sensation of the latch moving away. The window cracked open and he eased it out towards him. Putting his tool away, he brushed aside the curtain and clambered in, pulling the window closed behind him. The process had taken only the briefest of moments.

The room was as he had found previously, spartanly furnished and stale, desperately in need of some fresh air. Inspecting the dining table, he scanned a magazine that had been left open upon it, this month's *National Geographic*. Alongside that was a book on the fundamentals of economics.

A clock ticked on the wall in the narrow kitchen. A cat stretched out on the sofa, eyeing him suspiciously. He ignored it and walked towards the hallway.

Off to the left was the bathroom and another door to the one and only bedroom. To the right, three metres away, was the front door, accessed from the communal entrance. Glancing at his watch, he knew there wouldn't be long to wait.

As if on cue, a key was inserted into the lock, apparently in somewhat of a rush as the bearer struggled to get it into place. A vision of a flustered man came to mind as the latch disengaged and the door flew open. Taking a step back from view, he held his breath so as not to make his presence known, becoming one with the wall. He was a picture of measured calm, despite the adrenalin rush. The sound of someone entering and swiftly closing the door behind, dropping the latch and hastily attaching the security chain assured him that their quarry was aware of his presence.

Reaching into his coat, he withdrew the weapon, no more than six inches in length and easy to conceal. Depressing the power button, he allowed it a moment to activate. Stepping back into the hall, the resident was startled to find a man standing before him, gun raised. The red laser, levelled a dot directly to the centre of his midriff. He raised a hand in supplication.

"No, wait—"

The request was never completed. The barbed probes were deployed, punching through his heavy winter clothing and delivering their burst of energy. Both sensory and motor nervous systems were overwhelmed and the target dropped to his knees with a barely audible grunt, wide-eyed and straining every visible muscle. Covering the distance between them with speed, he pressed the Taser against the bare skin of the man's neck. Deploying the second charge incapacitated him yet further. The target slumped sideways to the floor, losing consciousness.

With a large stride, he stepped across the fallen man and over to the door. Activating the button to override the security lock to the communal entrance, he heard the outer door click open via the intercom. Next came the sound of the others moving through. Leaving the door to the flat ajar, he returned his focus to the man lying prostrate at his feet. Grasping him unceremoniously by the collar at the back of the neck, he dragged him down the hallway and into the living room.

The door to the flat was pushed open. A group passed, their footsteps echoing from the polished floor of the communal passageway. He closed the door to the flat behind them. It was time to get to work.

ALSO BY J M DALGLIESH

The Dark Yorkshire Series

Divided House

Blacklight

The Dogs in the Street

Blood Money

Fear the Past

The Sixth Precept

The Hidden Norfolk Series

One Lost Soul

Bury Your Past

Kill Our Sins

Tell No Tales

Hear No Evil

The Dead Call

Life and Death*

*FREE eBook - A Hidden Norfolk novella

Visit jmdalgliesh.com

Audiobooks

The entire Dark Yorkshire series is available in audio format, read by the award-winning Greg Patmore.

Dark Yorkshire

Divided House

Blacklight

The Dogs in the street

Blood Money

Fear the Past

The Sixth Precept

Audiobook Box Sets

Dark Yorkshire Books 1-3

Dark Yorkshire Books 4-6

Hidden Norfolk

One Lost Soul

Lightning Source UK Ltd.
Milton Keynes UK
UKHW010910260822
407817UK00006B/455